Kate Scott,
The Decoy Detective

New York, The Bay, looking towards the Narrows.

Kate Scott, The Decoy Detective;
or,
Joe Phenix's Still Hunt.

By Albert W. Aiken

Published 1884, Beadle's Weekly
Edited 2018 by Mark Williams

*Cover Design and Cover Illustration by
John Coulthart*

Dark Lantern Tales
Charlotte, NC

Copyright Information

Kate Scott, The Decoy Detective was originally published by Beadle and Adams in 1884.
Dark Lantern Tales has edited this story and added new material, including historical information, a glossary of slang and period terms, and illustrations.

Table of Contents

Joe Phenix's Silent Six;

or,
The Great Detective's Shadow Guard

Sample Chapters:

Order It Today!

THE GREAT EAST RIVER SUSPENSION BRIDGE.

CONNECTING THE CITIES OF NEW YORK AND BROOKLYN   VIEW FROM BROOKLYN LOOKING WEST.

01. *Kate Scott, The Decoy Detective* begins in the evening among some stylish strollers on the newly opened New York and Brooklyn Bridge, or East River Bridge, which is now known simply as the Brooklyn Bridge.

Editor's Introduction

Detective Joe Phenix encountered the woman who will be his new assistant when the first serial installment of *Kate Scott, The Decoy Detective,* hit the streets on February 9, 1884 in Beadle's Weekly.

The first scene is set in the evening among some stylish strollers on the newly opened New York and Brooklyn Bridge, or East River Bridge, which is now known simply as the Brooklyn Bridge. Nearly 14 years were needed to construct the innovative span, all in view of the two cities it would connect. Yet there were some people concerned about the safety of crossing on it, and a panic caused a dozen people to be killed during a stampede to get off of the bridge. A few months after *Kate Scott, The Decoy Detective* was first read by New York mystery fans, P. T. Barnum responded to fears about the bridge by having twenty-one of his elephants, led by the famous Jumbo, walk placidly across to demonstrate how durably it was built. And of course the bridge stands solidly in place today, but in 1884 the Brooklyn Bridge was the subject of rumors, and also a novel place to begin the fifth story of the the Joe Phenix Detective Series.

Kate Scott turns out to be quite a sturdy character in this story; self-possessed and bold. She also challenges some social rules of the time when she finds an excuse to talk with a couple of young men to whom she hasn't been introduced. Some readers in 1884 may have been further astonished when Kate offered these men cigarettes, and even matches for lighting them.

Cigarettes, sometimes called "Turkish Cigarettes," began to gain popularity during the middle of the 19th century, but were considered a lower class preference initially. Gentleman smoked cigars and ladies of breeding didn't smoke anything. At least, that was the popular consensus, though the fashion-conscious young men enjoying Kate Scott's smokes seem to think they are stylish.

Albert W. Aiken wrote *Kate Scott, The Decoy Detective* and all of the Joe Phenix Detective Series stories. His parallel career as a playwright, actor, and even theatre manager, is the source of the theatrical elements in his published stories. In 1881, Aiken is reputed to have retired from the stage to focus on writing for Beadles, but would return to the theatre three or four years later and continue to create for both print and performance.

At about 38 years of age when *Kate Scott, The Decoy Detective* was published as a serial, Aiken had become one of the literary mainstays of Beadle and Adams' publishing house. His new stories for adults were heralded prominently with his name in serials for Beadle's Weekly, which replaced The Saturday Journal. The serials were published again in the Beadle's New York Dime Library as complete stories in a single issue. Earlier tales by Albert Aiken were reprinted in various other Beadle and Adams publications, and he wrote new stories for the growing young adult market that appeared in the Beadle's Half-Dime Library.

This novel includes a family named Grimgriskin. The name was applied to a mercenary landlady in some Irish stories by John Brougham that were published in the mid nineteenth century. Albert Aiken wrote a number of Irish dialect stories early in his career, and must certainly have been familiar with Brougham's books. The Grimgriskins in *Kate Scott, The Decoy Detective* have a comparable character in the patriarch, who came into wealth when his property in Pennsylvania yielded oil.

By the late 1800s, Pennsylvania was producing oil that was sold world wide, and wealth from oil discoveries must have created a number of newly rich people.

To help understand the dollar amounts mentioned in *Kate Scott, The Decoy Detective,* especially the winnings in some card games, $1.00 in 1884 would have the equivalent value today of about $28.00.

But that's enough background - it is time to join Kate Scott for a stroll on the New York and Brooklyn Bridge for a breath of fresh air in novel surroundings.

Her evening is not destined to remain peaceful!

02. Beadle's Weekly of February 9, 1884, with the first
serial installment of *Kate Scott, The Decoy Detective,
or, Joe Phenix's Still Hunt.*
The original size was 14 inches wide and 21 inches tall.

Kate Scott,
The Decoy Detective;

Or, JOE PHENIX'S STILL HUNT.

*A Romance of the Upper Crust and Lower Crust
of New York Life.*

BY ALBERT W. AIKEN,
Edited by Mark Williams

CHAPTER I.
ON THE BRIDGE.

Through an almost unclouded sky sailed a glorious full moon, and the silver queen of night looked down upon about as fair a scene of land-scape beauty as this world can show.

New York Bay with its magnificent expanse of almost land locked water, wherein the navies of the world might ride at anchor.

From the far-famed suspension bridge, but recently completed, which connects the great city of New York with its neighbor, Brooklyn, on the Long Island shore, a fine view of the bay can be obtained. And on the pleasant summer night of which we write, hundreds of people were passing over the airy way, enjoying the pleasant promenade.

It had been a very warm day, but with the coming on of the night a balmy ocean-breeze had come up laden with the ozone of the great Atlantic sea, and nowhere

1

could the refreshing breeze be better enjoyed than on the spider-web-like bridge which practically makes the two cities one.

The elevated pathway was a favorite resort for young people of both sexes, and many a flirtation has been carried on there when the mantle of night covered the earth.

And on this evening of which we write, two young men made themselves conspicuous by the glances they cast at every attractive-looking girl who came anywhere near them.

The young fellows, too, would have certainly attracted attention by their peculiar appearance.

They were dudes in the fullest sense of the word.

"Tooth-pick" shoes, the tightest of pantaloons, white silk hats, with odd-shaped bell-crowns and curling brims; all in fact, got up regardless of expense. To complete the effect, swinging in their hands were dainty little switch-like canes with golden heads.

Both of them good looking young men, too, well worthy to catch a woman's eyes, in spite of the ridiculous style of their dress.

Curled and gilded darlings were these dainty young men, so careful of their precious persons, if there were any youths in great Gotham fit to be so termed.

Scions were they of two of the oldest and best families in the metropolis. No modern upstarts, but ancient Knickerbocker stock, who assumed to look with contempt on the mushroom millionaires of to-day.

The taller one of the two, a well-built young fellow with yellow hair, parted in the middle of the head, after the English style, and sleepy-looking blue eyes, was called Charles Van Tromp, the only son of a widowed mother and the heir to a half-dozen millions, besides being worth a couple in his own right.

His companion, younger by a year or two, also slighter in build, with brown hair and eyes and incipient side-whiskers, was the only descendant of one of the branches of the great Clinton family, so renowned in the history of the Empire State.

Alexander Clinton he was called, and though he had no property he could really call his own, yet as he had a life-income of twenty-five thousand dollars a year, he managed to get along tolerably well. By a whim of his father, who rather distrusted the ability of the son to take care of the wealth he had accumulated, the family estates were all tied up for the benefit of his son's heirs.

The two were fast friends and were seldom seen apart.

This was the first time they had ever condescended to "do the bridge," but as the fellows at the club that evening had assured them that it was the proper thing to do, they had taken a cab and ridden to the bridge entrance. Then, for the novelty of the thing, they had decided to cross the structure on foot.

"We must really give the ladies a treat, my deah boy!" Van Tromp had exclaimed. He assumed an English air as much as possible, and there wasn't anything pleased him better than to be taken for a son of Albion's sea-girt isle.

"Certainly—the charming creatures—the dear little ducks! I fancy they don't often get a chance to admire such perfectly stunning bricks as we are every day in the week," his companion replied.

And so arm in arm the two had sauntered over the bridge, feeling perfectly satisfied with themselves and all the world.

As we have said, they favored every good-looking girl that passed with a patronizing stare, and were duly stared at in return.

And just before reaching the center of the structure, an incident occurred which gave the pair something to talk about.

A well dressed girl, about the medium height, an extremely graceful walker with a finely proportioned figure, overtook the two and passed them as they were proceeding in a languid way.

"I say, Alex, there's a deuced fine creature!" exclaimed Van Tromp, calling his companion's attention to the lady in a tone intended to reach her ears.

"I don't really know, deah boy, I was not lucky enough to see her face, but her figure is perfection itself!" Clinton replied.

And then to the delight of the pair, the girl turned her head and smiled.

The young man was right; she was a fine creature, although she could not be called strictly beautiful according to the rules of art, for her features were rather irregular, although finely-cut. But there was an air of vivacity—of smartness to the face which was extremely charming.

She had brown-black eyes, and brown-black hair, worn short, and clustering in little crispy ringlets to her shapely head, and she had a coquettish way about her which decidedly impressed the two young men.

"Deah boy, I believe you have made a conquest," Clinton hastened to whisper to his companion, as he perceived the girl's movement.

But in matters of this kind Van Tromp needed no prompter, and he hastened to raise his hat and bow in the most courteous manner to the lady.

4

And to his delight she acknowledged the salutation with a slight nod, accompanied by a pleasant smile, and slackening her pace allowed the pair to overtake her.

"Very pleasant evening for a promenade," Van Tromp remarked, as he came up to the lady.

"Yes, very pleasant evening, indeed," she replied, without the least embarrassment, and just as if the two were old acquaintances.

"I don't think I ever saw the moon look more beautiful," Clinton hastened to observe, eager to place himself on familiar terms with the pretty unknown. "Just cast your eyes down the bay too, and observe what a truly lovely view you have from this elevated position."

The three were exactly in the center of the bridge at the moment and, as with one accord, they halted and leaning against the rail surveyed the scene which, as the young man had observed, was really beautiful.

"It is perfectly superb!" Van Tromp exclaimed. "I don't think I ever saw anything handsomer in all my life, present company of course excepted," and he bowed gallantly to the lady, who laughed merrily in return.

"You are inclined to be complimentary, I see," she rejoined.

"On, no, honest truth, I assure you," and Van Tromp bowed again.

"Oh, yes, not the slightest, doubt of that," Clinton hastened to add, and he too bowed as elaborately as the other.

Both the young men were decidedly impressed by the girl who had been foolish enough to allow them to become acquainted with her in this manner.

She was no common young woman, no poorly-paid working-girl, depending for her bread upon the labor of her delicate hands, no daughter of the under-crust, ground down almost to the dust by the pressure of untoward circumstances, nor was she either a scion of the upper-ten, a child of shoddy, who had been sedulously educated to believe that she was something better than the common herd.

In fact, although both of the young men prided themselves with the belief that they were "deuced knowing fellows you know," men who had seen a deal of life and were completely up to snuff, yet in the present instance they did not know exactly what to make of the girl.

In all their "wide" experience they had never encountered any one like her.

She was evidently a lady, well educated and used to good society, and yet she had permitted them to make her acquaintance in this extremely reprehensible manner. Still, there wasn't anything forward about her; nothing to encourage a flirtation.

"By Jove! I think I could stand here for hours and gaze upon this beautiful view!" Van Tromp exclaimed in admiration.

He was evidently referring to the moonlit face of nature, but he had his eyes fixed upon the pretty features of the girl.

"Oh. yes, it's really, truly, too awfully charming," Clinton observed, languidly. "But I think if I had to spend much time here. I should like a cigarette to while the minutes away."

"Allow me to offer you one," said the lady, with a brisk, business-like air, producing a dainty little cigarette case and proffering it to the gentlemen.

"Good gracious! You don't mean to say that you smoke!" Van Tromp cried, pretending to be horrified, while Clinton also assumed an air of intense amazement.

"Oh, no, I don't smoke myself. I only carry a weed for the accommodation of my friends," she replied, laughing. "Take one; I'll warrant you will find them as good as can be procured in the city. They are genuine Havana and no mistake!"

It was quite an odd picture, and none of the parties to it noticed a muscularly-built, stern-faced, plainly-dressed man who had carelessly halted in his promenade a short distance away, and, leaning on the opposite railing, was watching them.

"I am really too awfully pleased!" ejaculated Van Tromp, as he helped himself to a cigarette.

"Yas, too awfully, awfully!" simpered Clinton.

The girl had made an impression.

" Allow me to offer you one." said the lady, with a brisk, business-like air, producing a dainty little cigarette case and proffering it to the gentlemen.

03. "Allow me to offer you one," said the lady with a brisk, business-like air, producing a dainty little cigarette case and offering it to the gentlemen.

CHAPTER II.
THE EAVESDROPPER.

"Oh, don't mention it," replied the young lady, in the most matter-of-fact way. "I am always glad to oblige a friend. Have a light?" and then she produced a little ornamented box containing some tiny wax matches.

The young men hastened to avail themselves of the offer, and when their cigarettes were lighted, Van Tromp resumed the conversation.

"It seems to me that I have met you somewhere," he said, "for your face is very familiar. Isn't your name— upon my word, I believe I can't recall it," and he beamed insinuatingly upon the girl.

"Flora—Flora Muir," the girl replied, and then she added, in the most innocent manner possible:

"It seems to me that I have met you two gentlemen, but I don't remember where it was."

"Oh, there isn't a doubt of it!" Clinton exclaimed. "I'm sure we're old acquaintances, but I never can trust my memory about any such things. I never can remember places, but when it comes to features they always stick by me."

"I think it must have been up in the Catskills where I live when I am at home." the girl remarked. "I am only here on a visit. I live in Tannersville."

A perceptible shade passed over the faces of both the young men, and they cast furtive glances at each otter.

It was evident that something in the speech of the girl made them uncomfortable.

"Tannersville?" Van Tromp drawled, "yes, I think I have been there, but I don't remember much about it.

That's near the Catskill Mountain House, isn't it?"

"Yes; only a short distance."

I think I have driven through it." and then Van Tromp looked askance at his companion, and Clinton coughed slightly as though embarrassed and turned his attention to the view.

"It is a lovely place in summer time and is always crowded with visitors, and as your faces seemed familiar I thought perhaps I might have met you there," the girl observed, apparently not noticing the slight uneasiness of the gentlemen.

"Yes, it is possible, but I don't remember the circumstance. But I am just as delighted to see you now, and if you will permit the acquaintance to continue I am sure we will be very good friends indeed," Van Tromp remarked, in his most gallant manner.

"Well, I can't really ask you to call upon me because I am stopping with some friends in the city who are dreadfully strict, and they would pack me off home to my friends in a twinkling if I should be so imprudent as to have any gentlemen callers. But I go out walking in Central Park every pleasant morning, and I generally enter the Park at Fifty Ninth Street and Fifth Avenue, just about ten o'clock. So, if you should happen to stroll in that direction we should meet beyond a doubt. Mr.—Mr.—?"

"Thomas; Harry Thomas, at your service," replied Van Tromp, with unblushing assurance. "And this is my bosom friend, Robert Jones," he continued, introducing Clinton, who could hardly refrain from a smile at his chum's audacity.

"I should be pleased to see you to-morrow, gentlemen, and no doubt we can have a delightful walk. I'm only a country-girl, you know, and need guides and protectors, so I shall look for you to morrow.

"I am on my way to see some friends of the folks with whom I am staying, who live about a block from the end of the bridge on the Brooklyn side, and they are to see me home tonight, so I am obliged to bid you good-bye now. Ta! Ta!"

And with a charming smile she bowed and went on her way.

The young men returned the salutation in the most elaborate manner, and then when the girl's back was turned, winked at each other significantly.

"What do you think of it, old chappie?" Van Tromp asked.

"Oh, you've caught the girl for all she is worth, there isn't the least doubt about that," Clinton replied. "But, I say, old fellow, she made a cold chill run all over me when she mentioned the name of that infernal place."

"Yes; it was as much as I could do to keep my countenance. In fact, I never even hear the Catskills spoken of in common conversation without wishing that I had never been unlucky enough to go there," Van Tromp replied, as he turned, as also did the other young man, and began to retrace his steps.

"But it wasn't our fault, old fellow; we really didn't have anything to do with it. We were not to blame for what occurred."

"Yes, I know that, but in a measure we were mixed up in it, although really as innocent as a couple of lambs. And if there should ever be any row kicked up about the matter, the chances are about ten to one that it would cause us considerable trouble," Van Tromp observed, and from the earnest way in which he spoke it was plain he regarded the matter as being a serious one.

Clinton being much more of the butterfly order was

not so much impressed.

"It would be deuced awkward, of course; all such things always are and extremely disagreeable; but by the aid of the potential article, cash, we should be able to smooth things over."

"Perhaps," replied the other, with a dubious shake of the head.

Leaving this representative pair of the gilded youths of great Gotham to pursue their way, we will follow in the footsteps of the girl.

After parting with her admirers she had hastened with light and springy footsteps toward the Brooklyn shore, never noticing that the quiet-looking, sober-faced man who had been leaning on the opposite railing, near enough to overhear the conversation indulged in by the three, was following her.

He came close behind her, and after she had passed through the archway formed by the granite towers and began to descend the approach on the Brooklyn side, quickened his pace, then took advantage of the fact that no one was near enough to them on the footpath to notice what was happening, to address her.

"I beg your pardon, miss, for speaking to you," the stranger said, in the most respectful manner, "but as I have something important to say to you, I trust you will pardon the intrusion."

It would have been impossible for any woman not utterly and thoroughly a fool to take offense at the man, and the girl was by no means deficient in common sense, so after rapidly surveying the speaker with her sharp eyes, she replied:

"I shall be pleased to hear you, sir."

"In the first place I overheard the conversation between you and the two young men which took place on the bridge a few moments ago."

"Yes?" queried the girl, seemingly not at all surprised.

The two were now walking slowly along, side by side.

"The part of an eavesdropper or spy is not a particularly pleasant one to play," he remarked, "and if it were not for the peculiar circumstances of the case, most certainly I should have been the last man in the world to listen to a conversation not intended for my ears.

"But I happen to know both of those young men, and when I saw them accost you I knew that they meant you no good, and so I thought it was my duty to keep an eye upon them.

"I gathered from your conversation that you are a country girl and possibly not aware of the dangers that threaten an innocent maid in this great, overgrown city. Both of the names that those young men gave you were false."

"Is it possible?" she replied, and yet she did not seem to be much amazed at the intelligence.

"Yes, I am acquainted with the pair, although neither of them know me personally. They are good representatives of a large class common to all our big cities, rich young men with more money than brains, who stoop to follies which if indulged in by a mechanic would be termed crimes.

"I think that they have marked you for a victim, and so I deem it my duty to warn you against them. I overheard you make an appointment to meet these gentlemen in the park. Be guided by me, do not keep that appointment, and not only that, acquaint your friends with all the particulars of this affair. Do not walk heedlessly into the snare that these young wretches design to lay to entrap you."

The face of the girl did not betray the least emotion, for she listened with perfect calmness to the rather startling explanation.

"I am very much obliged indeed to you for your trouble." she said. "Indeed I am sincerely grateful, and I assure you I shall heed your warning. Will you favor me with your name, please?"

"Certainly; Joseph Phenix."

And it was indeed the renowned detective whose thrilling adventures and hairbreadth escapes we have so frequently chronicled.

And now for the first time a look of surprise appeared upon the face of the girl and she gazed earnestly at the features of the gentleman by her side.

"Phenix — Joseph Phenix," she repeated, slowly; "it seems to me as if your name was familiar to me. It is an odd appellation, and one that when once heard is not soon forgotten."

"My name gets into the newspapers once in awhile, although I do my best to keep it out, for in my business newspaper notoriety is about the last thing to be desired."

"And what may your business be, pray?" and as she put the question it was evident from her manner that she was deeply interested.

"I am a detective officer, and that is the reason why I made bold to interfere in your case. Knowing these young bloods, and ascertaining from your conversation that you were a stranger, and probably not familiar with city ways, I determined to spoil their little game if I could."

"You are one of the police detectives?"

"No, miss, not now, although the authorities do me the honor to ask my aid once in awhile when a difficult case comes up. I am in a private line."

"You are the very man I wish to see, then!" cried the girl, with sudden energy. "Heaven has surely sent you to my aid. It is I who will be the trapper, not those two silly fops!"

CHAPTER III.
KATE SCOTT'S STORY.

As a general thing, it was not easy to surprise a man like Joe Phenix. He had seen too much of the world, had been engaged in too many startling adventures not to take with composure whatever might occur.

Generally, too, he was able to make a shrewd guess at the character of the people whom he encountered and it was seldom that he was far from the truth. But in the present instance he was wide of the mark, to judge from the girl's exclamation.

He had taken her to be a country maid, a village coquette given to flirtation, and flattered by the attention bestowed upon her by the two well dressed city bloods. In order to save the girl from their wiles he had interfered.

But low and behold! The dove had suddenly turned into a hawk. Instead of a victim she intended to become the executioner.

"I must have played my part to perfection to deceive such a wonderful judge of humankind as you are, Mr. Phenix," the girl continued, rapidly. "I am no country girl, sir, no maiden innocent of the traps and pitfalls of this world, for I have fought for my daily bread and gained my own living ever since I was ten years old. And not only supported myself, but since the time I was fifteen I have also taken care of my younger sister, who has resided with some of our relatives in Tannersville, a village up in the Catskill mountains."

Phenix nodded.

"I know the place. I visited it on business, once. It is a charming country."

"Yes, it was a Paradise in which my beautiful sister dwelt until the serpent came and tempted her away," the girl remarked, with bitter accent.

"But it is quite a long story, and perhaps you will not care to hear it," she added.

"If you choose to honor me with your confidence, I shall only be too glad to listen," Phenix replied.

It was but seldom that the iron hearted, stern-minded detective ever took a fancy to any one, but in the present case he had been attracted to the girl from the moment when he had first beheld her face, and now that she had abruptly revealed she was capable of playing a part well enough to deceive even such an experienced judge of human nature as himself, his interest in the girl deepened.

"Oh, if I could only hope to arouse your interest so that you would aid in the terrible task which I have undertaken!" the girl exclaimed, her face flushing with an eager look born of the hope which had suddenly sprung up in her heart.

"I am not a man to make any rash promise," he said, in his sober, stolid way, "but I am ready to admit that I already take a great interest in you, and if I can be of any service I feel sure you will not have to call upon me in vain."

"Oh, sir, if you would only aid me!" she exclaimed. "You are all-powerful, and I have taken upon my shoulders a task of vengeance which might appall the stoutest-hearted man.

"It is the old, old story, the tale of man's perfidy and woman's weakness which has been rehearsed so many times since the world was young.

"You overheard the conversation between myself and those two young men?"

The detective nodded assent.

"They gave me false names, and I paid them in their own coin. I knew them well enough, and was not deceived by their falsehoods.

"The latter one is called Charles Van Tromp, and his companion answers to the name of Alexander Clinton."

"That statement is correct. I am well acquainted with both of them by sight, although not personally."

"My name is not Flora Muir, but Kate Scott. I was born at Tannersville, in the shadows of the Catskill peaks, just twenty-one years ago.

"When I reached my tenth year I had the misfortune to lose both of my parents. With an only sister four years younger than myself I was cast upon the mercies of a cold and often times cruel world.

"We were not absolutely helpless, as we had relatives, honest people enough, but poor, narrow-minded and grasping.

"It was in the summer-time when my parents died. The mountains were full of visitors, and I was lucky enough to find favor in the eyes of a rich lady, who, with her husband, was sojourning at the Mountain House."

"That was fortunate indeed," observed the detective, who was listening to the tale with the deepest interest.

"Yes, she said I was a bright, sharp little thing, and took me into her service as a sort of lady's maid.

"I had received a good education for one of my age, and my mistress made a sort of pet of me, treating me more like a companion than a menial.

"She paid me liberal wages besides providing all my clothes; she was rich, and could afford to indulge in her caprices. From my wages I paid my sister's board.

"With the lady I remained for five years, and then death removed my benefactress, but as a reward for my faithful services she bequeathed me a thousand dollars.

18

Her husband exerted his influence and procured a situation for me in one of the leading photograph galleries of the city, where I remained until about a month ago. I gave up my position to enter upon this task of vengeance which has fallen to my share.

"My sister, who was called Louise, grew up to be a beautiful girl. She was a blonde, with the most beautiful blue eyes and hair like threads of beaten gold.

"She had artistic talent, and I spent my money freely to develop her genius.

"All went well until about a year ago; she was just sixteen then and, oh, so beautiful! We were accustomed to exchange letters weekly. I wrote every Sunday, and she answered so that I would get the letter either Friday or Saturday.

"The letters never failed to come by Saturday until one week, then none arrived.

"I did not feel at all alarmed, for I imagined the letter had miscarried, but when Monday, Tuesday and Wednesday passed and no tidings reached me, I became alarmed. I telegraphed to Tannersville and received a reply that my sister was not there.

"In hot haste I took the first train for the Catskills, and when I arrived at Tannersville hurried to the house which had sheltered my sister so long. And when I questioned my relatives as to what had become of my sister, I found them as astonished as myself when they learned that I did not know anything about my beautiful Louise.

"They had been led to suppose that I knew all about the matter.

"One of the summer visitors, a young, handsome, and rich New Yorker, had become acquainted with my sister, and it seemed to be a case of love at first sight on both sides. After a courtship of just a couple of weeks, the two went to a minister one night and were married. Then they departed to the city, where they were to meet me.

"My poor, misguided sister had said I was aware of the affair, but was so busily engaged in the city that I was not able to come to the mountains.

"Henry Tappan was the name by which the New Yorker was known."

"It is an old New York name," the detective observed.

"But it was a false appellation!" the girl exclaimed. "I returned immediately to the city and set to work to discover what had become of my Louise. I feared for the worst despite the fact that there was not the least doubt she had been legally married, but her keeping me in utter ignorance of the entire affair I regarded as being a very bad sign.

"As I feared, I could not discover the least trace in New York of the young man who in the Catskills had called himself Henry Tappan.

"None of the Tappans who resided in the city knew aught of him; both he and my sister had disappeared and left no more trace behind than if the earth had opened and swallowed them.

"I spent money like water, employed the detectives, advertised, but all to no purpose. For a year now I have not wavered in my purpose, but not the slightest clew have I gained until this afternoon.

"I attended a matinée at the Academy of Music, and as I was coming out after the performance, in the crowd I happened to be immediately behind two young men.

"A fragment of their conversation reached my ears.

"One said to the other, 'I saw that Catskill fellow to-day.' 'Did he have the girl with him?' the other asked.

'No,' was the reply, and then from what followed it seemed as if they had a knowledge of some wrong which had been done by a fast young man in the Catskills to a country girl.

"Of course it was but a chance that they referred to my sister's sad affair, but I determined to follow it up and ascertain beyond a doubt, and when I gathered from their conversation that they intended to visit the bridge, I managed to meet and ensnare them there."

"It was cleverly done, and the clew is worth following up. You ought to join the detective force; there is a dearth of good female detectives," Phenix remarked. "I need a decoy detective myself. Often there comes a bit of work which only a woman can do."

"Will you take me?" cried the girl, eagerly. "It is the life beyond all others that I desire, and I am sure, too, that I have natural talent for such a vocation."

"Yes, I will, and gladly, and I will give you my aid in solving your riddle," Phenix answered, promptly. "I have a job on hand tomorrow night. Can you come to my office— here is my card—disguised as an Italian boy, one of the street bootblack boys, you know? If I need to change the place of our meeting, I will contact you."

"Oh, yes, I will be there, and I am sure I shall be perfectly at home in any disguise."

And so the compact was made which turned Kate Scott, the avenger, into Joe Phenix's Decoy Detective.

CHAPTER IV.
THE ASSAULT.

The girl went on her way with light steps and a cheerful heart.

The unexpected meeting with the detective, and his assurance that he would aid her in the task to which she had resolved to consecrate her life, was a most welcome piece of good fortune, and she felt greatly encouraged.

Since she had begun her search for her sister and had mingled with the detectives, she had often heard Joe Phenix spoken of in the highest terms.

In fact, there was hardly a man in the detective line who did not regard the cool, quiet, massive-formed detective as being the greatest thief-catcher who had ever flourished in New York.

And now since she had succeeded in forming an alliance with the most renowned detective of them all, she felt convinced she would succeed not only in discovering what had become of her sister, but in punishing the villain who was responsible for her flight, for Kate felt sure that there was something wrong about the matter.

True, her sister had been legally married to the young man who called himself Henry Tappan. There wasn't any doubt about that matter, for the marriage was performed by a regularly-ordained minister in the presence of witnesses. But that there was something wrong was evident, for if there wasn't, why had she been kept in ignorance in regard to it; she who had toiled that her sister might be comfortable ever since she had been big enough to work?

Then, if her suspicions were unfounded and everything was all right, if her sister had contracted a happy marriage with the man of her choice, why should there be any mystery about the affair? Why should both husband and wife hide themselves so sedulously from all the world that a year's search by some of the most expert detectives in the city, urged by the inducement of a large reward, did not result in a discovery of their whereabouts?

No, Kate Scott was sure her sister had been betrayed and foully dealt with.

The villain who passed by the name of Henry Tappan—Kate felt satisfied it was a false appellation—had managed to fascinate the innocent country girl, unsuspicious of the villainy that existed in this great world, and not being able to gain possession of her in any other way, had married her and taken her to the city and there probably tired of and deserted his victim.

But, if this was the truth, why was it that the unfortunate Louise had not sought out her sister, the unselfish heart who had watched over her since childhood with all a mother's devotion ?

It was a mystery, and the more the girl reflected upon it the more bewildered she became.

Only one explanation had occurred to her during all these long months when she had been as persistent in her search as the hound on the scent of blood.

Her sister and the villain who had lured her away had not remained in New York, perhaps had not come there at all, but had fled to some distant locality. To another country beyond the seas, perhaps, and the unfortunate Louise, when deserted by the serpent who had lured her away, had not been able to either return to the city or to communicate with her sister.

Of little consolation is the empty marriage-rite to a young girl when she makes the terrible discovery that the man to whom she has given all that she can give, is a scoundrel who has basely deceived her, a vile wretch, unworthy of the affection of any self-respecting woman.

Kate had almost given up all hope of ever again seeing her sister. She feared that she had found rest from her misery in the cold damp grave, but even if that was true, a task of vengeance yet remained.

The villain who was responsible for all this wrong must be sought out and punished.

The girl had not deceived the young men when she had said she was on her way to visit some friends in Brooklyn.

It was the truth, and after leaving the bridge Kate proceeded directly toward her destination.

She proceeded up Washington Street to Nassau and then turned into that thoroughfare, intending to go through it to Fulton, upon which street her friends resided.

Nassau Street between Washington and Fulton is dimly lighted, and is not an inviting spot after nine o' the night.

The street is but little used by anybody, and pedestrians are few and far between.

Into the street on the lower side were two narrow alleys populated by an extremely poor class of people.

The alleys are as dark as a pocket at night, and afford a convenient lurking place for any evil-disposed person.

The girl went on without a thought of fear, but, just as she crossed the first alley, out from the darkness of the narrow thoroughfare bounded two muscular fellows, and they seized upon the girl in a twinkling.

One grasped her from behind, and in the most dexterous manner passed his arm around her neck, put one of his knees in the small of her back and jerked her from her feet.

It was the ruffian's trick known as "garroting," from the similarity to strangling with a cord. When it is performed by an expert, as it was in the present instance, for the moment it renders the victim entirely helpless, so much so that it is impossible for the person thus rudely assailed to utter even a single cry.

And the second ruffian, too, was as prompt to play the part which had been assigned to him in this evidently carefully planned outrage as his companion.

He was provided with a sponge saturated with chloroform, and simultaneously with the garroting of the girl by the first scoundrel he applied the sponge to her nostrils, and then both of them dragged the hapless maid into the dark recesses of the alley.

This movement occupied far less time in its execution than we have taken to describe it.

All the surroundings were favorable, too. There was not a single soul near enough to the scene of the outrage to detect what had transpired, although Fulton Street, Brooklyn's main artery, with its constant stream of pedestrians, and Washington Street, the direct means of communication with the bridge, were only half a block away.

But the operation was performed so quickly and with so little noise that not the slightest disturbance was raised.

Within the alley stood a hack, its lamps un-lighted, so as not to attract attention.

Into that carriage the now senseless girl was placed.

The potent drug had done its work only too well, and Kate Scott was as helpless as an infant in the hands of the villains who had so roughly and unexpectedly assailed her.

The ruffian who performed the garroting operation was tall and thin, although extremely muscular. His companion was short and stout.

"Now, Stingy Bill," said the tall, thin man, who seemed to be the leader of the two, after the girl was safely bestowed in the coach, "light the lamps and get on the box. I'll go inside with the gal. Give me the sponge and the bottle, so I will be able to give her another dose if she gets her senses back and is inclined to squall."

"But that ain't according to the program, Four Kings," remonstrated the other. "The boss said that she was to be blindfolded so she would not be able to see where she was going, and have a gag put in her mouth."

"Blamed if I didn't forget all 'bout that," responded the other. "You're right, you duffer, for a thousand dollars. And I've got the gag in my pocket, too, as well as the veil to go over her eyes, so that she won't be able to spy out the lay of the land.

"Durn me, if I see how I come to forget it."

"Oh, you ain't got the head on you for biz, like your uncle!" exclaimed the stout man, complacently.

"Ain't got so much jaw, anyway," retorted the other, "But you get to yer lamps, and then heist onto that box and git', while I attend to the gal."

Then he entered the coach, drew the gag from his pocket—it was a curious contrivance, about the shape and size of a large pear, made out of a cork wound around with cloth, and with strings attached to it so that it could be held in the mouth after being placed there.

"No use to gag or blind her until I see she is coming to her senses," the man muttered, as he got the "tools" ready.

But he thought it necessary to securely bind both her hands and feet, so she was rendered perfectly helpless.

By the time this operation was completed the coach had started.

The seizure had been so adroitly performed that the girl had hardly time to realize that she had been assaulted before her senses fled.

How long she remained insensible she knew not, but when she recovered consciousness again she found herself in utter darkness, lying upon what seemed to be a lounge.

She was evidently in a room, for the air seemed close and musty.

Rising to a sitting posture, she endeavored to discover where she was, but the darkness was too intense.

Then a soft light began to illuminate the room, and when it partially dispelled the darkness, she saw she was in an apartment without either windows or doors and about twelve feet square by seven high.

The light came from a glass fixed in the center of the ceiling, through which the light of the moon flowed.

The room was comfortably furnished with a table, two chairs, the lounge, and in one corner an iron sleeping-couch like those used in hospitals.

The girl sprung to her feet and advanced to the center of this strange apartment, utterly bewildered.

Then a sharp click fell upon her ears. She turned to ascertain the reason of the sound and was confronted by a figure robed from head to foot in a black cloak, rising through the floor.

Kate started back in horror as her eyes fell upon the strange sight.

04. Kate started back in horror as her eyes fell upon the strange sight.

CHAPTER V.
A STRANGE DISCLOSURE.

When the girl turned only about half of the black robed figure was visible.

Kate started back in horror as her eyes fell upon the strange sight, for she guessed at once that she was in the power of a foe, completely helpless too, and yet she could not imagine why any one should take the trouble to injure her, as she had never wronged any one in her life, nor ever made an enemy to her knowledge.

It was little wonder that the girl was for the moment a prey to a sudden terror despite the stout heart she carried within her bosom, for the cloaked figure made its entrance into the room with almost as much celerity as the demon imp bounds through the stage in the pantomime.

And the machinery by means of which he made his appearance was borrowed from the theatrical world.

No yawning trap-door disclosed itself, but the floor seemed to cling to him as he rose, merely yielding enough to let him pass through.

Among the skillful stage artisans this clever mechanical contrivance is known as a "vampire trap."

When the figure reached the level of the floor he stepped forward, and the pointed sections of the trap shut again with a snap.

It was a man evidently, although thoroughly concealed from head to heel by the black cloak which was arranged to fall in folds from his head, thus rendering it impossible for any one to distinguish the outlines of his figure.

Through two holes in the head part of the cloak

shone a pair of brilliant eyes, eyes so black and piercing that the captive felt sure she would be able to recognize them again, no matter where she might behold them, nor how long the lapse of time.

And now that the first moment of surprise was over, the natural coolness of the girl came to her aid, and she stood erect and faced the intruder, a questioning look upon her features.

"Rather took you by surprise, I suppose?" said the man, in a gruff voice, evidently assumed for the purpose of disguising his own natural tones.

"You didn't expect visitors to make their appearance in this unceremonious way," he continued. "But this is a sort of Liberty Hall here, and we don't go much on style and ceremony."

"What is the meaning of this outrage that has been perpetrated upon me? Why have I been assaulted and brought here?" cried our heroine.

"Don't get into a rage, for it will not do you the least bit of good," the man responded, coolly. "Just help yourself to a seat, for I've something important to say to you, and I hate to see you standing like a servant."

Without a word the girl obeyed.

"There, that's better," the mysterious unknown remarked, approvingly. "Now we'll get right down to business. Your name is Kate Scott, I believe?"

"Yes, sir."

"And you used to live up in the Catskills?"

"I did—I was born there."

"You are the girl I want to see then. I thought you were the party, but it is always better to be certain in such matters. If I understood you correctly you complained in regard to the way in which you were brought here."

"It was a foul outrage!" Kate cried, spiritedly.

"There is an old adage that the end justifies the means," the unknown replied, "and in this case it most certainly does. I wanted to see you on a little personal matter, and as I have something particularly important to say to you it was necessary that the interview should take place in a quarter where we could not possibly be disturbed.

"I think you will admit that this cozy apartment fills the bill exactly in that respect," and he chuckled hoarsely, as though he thought he had given utterance to a good joke.

"Then too," he continued, "I wished to arrange the matter so that I could control all the details of the interview. I did not intend that you should have the power to either shorten or lengthen the duration of the conversation. I have something particular to say to you and you may not like it—you may become angry and feel like kicking up a row, but, as you are situated at present, it will not do you much good."

"What can you possibly have to say to me?" exclaimed the girl, not knowing what to make of this strange affair.

"Your name is Kate Scott and you originally came from the town of Tannersville in the Catskills—you had a sister there named Louise—"

The girl started as though thrilled by an electric shock.

Imploringly she extended her bands toward the disguised man.

"Oh, sir, can you tell me aught of my sister?" she cried.

"Yes, yes; you are at the right shop for information here," he replied, and then he laughed—laughed in a manner that sent a chill to the heart of the girl, for there was more menace than merriment in the sound.

"There isn't a person in the world who can tell you more about Louise Scott than a gentleman about my size, for I was nearer and dearer to her than all the rest of the world. In fact, I am the man for whom you have been searching so diligently—I am Henry Tappan."

Kate gazed at the speaker with straining eyes. She had not expected this disclosure, although when her sister's name was mentioned she suspected that the man might be an accomplice of the villain who had lured her idol away.

But the announcement that she stood face to face with the villain for whom she had searched so long and earnestly took her completely by surprise.

Tappan, to give him the name which he had claimed, noticed the surprise which his words had produced and again indulged in the low, jeering chuckle of which he seemed so fond.

"You are a little astonished," he remarked. "I suppose I am about the last man in the world whom you expected to see. Here you have been in search of me for about a year now, wasting your money on detective officers, who are generally nothing but a lot of beats, and you haven't been able to get the slightest clew to my whereabouts. You see, I have been well informed in regard to your movements.

"I didn't trouble myself much about the matter, for I reckoned that in time you would get tired of the thing and give it up."

"Never, while life remains!" the girl cried, impulsively. "I had made up my mind to find you, and in the search I should never have tired."

"That is exactly the conclusion I formed," he replied. "And that is the reason why I went to the trouble of bringing you here. I thought your desire might as well be gratified since you were so earnest in the matter.

"Now then, we are face to face; I am Henry Tappan; what do you want with me?"

"What have you done with my sister—my beautiful Louise?" Kate exclaimed.

"Of course it will be useless and only a waste of time for me to pretend that I don't know anything about her; for I am aware you have succeeded in getting at the facts in the matter," he observed, slowly. "Consequently I will tell you the truth about the matter. Your sister and I fell in love. There were certain reasons why it was not advisable to allow the matter to become public, so, owing to my solicitation, your sister did not even take you into her confidence.

"We were married, taking care to keep the marriage as secret as possible, and then came to New York, intending to sail for Europe, by the Inman Line steamship, City of Berlin.

"The steamer was to sail at six in the afternoon. We went on board about noon, and then I was compelled to leave my bride to attend to a little urgent business which I had somehow neglected, and owing to my watch being out of order I missed the steamer and she sailed without me.

"I immediately sent a cable message to the agent of the line in England detailing the circumstances and requesting that all possible attention should be given to my wife until I could join her, crossing by the next steamer.

"And this program I carried out, but upon my arrival in England, judge of my consternation when I was informed that my bride of a day had been lost overboard from the steamer on the first night out.

"Whether it was an accident or because a sudden fear had taken possession of her on account of my absence and she had yielded to the belief that she was betrayed and deserted it is impossible to say."

"And was it not the truth?" Kate demanded. "Is not this story of your missing the steamer all a lie from beginning to end?"

"It is only natural that you should jump to that conclusion, but it is not the truth," he replied. "The passenger lists of the steamer will prove that Mr. and Mrs. H. Tappan were booked to sail by the City of Berlin on a certain date, and that Mr. H. Tappan, alone, did sail by the steamer which was dispatched after that one.

"Then, too, an account of the death was published in the daily journals at the time, although as I had good reason for wishing to keep the fact of my marriage secret, I furnished as few particulars as possible."

"It is strange I did not see it or that the detectives I employed did not discover it," the girl remarked.

"Not at all; the publication was just about a month before you began your operations, and in the whirl of New York life a month is a great while.

"Your detectives, the blundering fools, looked forward; not backward. Here is the account," and he handed her an old newspaper.

It was only a brief item relating how a lady passenger on the City of Berlin fell overboard in the lower bay and in the darkness perished, although every effort was made to rescue her, and the name was given as Mrs. H. Tappan."

"Dead, dead!" moaned Kate, in heartfelt grief, letting the newspaper fall from her listless hands.

"Yes, 'gone to that bourne from whence no traveler returns.' The body was never discovered, although on my return I tried to trace it."

"I loved your sister, Kate, and truly mourned her death, and until I saw you I did not believe that I could ever find it in my heart to love any other woman."

34

CHAPTER VI.
THE CAPTIVE'S REPLY.

Our heroine started in surprise, for this avowal was entirely unexpected.

"I perceive you are astonished and no doubt you hardly know what to make of my speech, but I am a plain, blunt man, and I believe it is always best for a man to speak out when anything important is at stake," Tappan replied.

"I have been watching you now for nearly a year; ever since the time, in fact, when I got wind that you were hot on my scent. And since that discovery I have made it my business to keep my eyes upon you."

"I had no idea that I was being watched," Kate observed, hardly knowing whether to place credence in the statement or not.

"Of course, it was not my game to allow you to know it. You see, I play my cards much better than the blundering detectives whom you employed to hunt me down."

"But I do not understand the reason for this mystery!" the girl exclaimed. "If the story you have related to me in regard to the death of my unfortunate sister is true, and it seems to bear the impress of truth, why did you not come to me when you learned that I was in search of you? It would have lifted a terrible load from my mind!"

"Well, I had good reasons for acting as I did," the man replied, after a moment's pause, as if he was debating about the matter in his mind.

"In the first place, as you have doubtless guessed, Henry Tappan is not my real name."

"I did not think it was."

"I give you credit for being shrewd enough for that. Now, if I came to you in my own proper person you, of course, would know me if you saw me again, and I have good reasons for wishing to remain unknown.

"Money, you know, can accomplish almost anything nowadays, and money, judiciously expended, brought you here.

"Two reasons actuated me; in the first place I wanted to tell you the true story of your sister's unaccountable disappearance, and in the second to make known to you that you have inspired me with an ardent affection.

"As I have told you, after the loss of your sister I was so deeply affected by the calamity that I did not believe I should ever meet a woman whose charms could make my pulse quicken in the least degree. But when my attention was drawn to you by the earnest attempt you were making to discover what had become of the ill fated Louise, after a time I suddenly realized that you were beginning to occupy the place in my heart which she once enjoyed.

"I fought against this feeling for some time, but finally it grew so strong that I was obliged to give way to it, and so I planned to bring you here, that I might not only make known to you the sad fate which had befallen your sister, but also reveal to you the passion which has grown up in my heart."

With all her shrewdness the girl was puzzled, unable to guess the motives which animated the man, and caused him to act so strangely.

The reason he had assigned, that of having become fascinated by her charms, she did not believe was the true one.

It was possible that, finding she was not disposed

to give up the chase, and fearing in time she would hunt him down, he adopted this device to make her give up the pursuit.

But if the story of her sister's death was true, and he was not to blame in the matter, why should he fear?

She was satisfied there was something hidden; that the man had not revealed all the particulars, and immediately she gave utterance to her doubts.

"I do not credit this tale which you have told," she said.

"The proof that I have told you the truth in regard to the loss of your sister was in your hand, and if you doubt the truth of it, and believe that by some hocus-pocus the newspapers were imposed upon to publish a falsehood, you can easily satisfy yourself by visiting the office of the steamship company."

"Oh, I have no doubt that the account you give of the death of my poor Louise is correct, but the reason you give for the strange conduct on your part is not at all satisfactory," she replied.

"If you had come to me in your own proper person, and required me to pledge myself to keep secret whatever you might reveal to me, I would gladly have given such a promise; but after what has occurred, my mind is tormented by doubtful fears.

"Who and what are you? Why do you assume this strange disguise, and why was this mysterious apartment constructed? In fact, all that has transpired seems more like a leaf torn out of an old-time romance than anything else."

"Ha, ha, ha," laughed the masked man in his disagreeable, jeering fashion, "you are like all your sex, and can ask more questions in a minute than an ordinary man can answer in a week."

"You cannot expect me to walk blindfold in an un-known path," she retorted.

"I am afraid you will have to accomplish that feat for I am not at liberty to reveal to you any more than I have already done. You must take me blindly, and trust to luck.

"One thing I will tell you, and that is that I can give you a life of luxury such as few women in this world are able to enjoy.

"Your lightest wish shall be gratified, and you shall pass as the wife of one who stands as tall in New York as almost any man in the metropolis.

"All I require in return is implicit trust and exact obedience."

"Oh, you want me to take a leap in the dark and shut my eyes besides!" Kate exclaimed.

"Yes, that is about the idea, but by daring the risk you will receive a rich reward."

"I put very little faith in that assurance, and I think I am beginning to understand what kind of a man you are.

"Your strange disguise, the manner in which I was brought here, this mysterious apartment, your incompre-hensible offer, and the fact that you say you have been able to keep a watch on me ever since I came to the city, without my having the slightest suspicion of the fact, all serve to convince me that you are not a man whose deeds can bear the sunlight, but on the contrary you seek the shadow to hide evil purposes."

"Not a very flattering estimate this that you have formed of my character!" he exclaimed, seemingly more amused than affronted by the girl's remarks.

"What other opinion can I have under the circum-stances?" she asked. "If you are an honest man, and there are good reasons why you do not wish me to know who you are for fear that I might betray your secret, the matter can be easily arranged.

"Your name is not Henry Tappan, of course. I understand that appellation is an assumed one. But you can be known to me by that name and I will not trouble myself to discover what your real name is. If you wish to see me you can come at night, and I will so manage that you will not meet any one; but I tell you, frankly, right at the beginning, I do not think I shall ever be able to bring myself to like you.

"You may be innocent of any guilt as regards my sister's death, but I cannot forget that if it had not been for you, in all probability she would be alive and well to-day, safe and happy in her mountain home.

"You came between my sister and myself, stole her away from me, and that fact I shall never be able either to forget or forgive."

"It is true enough. I did take your sister, but she went of her own free will."

"Lured by your dazzling promises, no doubt!" Kate exclaimed, bitterly. "Just as you have tried to dazzle me with a brilliant prospect. I may wrong you, but I can think of nothing else but the Fallen Angel trying to tempt the Holy One by promising a world which was not his to give."

"Oh, I can make good my offer," Tappan asserted.

"Perhaps, and yet I do not believe it. Your words are fair enough, but something whispers to me that you are not to be trusted."

"Then you do not choose to accept me in the guise of a lover?"

"No, I do not."

"Well, I'm sorry for that, for you are just the woman for me; keen-witted, sharp as a steel trap and no doubt not devoid of courage. In this chase of me, too, you have displayed the dogged determination of a bloodhound. Oh, decidedly, Kate, I shall have to have you, and there's no two ways about it."

"Whether I will or no?" and an angry light shone in the girl's eyes, although she put the question in the most matter of-fact manner.

"Yes, I suppose so," he answered, carelessly. "You see you force me to such a course, and I must adopt it, although it certainly is most distasteful to me: but under the circumstances what else can I do? You tell me that there isn't any hope for me to win you, supposing I lay siege in the regular way, and so I am compelled to try a novel kind of courtship. You are here in my power, completely isolated from all the world, and here you will remain until you consent to become mine."

"And that I will never do under such degrading conditions!" Kate cried, spiritedly. "You may keep me here until I die, but never will I agree to say yes, when my heart tells me that I ought to say no!"

"You think so now, but you may change your mind after a week or a month elapses," he rejoined. "Solitary confinement, even in such a cozy apartment as this, is not the pleasantest thing in the world, as you will discover after a week, a month or a year."

"A thousand years will not make me yield!" the girl exclaimed.

"We shall see; and so for the present, adieu!" Then he stamped his foot thrice upon the trapdoor.

There was a moment's interval, and then Tappan sunk specter-like through the floor.

CHAPTER VII.
A BOLD ATTEMPT.

The girl stood like a statue until the man disappeared and the trap closed over his head.

For the moment she was bewildered; she did not know what to make of this strange affair.

Was she in the power of a wealthy young man who took this strange mode of compelling her to accept his attentions, or was he a desperate and determined villain who had fixed his eyes upon her, regarding her in the light of a convenient tool?

Possibly the man was not in his right mind, a lunatic gifted with the peculiar cunning common to some madmen.

The assault upon her, which had resulted in her capture, had been performed so adroitly that she had no idea of how many had taken part in the attack.

For all she knew a single man might have accomplished it.

Take it for all in all it was the most mysterious affair, and the more she reflected about the matter the greater became her perplexity.

One thing seemed certain though and that was, no matter what the man might be, he intended to keep her a close prisoner.

The first thing to be done then was to endeavor to escape.

She looked around her carefully.

As we have said there were neither doors nor windows to the apartment.

The only break in the room was where the light in the center of the ceiling shone through a small pane of glass.

The glass was only about eight inches square, and even if the captive could succeed in reaching it the aperture was not large enough to allow her to pass through.

Then she proceeded to examine the trap through which the man had ascended and descended, although she had very little hope that she would be able to make use of it, for it would, in all probability, be securely fastened.

Now that she knew exactly where the trap was situated she was able to locate it without difficulty, although the contrivance had been arranged with so much skill that the cracks in the carpet caused by the trap could only be discovered by a most careful inspection.

But, as Kate had expected, the trap was fully as solid as the rest of the floor, and she could not produce the slightest impression on it.

In fact, if she had not known that there was a trap there she never would have suspected it.

Rising to her feet she proceeded to carefully inspect the walls of the apartment.

They were not like ordinary walls composed of laths and plaster, but solid wood, wainscoted in the olden style, and the ring which the wood gave back when she pounded on the walls with her clinched hand convinced her that nothing short of a crowbar or an ax would make any impression upon them.

"Surely there must be some other way of gaining admission to this room besides the trap door," she murmured, as she retreated to the center of the apartment and gazed anxiously around her.

"This is evidently a very old house," she continued, "for the wood is brown with age. This is no secret chamber lately arranged but one of the odd contrivances due to olden times. I have read of such things, although I had no idea that any of them existed in this country.

"And all such secret apartments, originally designed to hide the owner of the mansion from secret enemies, always had more than one mode of entrance, so if the pursuers chanced to hit upon one, the fugitive might escape by another.

"And, now, since the trap door is one way, the probabilities are great that a secret passage through one of the walls is another.

"And in the old-time stories which I have read such panels were operated by a secret spring concealed in the wood-work.

"I must examine every inch of the walls, and if there is a secret spring the pressure of hands upon it ought to have slightly discolored the surrounding wall so I will be able to discover it."

Kate was as good as her word.

She examined the wall so thoroughly that not a square inch of it escaped her scrutiny, from the floor to as high as her eyes could reach.

The girl reasoned that the spring would in all probability be located about the height that a door-knob usually is, and so she devoted particular attention to that part of the wall.

Small discolorations were plentiful enough on the walls, but none of them yielded to the power of the girl's eager fingers.

At last, just as she was about to despair— having made the circuit of the room and returned to the point from whence she started, she caught sight of what looked like the head of a small nail imbedded in the wood, six inches from the corner of the room and about two feet from the floor.

The head projected just a little, and there was a thick coating of dust upon the upper side, proving that no one had disturbed it for some time.

Kate surveyed the nail with a dubious expression.

It did not seem to be a promising discovery.

She tried her thumb upon it, thinking that if it was the spring which she sought it would yield under the pressure, but it did not.

It was only a common nail after all.

The heart of the girl sunk within her.

"Is it possible that I am doomed to remain here a helpless prisoner?" she exclaimed. "Is it fated that this villain, not content with the ruin he has already wrought by luring my unfortunate sister away from her quiet country home, will also be able to inflict misery upon me?

"It cannot be that a just Providence will permit such a thing."

She was on her knees, her thumb still resting on the head of the nail, and as she uttered the last word of the sentence she made a motion to rise to her feet, and as she did so the nail of her thumb catching upon the head of the iron fragment seemed to stir it.

It was as much as the girl could do to repress the loud cry of joy which sprung to her lips.

She had discovered the secret spring, but the way to work it was not to press it in, but to *pull it out*.

Quick was she to try this.

And it worked to a charm.

Out came the nail, which was a small iron rod about six inches long with a nail head on the end, and then a section of the wall, about two feet by three, swung noise-lessly inward, disclosing a narrow passage about two feet squire, only extending downward.

The passage was as dark as Egypt, and a stream of cold, damp air came pouring up from it.

It was more like a well-hole than anything else.

The girl peered down, not a ray of light could be distinguished, and from the damp air which ascended she came to the conclusion that the passage led to the cellar.

The shaft was built of brick, and in the side opposite to the opening through which the girl was peering, some strong iron spikes were driven into the wall, one below the other, in regular succession.

The reason why the spikes were driven into the wall flashed upon the girl immediately.

They were to serve as a ladder, so that any one sufficiently agile, and with nerves strong enough to attempt the feat, might either ascend to the apartment or descend from it.

Kate was no coward, and she had perfect confidence that she could accomplish the task, although she was a little doubtful as to where the passage would lead.

"Never mind!" she exclaimed, after debating the matter in her mind for a moment. "I will risk it. I cannot very well be any worse off than I am here.

"Almost any change must improve the situation."

Into the dark passage then she fearlessly went.

Her woman's garb was an impediment, but she was strong-armed and agile-footed.

The task was not so difficult as it seemed for the passage was so small that it was possible for the climber to rest and take, partially, the weight from the hands and feet by pressing against the wall.

This fact Kate discovered before she had descended a dozen steps, and it cheered her exceedingly.

"No danger now but that I will reach the bottom in safety," she muttered.

Hardly had the words left her lips, when she felt the spike on which she had just placed her right foot give under her weight.

An exclamation escaped from her lips and she clung for dear life with her hands.

The alarm was a false one, though, for the spike only yielded a trifle and at the same time the door above, through which she had gained entrance to this mysterious shaft, closed noiselessly, plunging the passage into utter darkness.

The girl immediately comprehended why the spike had yielded.

It was connected by a wire, probably, with the secret door, and when sufficient weight was brought to bear upon it the door was forced to close.

"Perhaps it opened in the same way, too," the girl murmured, as she resumed her downward passage, "but I am not sure of that, and now I must go on, for I may not be able to retrace my steps."

It was a long and weary climb and more than once the girl was forced to stop and rest, and each time she peered into the darkness beneath, anxious to behold the end.

The air seemed to grow damper and more dense.

"If I was at the very top of the house, I must be near the cellar now," she soliloquized.

The words were hardly spoken when to her ears came the sound of hoarse voices apparently raised in anger.

She halted for she feared that danger was near.

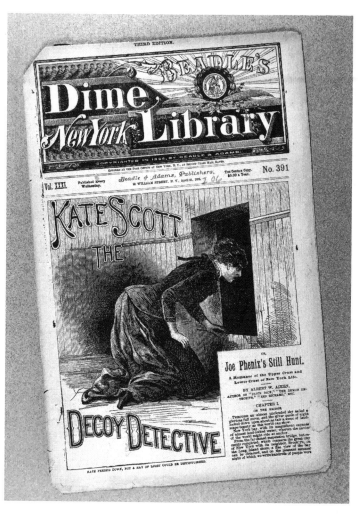

05. "Kate peered down; not a ray of light could be distinguished." *Kate Scott, The Decoy Detective, Or, Joe Phenix's Still Hunt*, was published as a complete story in the Beadle's New York Dime Library issue of April 21, 1886. This copy is a "Third Edition" printing, probably from around 1891. Original size 9 inches wide and 13 inches tall.

CHAPTER VIII.
A TALE OF MURDER.

It was a fortunate circumstance for our heroine that the voices reached her ears at the time they did, for she was within four feet of the ground, and her foremost foot rested upon the last spike, as she speedily discovered when she attempted to find the one beneath it.

It was just at this moment that the coarse, hoarse voices fell upon her ears, and glancing downward she saw the glimmer of a light below.

She had evidently descended to the cellar, and now, that she took time to reflect upon the matter, she understood the nature of the secret passage by means of which she had escaped from the prison pen.

It was a chimney flue leading from a fire-place in the cellar and some inventive genius had utilized it so as to open a means of communication with the secret chamber that must be at the very top of the house.

The idea too came into the mind of the girl that the secret passage was not known to the people who were now in possession of the mansion, for there were no signs that the passage had been recently used.

The men in the cellar were so near that the girl could plainly hear every word that passed between them, and she was almost afraid to breathe lest it should lead to her discovery.

There were two of them only, and they had evidently just descended into the underground apartment,

"Look a'here, Four Kings, I don't exactly git the rights of this thing through my hair," said one of the men.

"Stingy Bill, you never did have any brains," responded the other, in contempt.

As the reader will perceive the men were the same two ruffians who had captured the girl, but she was not aware of this fact, for the assault had been committed so adroitly that she had not been afforded a chance to identify either of the men.

"Oh, well, I've got enough to swear by, I reckon," rejoined the other, placidly. "It's sich smart cracks as you what are always gittin' into musses. I know enough to get along, but I must say this here business is too much for me. Of course, I s'pose the captain knows what he's up to, but I'm blessed if I do."

Kate listened intently, for she perceived there was a chance that she might pick up some valuable information.

The reference to the captain impressed her particularly, for she had an idea that the captain was the man who had called himself Henry Tappan.

"Don't you make any mistake about that," observed the other. "The captain wasn't born yesterday, and you can bet all the money you can get your hooks on that he knows the time of day as well as any man going."

"But see here, Four Kings, it 'pears to me as if the boss was takin' a deal of trouble for nothin'. What's the use of all this bother 'bout the stiff?— why not get rid of it in the usual way?"

"Stingy Bill, you've got a thing that looks like a head on your shoulders, but when it comes to doing any thinking, it ain't of much more use to you than a pine knot. There's money in this business, and don't you forget it."

"Well, I'm blamed if I kin see it !" responded Stingy Bill.

"I can put it to you in a minute," said Four Kings. "Do you ever read the newspapers?"

"No, I can't say as how I do as a general thing."

"Then I suppose you don't know that there is a reward offered for the recovery of the body?"

"No! Is there?"

"Yes—five hundred dollars, and the captain, after thinking the matter over, came to the conclusion that he was just as good a man to collar that little five hundred as could be found. But the trouble was to deliver the body up so as to get the reward without betraying how the man came to die."

"I see—I see! I've got brains enough to understand that."

"Wonderful!" the other retorted. "Well, the captain put on his thinking-cap, and at last hit on a plan.

"You know, it wasn't in the programme for this old duffer to be put out of the way at all. His death was an accident.

"He was lured away and then drugged so we could get at the five thousand dollars that he very foolishly carried around with him, instead of putting it in a safe place as soon as possible after he received it.

"Through some mistake the dose was made too strong and it killed the man.

"The captain reckoned that he must have been troubled with heart-disease or something of that kind or else it wouldn't have laid him out. We hadn't any idea of doing him in as there wasn't the least bit of use to kill the old fellow, seeing that we could easily get at his boodle without taking much risk.

"But I reckon his time had come and so he made a die of it. His folks took the alarm when he was discovered to be missing, and as I said, offered five hundred for any information of him if living, or the same amount for the recovery of his body if he was dead."

"And the captain thinks he would like to git his grip on the five hundred," Stingy Bill remarked.

"Now you are shouting, Bill," his companion replied, "and why shouldn't he go for the stamps? The old man's body is of no use to us, and of course we have to go to the trouble of getting rid of it. Now the captain's idea is, instead of committing the stiff to the water in the usual way, to take it in a box to some lonely spot and then have one of the gang accidentally run across it so as to claim the reward offered for the discovery of the body."

"Ain't it risky?" asked the other, in a doubtful sort of way. "S'pose the police take it into their heads that the man who discovers the body had something to do with the old cove's death?"

"Don't you worry 'bout that. I can just tell you that what the captain don't know ain't worth knowing. He's as full of tricks as a monkey.

"Jackey Candorson, you know, Jackey the Milkman, is the party who is to discover the body. His record is just as square as can be; the police never had reason to put their flippers on him yet.

"That's the captain's little game, you see. Jackey is a mighty useful man in spying out cribs worth cracking, and the Cap has always been careful not to have him mixed up in any jobs."

"I see now, and I've often wondered why Jackey never took a hand when there was work to be done."

"That was so the police should not be able to get onto him. If he once fell under suspicion of being crooked, his peculiar usefulness would be destroyed. Now this little trick is just as simple as can be.

"Jackey lives on the outskirts of the city, near his cow-stable, and it is quite a lonely spot, particularly after nightfall, for it is beyond the gaslight region, and there's no travel at all out there to speak of after nine o'clock."

"That's just the spot for such a job as this. "

"Exactly. Well, five or six hundred yards beyond Jackey's place there's an old barn that he has been dickering to buy for five or six months.

"It hasn't been used for a year or so, and has been tightly locked all the time.

"Jackey came to terms with the owner, and bought the property this afternoon. Of course, as is only natural under the circumstance, he with a couple of his boys will go to examine the property to-morrow, and in the barn they will find the body, do you see?"

"It's jest fixed splendid, ain't it?" cried the other in a burst of admiration.

"Oh, I tell you, the captain's got a head on his shoulders. Or course, everybody will wonder how the old man got into the barn, but in his pocket a key will be found which will fit the lock of the side-door, and as there isn't the least sign of violence on his person, the thing will be the biggest mystery that anybody has known for a long time.

"But how 'bout getting the stiff to the barn?"

"That will be the only difficult and risky part of the job, but the captain has arranged it so nicely that it's a hundred to one against failure."

"There's a covered express wagon in the stable, a common-looking concern with the roan mare hitched to it. That box yonder will just about hold the body."

"We'll put it in the box, carry it by the underground passage to the stable and place it in the wagon, then drive to the barn. We can cover the distance in an hour easily enough."

"I see, and if there isn't anybody 'round, we h'ist

the thing into the barn."

"Just so and bring the box back, so as to cover up the trail."

"I don't see why it won't work."

"It will unless some unlucky accident occurs. But come, we must get to work. Give me a hand to put the body in the box, and then we'll cover it over with the cloth."

Kate heard the men shuffling about the cellars as though they were carrying a weighty burden, and after a minute or so the man who bore the odd name of Four Kings said:

"Now, Bill, give me the hammer and nails for it will be as well to tack the cover down, for fear of accidents.'

"Blame me if I didn't forget the hammer!" the other exclaimed. "Here are the nails, hammer 'em in with the butt of my revolver."

"Oh, no; do you want to spoil the tool? I'll get the hammer and you take a look in the street so as to see if the coast is clear."

"All right."

Kate listened until the footsteps of the two rascals died away in the distance, and then she descended from her perch in the secret passage and emerged from the fire-place into the cellar.

A means of escape from her present dangerous position had flashed upon her mind.

06. "Four Kings"

CHAPTER IX.
THE ESCAPE.

The girl had been thinking deeply while listening to the conversation of the strangers.

That she was in the secret haunt of a desperate and determined band of outlaws was quite evident. She also suspected that the man whom the two referred to as the "captain" was no other than the man who had lured her sister away; the man who called himself Henry Tappan.

And as this became evident to her the darkest thoughts filled her mind.

She had believed that the account he had given her in regard to her sister's fate was true, but now she had learned what a consummate scoundrel he was, she wavered.

The story might be all a lie; her sister might be still alive and—horrible thought!—in the power of this vile ruffian.

At all hazards she must make her escape and seek the counsel of the veteran detective.

Possessed of the clews which she would now be able to give him, perhaps he would be able to guess at the identity of the captain of this murderous band.

It was a bold idea that had entered the mind of the girl.

She realized that it would be an almost impossible task to escape from the cellar without encountering some member of the outlaw band who would most certainly give an alarm which would lead to her recapture.

The scheme she had conceived was to take the place of the murdered man in the box and permit the ruffians to transport her to the old barn.

Then her idea was to rise up before them the moment the box was opened, enveloped in the cloth, trusting to inspire them with a sudden fright and so make them take to their heels in the belief that the ghost of the dead man had come.

Circumstances favored the bold girl.

The ruffians had left a lantern behind them, so Kate had ample light to see what she was about, and, what was still more lucky, the man who had proposed to hammer the nails with the butt of his revolver had left the weapon on the rude table where he had placed it for the accommodation of his partner.

It seemed like inviting discovery to possess herself of the weapon but the girl could not resist the temptation.

It was a seven-shooter, a small, but serviceable weapon.

The pistol secured she removed the dark cloth which the ruffians had flung over the remains of the murdered man, exposing to view the corpse of an elderly gentleman. The body was neatly dressed, and from the appearance was evidently that of a respectable, well-to-do citizen.

The girl was naturally strong and so she managed to remove the body from the box and concealed it in a dark recess under the cellar stairs.

Then she took its place, covering herself up with the cloth, endeavoring to assume as nearly as possible the exact position in which the body bad been placed.

Hardly had she comfortably bestowed herself when the footsteps of the returning ruffians fell upon her ears.

Both of them were returning, one coming down the cellar stairs, the other from the extreme end of the cellar where a secret underground passage led to the stable. They came up to the box.

The cover was placed upon it and a couple of nails, lightly driven in, held it in its place.

"We mustn't nail it on too strongly, you know," Four Kings observed, "for when we get to the barn the cover must be taken off so we can get the stiff out. The box comes back with us, for if we were to leave it there, it would be sure to excite suspicion.

"Now then, pick up your end and come on," continued the speaker.

"All right, but I say, what did you do with my revolver?" asked Stingy Bill, who had looked on the table for his weapon and found it not.

"I don't know anything about your revolver," responded the other.

"Didn't you take it off the table?"

"Nary take."

"I laid it there, you know, for you to use in hammering the nails in the box."

"Yes, I know you offered me the weapon but I didn't take it."

"The blazes you didn't!" growled Stingy Bill in amazement.

"Nary time."

"Well, if you didn't take it, what did become of it?"

"How on earth should I know?

"I'll swear I laid it on the table!" exclaimed the perplexed ruffian.

"If you did, it would be there, unless the stiff collared it while we were absent," replied the other, with a grim attempt at a joke.

"Blame me if this here don't bother me!"

"Oh, you took it up in the stable with you, and you'll find it there."

"Mebbe so," the other responded, although in his own mind he felt certain that he had left the weapon on the table, but it was possible that he was mistaken.

The two lifted the box and carried it through the secret passageway into the cellar of the stable and then ascended to where the horse and the covered express-wagon stood.

They placed the burden in the wagon and then while Four Kings mounted to the seat and took up the reins the other opened the stable doors.

Kate within her hiding-place was able to overhear all that passed.

"All serene, not a soul about," answered Stingy Bill.

"The captain has looked out for that," Four Kings replied, as he drove out of the building.

Stingy Bill closed the stable doors after the wagon passed through and hastened on ahead to open the gate.

When the wagon got into the road it halted until Bill closed the gate and mounted to the seat beside Four Kings.

"Go ahead!" said Bill, after he was fairly in position, and Four Kings immediately gave the lines a slap on the horse's back and away they went.

Luckily for the girl, cramped within the narrow confines of the box, the ruffians had placed the box in the wagon right side up, and so she was far more comfortable than she would have been if they had reversed it.

Hardly a word passed between the pair during the trip, which occupied about half an hour.

The time seemed terribly long though to the imprisoned girl and she thought the journey would never end.

At last, however, the wagon stopped, the destination being reached.

"We've had a regular streak of luck to-night," Four Kings remarked as he jumped out of the vehicle. "We haven't met a soul. Now if we can get the stiff into the barn and get off without being noticed by any one we shall be all O. K."

"Let's hurry then for I reckon this is the pull jest now!" Stingy Bill declared.

The barn was a hundred feet or so from the road, and in quite a lonely situation, the nearest house being fully three hundred yards away. And as there weren't any lights visible it seemed probable that the inmates had retired to rest.

The night was dark, no moon shining, although the heavens were liberally spangled with countless stars, and as the confederates had driven the wagon around to the rear of the barn there did not seem to be much danger of their being discovered.

Four Kings unlocked the barn door and the two carried the box into the building. Then, being provided with a dark lantern and a hatchet, Four Kings proceeded to pry up the lid of the box.

But just as he loosened one end of the lid an unforeseen event took place.

Neither one of the two had taken the precaution to fasten the horse, thinking she would stand without any trouble. But the beast was an old and sagacious animal and did not at all relish this night work. So, when she discovered that the humans who had her in charge had disappeared, and anxious to get home to her stable, she turned quietly about and set off for home.

"Blazes! There goes the horse!" cried Four Kings, dropping his tool.

"We ought to have fastened the cursed beast— 'tain't the first time the roan mare has tried it on; but we kin catch her easily enough, for she always goes along on a little jog-trot," the other replied. Then the two, in hot haste, ran out of the barn and gave chase to the horse.

It really seemed as if Heaven itself was taking the part of the captive girl.

Kate, who had overheard every word of the conversation, was quick to improve the opportunity.

The box cover being loosened at one end was no obstacle to her escape, and soon she was at liberty.

Hastening to the door, she could easily distinguish, thanks to the stillness of the night, the sound of the retreating horse and the rumble of the wagon-wheels, as well as the rapid footsteps of the men in pursuit.

She only paused a moment on the threshold, and then gathering up the cloth that had disguised her person in the coffin, she turned and fled in the opposite direction as fast as she could run, yet at the same time taking care that her footsteps should not be heard.

Down the road a few hundred yards another road crossed the first at right angles, and into this she turned. Five minutes more and she came to another cross-road.

This also she took, turning to the left this time, her idea being to baffle pursuit if any should be given, although it was not likely that the ruffians, upon returning to the barn and discovering that the body had disappeared, would be apt to think it had run away and set out in chase.

Ten minutes of active exertion, and then Kate relaxed into a walk.

She felt she was safe.

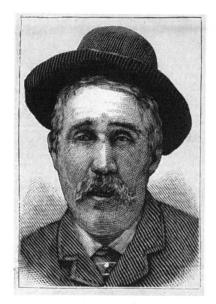

07. "Stingy Bill"

CHAPTER X.
IN THE NIGHT.

There was not a sound stirring save the usual noises of the night which prevail in the neighborhood of a big city—in the suburban districts.

The distant cry of a watch-dog rose on the air, answered almost immediately by the long-drawn howls of a dozen other curs, yelping, they knew not at what.

Then the distant whistle of a locomotive, "piercing the night's dull ear," resounded.

The shrill cry of the tree-toads, the crickets and the little insects that hold high carnival when the dark mantle of night falls upon the earth, rose clear and full.

On went the girl with sturdy step through the darkness, her heart full of gladness that she had so fortunately escaped the trap which had been set so cunningly for her.

There was not the least doubt in her mind in regard to Mr. Henry Tappan now.

The man was a thorough-paced scoundrel—no doubt at all that he was the captain of a band of desperate law-breakers, banded together to defy the power of justice.

And if her sister, the idolized Louise, had perished as this arch villain had described, it may have been through the kindness of a merciful Heaven when she discovered the truth in regard to the man to whose care she had committed her young life.

"I will avenge her—I will fearfully avenge her!" Kate cried as she walked along the lonely road.

Busy as she was in thought her senses were keenly on the alert.

She had not the slightest idea as to where she was

going. That she was in the suburbs of Brooklyn was probable, although it was possible that during the temporary insensibility produced by the use of the drug upon her at the time of the assault, she might have been transported to the upper part of New York and that she was now in the Westchester district, as the annexed portion of the great metropolis, north of the Harlem River is termed.

That she was in the neighborhood of some big city was apparent, although the country she was now traversing was as lonely as though it were a hundred miles from a populous town.

But Kate had a stout heart and went on without the least fear.

Then, too. she was amply armed against danger, for she had not relinquished the revolver which she had so fortunately obtained.

She was used to fire-arms and knew how to handle such a weapon from her young life in the Catskill Mountains. And having tried its workings, found it was in excellent order.

Pursuit being distanced, although she did not think there was much danger that any attempt in that direction would be made, all she had to do now was to find out where she was and then turn her steps toward home.

For all she knew she might be walking away from the city instead of toward it.

A man came shuffling along the road.

A rather undersized, thick-set fellow with a somewhat disreputable look.

Kate's eyes had by this time become accustomed to the gloom, so she had no difficulty in ascertaining the character of the new-comer, and the impression he produced was so unfavorable that normally she would never have thought of accosting him for information.

But it was Hobson's choice this time. This man or none.

Wayfarers seemed to be few and far between, and the girl felt that it would not do for her to go blindly on in the dark, for, although she was not certain in regard to the exact time, yet she felt sure it was quite late and she knew she could not go wandering in this uncertain way all night.

So, despite the repugnance that the man inspired, she determined to address him.

She took the precaution though to cock the revolver which she carried concealed in the folds of the cloth.

The cloth, which was a good-sized piece of coarse, dark stuff, she had wound around her head like a shawl, for she could not very well make her way through the open country bare-headed.

And now, thanks to its folds, she was able to prepare the pistol for immediate use, without exposing the fact that she had a weapon.

"Will you have the kindness to tell me if this road will lead me to Brooklyn?" she said, as the man approached.

The man halted, Kate followed his example, and he peered into her face in an insolent sort of way.

"Well, no, it won't. You're on the wrong track. You're heading now for Canarsie, but you kin git a train there, what will take you to Brooklyn. It's only a mile or so."

"Keep straight on?"

"Oh, yes. Follow your nose, and you can't miss it.

"Thank you," and Kate made a movement to go on, but the man got right in her way.

"Say, you ain't got no politeness! Ain't you going to pay a feller something? You might give me two or three kisses, anyway."

"Out of my path, you scamp!" cried the angry girl, and she thrust the revolver under his nose.

The man staggered back demoralized and it was lucky for him that he did so, for in her excitement Kate's finger bore heavily on the trigger, and the pistol was discharged.

Over on his back went the rascal with a howl of terror. He thought he was shot, although the bullet did not come within a yard of him.

Kate felt sure she had not injured the man, and so she hastened on her way.

It did not take her many minutes to walk the mile. No one molested her, and at Canarsie she took a train which carried her to Brooklyn. In due time she arrived safely at her boarding-house in New York, tired out but otherwise none the worse for her strange adventure.

Our heroine boarded on Fourth Avenue, near Twenty-third Street, in one of the old-fashioned three-storied brick houses so common in that locality.

Her room was a small, comfortable apartment on the second floor, and the window in it looked out on the rear yard.

There was a back piazza attached to the house and on the roof of the piazza the girl kept quite a collection of flowers in pots.

She had boarded there ever since she had been cast upon her own resources and had come to be regarded as one of the family.

Being provided with a latch-key she had no difficulty in entering the house and making her way to her apartment, although all the lights were out and everybody, apparently, in bed.

She knew it was late, for she noticed that the streets through which she had passed in coming home were almost deserted, but had not been able to ascertain the hour for she did not notice any clocks while *en route*.

After gaining access to her apartment and lighting her lamp, though, she was annoyed to discover that it was nearly half-past one by the little clock which ticked upon her mantle-piece.

"Why I hadn't the least idea it was anywhere near as late as that!" she exclaimed.

Despite the strange adventures through which she had passed, she did not feel fatigued, the excitement seemed to have given her unnatural strength.

And now that she was safely at home she sat down to reflect.

After a year of weary work and disappointment she felt that at last she was on the threshold of success.

As she had feared, the man, who with his wily ways and specious tongue had enticed her sister away, was a villain of the deepest dye.

Her persistent search and vigorous attempts to discover his whereabouts had alarmed him and he had concluded that such a tireless sleuth-hound must be made to give up the chase. So he had then schemed to get her into his power.

The attempt had not only failed but it had given her a clew upon which she might work.

Then too, she had faith that some good results would be obtained from her meeting with the two young bloods, the dudes, whom she had encountered on the bridge.

She believed that they were acquainted with the arch villain, although not posted as to his real character, for it was evident he was moving in good society, and so obtained a knowledge of the birds worth plundering. From what she had overheard while concealed in the cellar, it was evident the betrayer of her innocent sister was the captain of as desperate a band of men as had ever been known.

From the dudes she hoped to gain information which would enable her to identify the man she sought.

The threads of the mystery were in her hands, and now she had the promised aid of the most renowned thief-taker in the country, the famous Joe Phenix. Kate felt sure that the moment the information was made known to him he would be able to hit off the right trail, and in time revenge her wrongs.

The girl meditated over the matter until the hands on the clock pointed to the hour of two, and then, happening to notice how time was flying, she arose, disrobed, put out the light and retired to rest.

Nature at last asserted her rights and within ten minutes Kate was fast asleep.

How long she slept she knew not, but it did not seem to her as if she had hardly closed her eyes when she was suddenly awakened.

Some one outside on the roof of the piazza had knocked over one of the flower-pots and it had rolled off the roof crashing into the yard below.

The moment she awoke she sat up in bed and grasped the revolver which she had taken the precaution to place under her pillow.

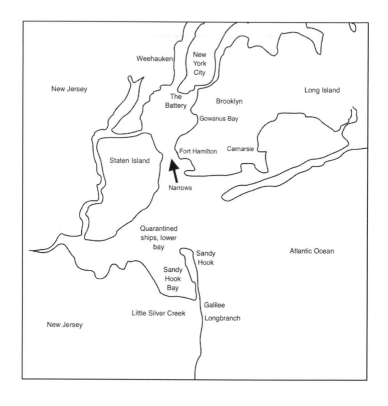

08. The areas near New York City where the story of
Kate Scott, The Decoy Detective takes place.

CHAPTER XI.
THE SPIDER CAPTAIN.

As the ruffians had anticipated, the overtaking of the horse was not a difficult matter.

The animal had not the slightest intention of running away.

He was far too well trained and entirely too lazy to do anything of the kind. He was merely hastening along, homeward bound, at his usual jog-trot.

And when he heard the men running after him—they did not dare to shout to the beast for fear of calling the attention of any one who might be in the neighborhood to their movements—the animal kept on just the same, neither increasing his speed or relaxing it, so they were forced to chase him some hundreds of yards before they succeeded in capturing him.

Stingy Bill was proceeding to swear at the brute for the trouble he had caused, but Four Kings, who was by far the shrewder of the two, stopped him.

"Oh, come, shut up!" he said. "It won't do any good to curse the horse. He don't know any better, and it serves us right for not tying him."

"I'd like to kick the stuffin' out of him, though!" Stingy Bill cried, viciously, as the two retraced their steps to the barn.

This time they were careful to tie the beast so that he could not repeat the trick if he felt disposed to be ugly.

"Mighty nasty trick, I tell you," said Stingy Bill. "If any country chumps had happened to come along and noticed the muss they might be curious as to what we was a-doing in this neighborhood, 'cos they would have spotted us for strangers instanter."

"It would have been ugly; you can bet high on that," Four Kings remarked. "But luck is with us to-night, for nary a soul has been along. Now let's hurry up and get through the job."

Then the two re-entered the barn.

The girl had been careful to replace the lid of the box so that everything looked exactly as it was when they had left.

So it was without the slightest suspicion of the discovery that awaited them that the two jerked off the lid of the box and peered into the empty receptacle.

"Blazes!" exclaimed Four Kings.

"Durn me for a sucker!" cried the other.

And then the two stared at each other for a moment in silent wonder.

They were stupefied by this unexpected discovery.

"What in thunder does this mean?" Four Kings exclaimed at last.

"Well, I'll never tell you, as they say in Kentucky," replied Stingy Bill.

"Can the old man have come to life and walked off while we were after the horse?" was the natural inquiry of the other.

"Durn me if it don't look like it."

"Oh, but the idea is ridiculous! The man has been dead for three days, and he was cold and stiff when we put him into the box."

"That's so—stiff as a red herring."

But in spite of these emphatic declarations, the two glared about them as though they expected to see the old man lurking in some dark corner of the barn.

"I say, Four Kings, he was in the box safe enough, wasn't he?" Stingy Bill observed dubiously, as though he was not so certain about the matter as he pretended.

"Of course! Didn't we put him in ourselves? There couldn't be any mistake about that."

"Yes, it seems to me as if we certainly did put him in. But I say, suppose we made a mistake about the matter?"

"Mistake how?"

"We might have thought we put him in and didn't."

"Oh, I'm sure we put him in; besides, lift the box," and Four Kings took hold of an end and tilted the case on one side. "Can't you see it that it isn't near as heavy as it was when we brought it in? And where's the cloth too? I'll swear that the cloth was in the box, whether the body was or not."

Stingy Bill tried the weight of the box, and being in a contrary turn of mind, took it into his head that it was almost as heavy as it was when they carried it into the barn.

"I don't see that there is any difference in the weight," he remarked.

"The blazes you don't!" cried Four Kings, enraged at the stupidity of his companion.

"Nary time!"

"Well, all I've got to say is that I wouldn't give much for your judgment," retorted the other. "To my thinking there's a big difference."

"Mebbe there is, but I don't see it."

"One thing is sure: the stiff ain't here now, whether he was or not."

"There ain't any doubt 'bout that."

"And the quicker we get back to the captain and let him set his thinking-machine to work on this puzzle the better."

Stingy Bill shook his head in a doubtful sort of way.

"Hadn't we better keep it dark?" he asked. "The captain is a reg'lar tornado when he gets going, and I reckon he'll be mad enough to cut us up, body and boots, when he comes to know the rights of the business."

"The captain is a good, square man, though, if you don't try to play any games on him. But if you do, then you had better keep your eyes peeled," Four Kings replied, slowly and with an air of great deliberation.

"Now I ain't a-going to get the captain after me if I know myself, and I think I do. I don't see as we have done anything wrong and I'm going to report the thing jest as it is."

"He'll blow the whole top of our heads off," Stingy Bill grumbled.

"If you're skeered and think you're going to get in over your head, you had better swim out," Four Kings suggested. "But one thing I can tell you, and that is, you'll have to make good time and put considerable ground between yourself and this 'ere section for to get out of the captain's reach.

"He's got a mighty long pair of arms when he's reaching for a man that he's got a grudge against."

"Oh, I was only talking for the sake of hearing myself talk," replied Bill, evidently alarmed by Four Kings' ominous words.

"I ain't afeared but what the captain will do us justice."

"Let's travel then; lend a hand with the box."

The two carried the box to the wagon, then got into it and drove to the house from whence they had come at the best speed of which the horse was capable.

Leaving the vehicle and horse in the stable they hurried into the house, using the secret passage leading into the cellar.

It did not take them long to discover the body of the old man and of course, when they found it, they immediately understood what had happened.

Or, at least, Four Kings made a shrewd guess at the mystery, for to solve any such puzzle was altogether too much for Stingy Bill's dull brains.

"I see how the trick was worked!" Four Kings exclaimed. "While we went for the tools some one who was hiding here in the cellar, took the body out of the box and got into it. Then while we were chasing the horse, he slipped out of the barn."

A new light suddenly broke upon Stingy Bill. "You're right, Four Kings, jest as sure as you are standing in sole leather!" he exclaimed. "And that is jest where my revolver went. The fellow lifted it, 'cos I'm certain I left it here when we went into the stable."

"I reckoned you was a little off your base, Bill," Four Kings observed, "but I see now that you were right about it."

"What's to be done?"

"Notify the captain at once."

Then Four Kings went to the wall just at the foot of the cellar stairs and whistled through a speaking tube which was there.

There was a moment's wait and then a sharp, imperative voice asked:

"What, is it?"

"That's the captain himself," Bill remarked.

"Yes, and it's lucky he's to the fore."

Then Four Kings answered through the pipe: "Something wrong down here. Can't you come down and look into it?"

"Who's down there?"

"Four Kings and Stingy Bill."

"All right, I'll be down in a minute."

"The captain will get to the bottom of the thing if any man can," Four Kings remarked, confidently, to his companion.

And then the two sat down on the stairs side by side to wait for the master spirit of the gang.

About ten minutes elapsed, and then they heard the key grate as it turned in the lock of the door above.

They rose to their feet, and a tall, well-built man, with a very pale face and a short black beard which covered the lower part of his countenance almost to the eyes, came down the steps.

He was rather poorly dressed in a dark, rough suit and wore a soft slouch hat pulled down over his forehead, almost to the very large, bushy, bristling eyebrows which overshadowed his piercing black eyes.

Take him for all in all, the Spider Captain, for so the captain of the band was termed, had an appearance so remarkable that no one who had ever had the opportunity to get a good look at him would ever be apt to forget his strange looks, though years and years intervened between the first view and the second.

The lantern upon the floor of the cellar dimly illuminated the scene.

"Well, boys, what's broke?" asked the outlaw leader, in a shrill, sharp voice, fully as peculiar as his appearance.

Four Kings took it upon himself to explain what had occurred, which he did at length, interrupted now and then by a sharp, short question from his chief, and soon the Spider Captain was in possession of all the facts.

CHAPTER XII.
A MURDEROUS DETERMINATION.

He was puzzled to understand the strange affair, and said as much after Four Kings finished his recital.

"I don't doubt that you have got the thing straight enough," he added. "There isn't any doubt in my mind that you have hit the truth and the job was worked just as you think, but what gets me is, who is the party that did the trick? Who on earth could have been hiding in the cellar?"

"Mebbe it was a detective," suggested Stingy Bill, with a nervous glance around as though he expected to see a police spy spring out of some dark corner.

"If it was, the quicker we get out of this the better," the captain replied. "But I don't see how any sleuth-hound could manage to penetrate into the place.

"Was everything locked and all right when you entered?"

Both answered in the affirmative.

"Well, boys, it's a conundrum, and as I'm pretty good at that sort of thing I'll try to smell it out. In the mean time, as I don't want to be surprised and taken here like a rat in a trap, you, Four Kings, take a scout out by the front of the place, and Stingy Bill, put yourself on post in the rear, and if anything suspicious occurs let me know immediately.

"If it was a detective who got away, and the game is to nab us here, it will not be likely that the cops will come in force strong enough to entirely surround the place, so if we are on our guard we will be able to get out."

Both of the ruffians protested that they would be as watchful as foxes, and then departed.

After they were gone the captain picked up the lantern and proceeded to examine the cellar.

"The first thing is to find out where the fellow hid himself, and that bothers me, for there don't hardly seem to be room enough here anywhere for a good-sized cat to stow himself away without being discovered," he remarked, as he stood in the center of the apartment and glanced around him.

"If some infernal police spy has got on the scent it will be 'extremely unfortunate,'" he continued, "for if the police come down on us it may lead to the discovery of the secret cage and the pretty bird that I have ensnared therein, although it is not probable that the secret would be discovered unless some one has a clew to it, and it does not seem possible that such a thing could be.

"Not a single one of the band suspects that the room exists, so cunningly is it hidden, and I should not have suspected it myself if I hadn't stumbled, just by accident, on the passage that leads to it.

"No, no, I do not think there is much danger of that cubbyhole being discovered until the old house is torn down.

"By Jove!" the exclamation came rapidly from his lips.

His eyes had just fallen on the old fire-place at the extremity of the cellar.

"There's a fire place there; I remember now, I noticed it when I first examined the cellar. There's a flue to the chimney, of course, and if it is like the majority of the old-fashioned houses, it is plenty big enough, to shelter a man.

"There's where the spy found concealment, beyond the shadow of a doubt."

The captain hastened to examine the chimney,

flashing the lantern into the dark cavity.

"Aha! There are the footprints, sure enough," he exclaimed, as he beheld the plainly visible marks in the thick dust which had collected on the hearth.

And then another cry of amazement broke from his lips.

He had made a most unexpected discovery.

The footprints were not those of a man, but the dainty imprint of a woman's feet.

"What does this mean?" he cried, for the discovery made the mystery deeper.

Then he directed the rays of the lantern up the chimney.

As he had expected, there was but a single big flue, and it afforded ample room for a human to ascend.

Then his eyes fell upon the spikes driven in the wall.

"Hallo, hallo!" he cried; "that looks as if those had been driven in there so as to make the ascent of the chimney an easy matter.

"This old shell is a regular house of secrets, for I thought I had explored it pretty thoroughly, yet I hadn't the least suspicion of this wrinkle.

"The dust has been rubbed off the spikes, too," he continued, as he went on in his examination, "and that shows that some one has made use of them lately.

"I guess I will have to try this novel ladder, and see whither it leads."

The purpose was immediately executed.

Thanks to the spikes, the Spider Captain found it an easy matter to ascend the chimney.

Up he went, examining the wall carefully us he progressed, for he expected to find a secret door somewhere, until he came to the spike which communicated with the machinery of the invisible door.

And the moment he put his weight on the spike, the door into the secret apartment, which was just on a level with his head, opened.

A cry of rage broke from the lips of the outlaw leader as he looked into the secret chamber, so carefully hidden away in the middle of the house, and discovered that the bird had flown.

"The curse of all the fiends light upon this unlucky chance!" he cried.

"What marvelous stroke of fortune revealed to the girl the existence of this passage which I, who thought I knew all the secrets of the house, never suspected?"

Then he entered the room and looked around to see if he could discover aught that would be of service to him.

The hat of the girl was on the table, but otherwise there was no trace of her.

The Spider Captain looked about the room for a moment and then knitted his brows fiercely together.

"This girl must die!" he exclaimed. "She is not like the other. I thought that like pliant wax I could mold her to my purpose, but it is quite evident that for once in my life I have made a serious mistake.

"Few women have ever made any particular impression upon me, foolish, shallow creatures the most of them, not worthy of my attention.

"But this one is dangerous, and she must be silenced. Her persevering chase of me proves that there is a good deal of bloodhound about her, and in the end, if she is not put out of the way, she may succeed in doing me serious damage—perhaps succeed in accomplishing more than the officers of the law have ever been able to do.

"It would only be the old story of David and Goliath over again. Cunning succeeds where strength fails.

"Decidedly I must not wait for her to administer the blow, but strike the first one myself."

Then he re-entered the secret passage and descended to the cellar.

"Mighty strange that I never even suspected the existence of this passage," he muttered, as he made his way down the shaft, "and yet the girl managed to discover it before she had passed a day in the room."

The existence of the secret chamber was known only to the Spider Captain.

He had discovered the long-forgotten apartment by accident, and perceived immediately how useful the knowledge might be to him, and so had taken particular pains to hide the matter from the rest of the band.

He understood now how the girl had managed to make her escape as well as though he had been a witness to the whole proceeding.

After he had arrived in the cellar be summoned Four Kings and Stingy Bill, and briefly explained to them the discovery which he had made, carefully, though, suppressing all mention of the secret apartment.

"It was the girl whom you treated to a surprise-party this evening, boys, that has done the trick," he said. "I had her in a room upstairs, and she managed to get out, and in some way got into the cellar. Then she hid here somewhere, under the stairs probably, and took the place of the stiff in the box. And when you left the barn to catch the horse, she made her escape.

"It's an ugly business, but it might be worse, for as far as I can see, she couldn't tell where she was, unless one of you were careless enough to let out something while you were talking in fixing the box."

Both of the men immediately fell to thinking.

Stingy Bill was the first to speak.

"Blamed if I think we said much of anything at all," he observed.

"Oh, yes, we did," Four Kings added. "Bill, here, was curious to know what kind of a trick we were up to, and I spit out the whole business, like a durned fool. There wasn't a word said about the house, but I blowed the trick with the stiff."

"That upsets that little game then, and the quicker we get rid of the body in one of the old ways the better."

"Bury it or give it to the fishes?" Four Kings asked.

"Bury it; let the worms have a feast. As long as we can't collar the reward, I don't see any use of putting the money in anybody else's way," the Spider Captain replied. "But I will attend to that. I have other work on hand for you, and it must be attended to this very night."

"All right; we're on deck!" Four Kings exclaimed.

"This girl must be got at and silenced. She knows too much now to be allowed to live. Before morning dawns she must join the majority and cross the dark river that sweeps all around the world."

CHAPTER XIII.
CRACKING THE CRIB.

The Spider Captain was no common rascal; the successful manner in which he had defied all the efforts of the authorities to capture him and to break up the criminal league which he had formed was ample proof of that.

He was well served too, for he had a regular army of spies, and kept a far closer watch on the authorities than the chief of police with all the detectives under his command was able to do on the captain.

Some of the private detectives of the city too were in his pay,

There are many honest and honorable men in this new line of business, a product of our advanced civilization, and then, too. some of them are as big rascals as can be easily found.

Men without the least skill in the business which they pretend to follow, but possessed of an uncommon amount of ability to extract money from gullible clients without rendering any service for the buyer.

The Spider Captain had contrived to let these gentlemen—whose sole idea of the detective business was to get all the money they could for as little work as possible—understand that any information of value would be liberally rewarded.

And to the firm of private detectives most intimately connected with the Spider Captain, Kate Scott had applied for assistance when she had entered upon her persistent search.

The chief of this desperate criminal band was always careful to cover up his tracks as completely as possible, and not to a single soul had he confided the fact that he had masqueraded as a rich New York blood up in the Catskill region under the name of Henry Tappan.

But when the girl had entered upon her search with such ardor the detectives thought it wise to send word to the Spider Captain in regard to the matter.

The outlaw leader was not known personally to the detectives, and in fact, few of his band were ever honored with a sight of his face, for by thus keeping in the background he rendered identification difficult, and put it out of the power of any of his tools to betray him to the authorities.

In all such secret bands it is the traitorous informer who is most to be dreaded, as the history of the world amply proves.

The detectives had an idea that the outlaw chief might know something of this Henry Tappan, for they felt sure from the account given by the girl that he was some New York crook in disguise.

If Tappan was one of the Spider Captain's band, the captain would be glad to know that there was an inquiry afoot in regard to him. If he was not in the gang, but the Spider Captain knew the man, he might possibly put the detectives on the scent. The leader of the secret band professed ignorance in the matter, but was careful to learn all the particulars of the affair, and from that time he caused a watch to be placed upon the girl.

He did not trouble himself much about the matter in the beginning, because he did not believe it would amount to anything.

What chance was there for a single girl, alone and friendless, to damage a man like himself so securely entrenched.

But as days lengthened into weeks, and weeks into months, and still she persevered, he awoke to the consciousness that if she succeeded by any accident in hitting upon a clew she would be apt to cause him considerable trouble.

Then, too, he had taken pains to make himself acquainted with the girl, and had become interested in her.

She was altogether different from her sister, possessing a dash and vivacity that was charming. and the idea came into his mind that she could be made to prove almost invaluable to him in his criminal career if he could succeed in bending her to his will.

The reader knows how signally the outlaw chief failed in his attempt.

But thanks to the watch he had caused to be placed upon her, he knew exactly where to find the fugitive.

His first idea when he discovered that the girl threatened to prove dangerous was to have her put out of the way, for the Spider Captain was a man who thought no more of taking a human life, if he could profit thereby, than of killing a worthless dog.

And he had caused a careful examination to be made of the premises where she resided, in order to ascertain if she could be "got at" and put out of the way, in the silent watches of the night when slumber chained the senses of the great city's denizens.

So, when he had come to the conclusion that the girl must die, the method by which the deed could be accomplished had already been decided upon.

Four Kings and Stingy Bill had been the men selected by the outlaw leader to watch the girl, and they had made all preparation to murder her when the Spider Captain had suddenly changed his mind and concluded to alter murder into abduction, therefore they were prepared to carry out the original idea.

"The girl knows too much now to be allowed to

live," the Spider Captain declared. "She has a clew which if diligently followed up, will be certain to lead to our detection.

"It is her life or ours, boys, and I don't know how you feel about it, but as far as I am concerned, I prefer to let her take the jump into eternity rather than try the leap myself!"

"That's me, every time!" Four Kings exclaimed, emphatically.

"You bet, it's me, too!" added Stingy Bill.

"Go ahead on the old programme, then," the leader commanded. "She's a plucky little imp and will not have any difficulty in finding her way home, but you ought to be able to get there about as soon as she can, for the girl has a long distance to cover.

"Make a sure thing of the job—don't half do it, you know, for that would be a deuced sight worse than to let the matter alone."

"Don't be alarmed about that, captain," Four Kings replied. "We'll do the work up in first class style."

"Oh, yes, we ain't no slouches!" Stingy Bill protested.

"Away with you then, for there's no time to be lost. The girl will be pretty well played-out after the adventures she has encountered tonight and ought to sleep like a top."

"No doubt about that. We ought to do the job with mighty little trouble, for we laid out the whole business and know exactly where to go and what to do," Four Kings observed.

"You kin bet all your wealth on that!" Stingy Bill exclaimed. "The thing is jest as fine as silk, and we kin send her kiting into the other world afore she'll have time to open her mouth and give a single peep."

"Be careful, you know, don't leave any telltale traces," the outlaw leader cautioned. "Let it be one of those mysterious, bloody deeds which puzzle the police and shock the public."

"Oh, it will be all right; we can get into her room from the roof of the piazza. There's only a common catch on the window and we can easily open it with a knife."

"At it at once then, for there isn't any time to be lost!" commanded the chief.

The two set out, after providing themselves with the proper tools.

This business was no new thing for either one of them, for there were no more experienced "cracksmen" to be found in all the country than Four Kings and Stingy Bill, as the police records amply testified.

As luck would have it the two ruffians arrived at the house in Fourth Avenue, the "crib" which they intended to "crack," at the very moment that the girl, their destined victim, came up the street.

The ruffians were upon the opposite sidewalk, as they desired to inspect the house fully upon all sides before proceeding to business, and they recognized the girl the moment she came up the avenue.

"We'll have to wait for a couple of hours so as to give her time to get asleep," Four Kings observed.

Bill immediately expressed his discontent at this prospect, but the other reproved him by asking if he "expected to get the earth every time just for wishing?"

Satisfied from the darkness that reigned within the house that all the inmates were buried in slumber with the exception of the belated girl, the two turned into the side-street and proceeded along it until they came to the end of the high board fence which protected the yard of the corner house.

It was an easy matter for the two to scale the fence and descend into the yard on the other side, after being careful to ascertain that there wasn't any one near enough to observe the movement.

Once they were inside of the first yard it was not a difficult matter for the cracksmen to progress from yard to yard until they reached the one which appertained to the house wherein the girl resided.

At the back of this yard was a woodshed. It was not locked, and there was a small window in it that commanded a view of the casement of Kate's apartment.

The gleam of a light within showed that the girl was there, for her shadow appeared every now and then on the curtain.

The ruffians took refuge in the woodshed and there made themselves as comfortable as possible.

In twenty minutes the light was extinguished.

"Now then, we'll give her about an hour to set sound asleep and then we'll do the job," Four Kings observed to his companion.

For a full hour the two waited, and then, satisfied that all was favorable for the attempt, they proceeded to the accomplishment of their murderous design.

Their plan had been well digested and they knew exactly what to do. It was an easy matter to climb to the roof of the piazza. The catch of the casement yielded to the knife of Stingy Bill, and Four Kings cautiously raised the window-sash.

CHAPTER XIV.
ONE RUFFIAN CAGED.

The two were extremely skillful at this sort of business, and the delicate operation was performed in such an adroit manner that it would have been a light sleeper indeed who could have been disturbed by the slight noise.

But Stingy Bill was careless enough to strike his foot against one of the flower pots on the roof and it rolled into the yard beneath.

The noise was a slight one, though—hardly enough to awaken a sleeper well wrapped in the embraces of Morpheus.

"You're a clumsy brute," Four Kings growled.

"I couldn't help it; don't make no difference anyhow, I guess."

"I'll try climbin' in the window, and if she is awake she'll howl and then we'll git."

The sash being raised, the two paused and listened before they attempted to enter the room.

They listened intently, but not a sound could they hear.

It was plain that the inmate of the room had not been disturbed, for if she had been, most certainly she would either have made a noise by stirring in the bed, or by calling out in alarm.

"It's all right," Stingy Bill muttered. "She's sleeping like a top and we kin do the job without any trouble."

It was a noiseless and easy death that the ruffians destined for the girl.

She was to be chloroformed as she slept, and then a strong dose of prussic acid poured down her throat while in the insensible state, unable to help herself.

The vial which contained the poison was to be placed in the girl's hand, so it might be found there when the body was discovered; thus the murder might be made to appear like an act of self-destruction.

The Spider Captain had planned the operation in this adroit manner in order to avert suspicion.

The girl being found dead in her apartment, the door securely locked, the window fastened —this was arranged by means of a fine copper wire attached to the catch and operated from the outside—an empty bottle which had contained poison in her hand, it would be a shrewd brain indeed to suspect foul play.

"Oh, yes, she's safe enough, and we shall be able to settle her hash without giving her time to give a single squeak."

The curtain was down—it was hung on a spring roller that worked without a cord—and Four Kings drew it up, cautiously, and as he did so Stingy Bill put his leg over the window-seat, and thrust half of his body into the room.

It was a rather dark night, the moon not being visible, yet there was light enough to enable one to detect large objects a short distance away, but when the two ruffians peered into the room, for a moment they could not distinguish the girl, although there wasn't any doubt in their minds that she was lying on the bed.

"Go ahead, Bill, everything is all serene," said Four Kings in a whisper to his companion, but no sooner had the words left his lips than the two were treated to a surprise that completely astounded them.

There was a flash of flame, which for a moment illuminated the apartment, followed by a sharp report.

Imagine the disgust and anger which filled the

breasts of the two midnight marauders when by the aid of the powder's flash they discovered the girl, whom they fondly believed to be sleeping the sleep of the righteous, sitting bolt upright in the bed, with a revolver in her hand and a determined look upon her face, just as if she felt confident of her ability to cope with all the scoundrels in the world.

And to add insult to injury, Stingy Bill, too, felt sure that the revolver with which she threatened their lives was the very one which had been stolen from him in the cellar.

It was of a rather peculiar pattern, and Stingy Bill was certain that he could not be mistaken.

The first shot fired by the girl went wide of the mark, passing between the heads of the two men.

"Out with your pistol—kill her!" Four Kings cried, infuriated at the failure of the carefully planned attack.

The two men were desperate. The orders of the Spider Captain had been to kill the girl at all hazards.

Had not such been the case—if the two were merely on a plundering excursion—they would have retreated as quickly as possible the moment they discovered that the girl was awake.

But in this instance, so eager were they to carryout the commands of their leader, instead of retreating they pressed forward, determined to kill the girl, although they knew their were putting their necks in jeopardy by so doing.

Before either of the two could get a weapon out the girl fired again, and this time with so true an aim that the bullet struck Stingy Bill in the breast, and with a groan he fell backward on the roof of the piazza.

Four Kings attempted to catch him as he fell but Stingy Bill was so bulky that he carried the lighter man down with him.

Both landed in the yard.

"Are you hurt, Bill?" Four Kings cried. The two were old partners in crime; they had been pals for many a year, and it was a severe blow to the younger ruffian when he saw his companion laid low.

"Done for, I'm afeard," the other murmured, striving with all his power to refrain from groaning at the acuteness of his pains.

"I'll murder the she-devil for this!" Four Kings cried, fiercely.

Just then a policeman, warned by the shots, sounded the alarm with his club on the sidewalk in the cross-street.

"The jig is up for the present, anyway," gasped the stricken ruffian.

"You had better give leg-bail, Four Kings, or else they'll have you in limbo with the darbies on your wrists afore you know where you are."

"I hate to leave you!"

"Oh, I'm all right, or all wrong, maybe, but you can't do me any good by staying, so git out while you kin. Perhaps I'll pull through."

There was sound sense in this, and Four Kings was quick to perceive it.

The neighborhood had been alarmed by the shots, lamps were being lit, and light was beginning to appear in quite a number of the windows.

"All right then, I'll mosey. But I'll warn the captain so that you'll be looked after."

"So long," muttered the wounded man, faintly, weak from the effect of his hurt.

The conversation had been a hurried one, and had not occupied as many minutes as we have taken to detail it, so little time had been lost.

"Keep your spirits up, there's a good time coming!" was Four Kings' parting salutation, and then he hurried away.

It was not the first time that the veteran cracksman had been caught in just such a scrape, and he set about making his escape with perfect coolness.

He was a man of brains, and in a second he had thought out a feasible plan to escape from his perilous position.

The policeman was in the side street by means of which the two had gained access to the back yards of the houses which fronted on Fourth Avenue, so escape was cut off in that direction.

The houses on the block were about the same size and all of them had back piazzas, the roofs of which joined, therefore it was an easy matter for the fugitive to pass along the piazza roofs, in the opposite direction from which he had come, until he came to the end house in the block; then he descended to the fence and from the fence into the street.

The people in this direction were so far from the scene of the disturbance that they had not been disturbed by the sound of the shots, and Four Kings reached the street without exciting any alarm.

Once safe in the street, with that rare good-generalship characteristic of the master-scoundrel, he hastened along Fourth Avenue to the scene of the disturbance, as though happening to pass that way by chance, he had been alarmed by the noise.

By the time he reached the spot there was a small crowd gathered. The policemen had discovered the wounded man, and were waiting for an ambulance, which had been summoned, as Stingy Bill was so badly hurt as to be unable to walk.

The ruffian, with the cunning of his class, pretended to be under the influence of liquor, and swore roundly that it was a shame to shoot a man just because he had drank a little too much and was trying to get into his house without waking anybody up.

"Too thin!" was the policeman's comment, and when the ambulance arrived the ruffian was carried off.

The police surgeon's examination disclosed that, although the ruffian had received an ugly wound, there wasn't much danger of it proving to be a fatal hurt.

Nevertheless it was serious enough to warrant his being taken to the hospital.

On the next day Kate's evidence in regard to the affair was taken and a formal complaint entered against the ruffian.

Of course there wasn't the slightest doubt in the minds of the authorities that the man was attempting to enter the house for the purpose of plundering the inmates.

The girl had expected to encounter Phenix during her visit to the temple of justice, but in this she was disappointed.

Intelligence of the affair had reached him, and he regarded it as unlucky that the girl should have become mixed up in such a public matter.

It was his idea that a detective could not be too careful in keeping in the background.

If Kate became well known to the criminal classes, she would not be useful as a decoy.

Therefore, the girl did not meet Phenix until the time fixed for their appointment.

CHAPTER XV.
DOWN THE BAY.

The night was not dark, nor yet could it be called light.

We say night, although the hour of twelve had long since been marked by the clocks of the city and the wee small hours of the morning were close at hand.

Quite a fog had rolled in from the ocean and hung heavily over the bay, and the air was damp and disagreeable.

Hardly a breath of wind was stirring, and with the exception of the all-night ferry-boats wheezing and puffing through the heavy banks of vapor as if it was hard work, there was hardly a sign of life visible upon the river.

The police patrol-boat, though, was making its rounds as usual, gliding through the inky current like some dark, uncanny thing that would vanish into thin air before a blaze of light.

A spectral boat with a spectral crew.

But this was the game of the patrol. They could not hope to surprise the "river-rats"—as the thieves who operate on the water and along the river side are called—without due caution.

If the marauders had the slightest warning of the approach of the police-boat, they would take to their oars and row for dear life.

And as the thieves were invariably well-boated, and expert oarsmen pulling with muffled oars so that the sound of the tools working in the locks was materially deadened, that if they secured anything like a fair start and were aided by a fog it was almost impossible for the police-boat to overtake them.

These river-rats were desperate fellows, too, and had been known, when surprised with a rich booty, to show fight, and cases are on record when the thieves were strong and skillful enough to beat off the patrol-boat and compel the officers to seek reinforcements.

Rarely though are the marauders disturbed in their operations, for the police have an immense amount of water front to cover, and the means placed at their disposal are entirely inadequate to do good service.

All the thieves have to do is to pull their craft into the dark shadows of some obscure pier, near to the vessel which they intend to attack, and remain concealed there until the patrol-boat passes. The police-boat passes that place at about the same hour every night, so, after allowing a sufficient time for it to get well out of the way, the river-rats can glide back out upon their mission of plunder.

None of the police care much for the patrol service for it is disagreeable work at the best, besides involving considerable toil, and glad enough are the crews generally when the first gray streaks begin to line the eastern skies, heralding the coming of the dawn.

Not at all sorry are they when they can say, in the words of the poet:

The moon, in russet mantle clad,
Walks o'er the dew of yon high eastern hill;
Break we up our watch awhile.

On this particular night of which we write, not a single episode had occurred to break up and enliven the monotony of the tiresome round.

The patrol-boat had started out as usual, gone on its

accustomed way, the policemen muttering in discontent every now and then as the disagreeable damp air of the night seemed to cut to their very bones. The men peered into the dark recesses of the docks as they swept along on the bosom of the tide, in search of skulking water-rats. Ever and anon they took a sweep out on the open water where the moving lights, dancing up and down with the action of the swelling bosom of the troubled deep, showed that vessels were riding at anchor.

The night wore away and not a single suspicious craft did the patrol-boat encounter until after three in the morning.

The patrol boat had just rounded the Battery, at the extreme end of Manhattan Island, which is wholly taken up by the great young monster of a city, New York.

Making their way up the North River, the vigilant, cat-like eyes of the sergeant in charge of the boat detected a small sail-boat coming down the river. The officer fancied that the strange craft had just altered her course as if those on board of her had detected the approach of the patrol-boat and were anxious to keep out of the way.

This suspicion was quite enough to make the sergeant decide that it would be as well to examine the other craft and see what brought her out on the river at such an untimely hour.

With the whispered command to his men, "Give way lively, lads!" the officer changed the course of the boat and headed it so as to intercept the strange craft. On the approach of the police-boat the sail-boat had veered in quite a suspicious manner over toward the Jersey shore.

If there had been any breeze worth speaking about, the police-boat would not have found it an easy matter to overhaul the other craft, but as it was the sail was small benefit.

"Hello! Come about, I want to talk with you," the sergeant exclaimed, as he came within easy hailing distance of the boat. And as the officer spoke he flashed the light of his bull's-eye lantern upon the suspicious stranger.

"What will I come 'bout for, an' what do you want with me, anyhow?" asked a coarse voice, coming from the small boat, evidently the voice of an old man, and an illiterate one.

"This is the police patrol-boat, and I want to have a little talk with you, so come about without making any more talk, or I shall be under the disagreeable necessity of making it warm for you."

The officer spoke in a determined tone, and he drew forth his revolver and allowed the light of the lantern to play upon its polished barrel.

"I don't see what call you've got to trouble yer head 'bout honest people, going their own way an' mindin' their own business," the man grumbled, as he obeyed the command of the metropolitan officer and brought his boat up alongside of the police craft.

"Yes, but I don't know that you are honest, and that's what I want to find out," replied the sergeant, sharply. "This is a rather queer hour for a man to be out on the river, and your business may consist of helping yourself to other people's property for aught I know."

Thanks to the light afforded by the lantern, the police had a good view of the boat and its occupants.

We say occupants, for there were two persons in the boat.

The craft was a small keel-boat, considerably the worse for wear, and the sail was browned by age, and patched in a dozen places.

There was a large open basket, half full of soft

clams, with a lot of fish lines on top. This, with a pair of oars, a small grapnel for an anchor and a boat-hook, was all that the boat contained, besides the two humans.

And these two were, first, the man who had held the conversation with the sergeant; a heavily-built, weather beaten old fellow, somewhere between fifty and sixty, apparently, with bristling, iron gray hair visible below his headgear, and a stubby, matted beard of the same hue.

He was dressed like a fisherman, in rough, woolen clothes, and wore a regular waterman's sou'wester on his head.

The old man was at the tiller, which was merely a broken oar.

Forward of him, attending to the "sheet," was a tanned, bright-eyed lad, a boy about fourteen or fifteen, who had the look of the lower class of Italian boys. With his bright eyes, black as jet, shining like a pair of glass beads when the lays of light fell upon them, he stared in stupid astonishment at the police-boat and its occupants. The sergeant was disappointed.

He expected to capture a prize.

From the mysterious movement of the boat he had jumped to the conclusion that it was the craft of a river rat returning from some successful expedition, and he hoped to capture not only the thieves but the "boodle" also.

There wasn't any doubt about the matter, for there was no possible place in the boat where plunder could be concealed.

"What are you doing out in the river at such an hour as this?" the officer asked sharply. He really cherished an animosity against the pair in the boat because they had not turned out to be rogues.

"Goin' fishin', don't you see? Hain't blind, are ye?" responded the old man, fully as arrogant as the policeman.

"Say, you had better keep a civil tongue in your head!" cried the officer, angrily. "I have known men to get rich by being civil."

"I reckon you don't stand much chance to git rich then," retorted the old man.

"None of your impudence, or I'll run you in anyway, just for greens!"

"Well, if you do, I reckon it will be the biggest joke of the season. Ho, ho!" and the old man indulged in a hoarse laugh. "Mebbe the rest of the boys wouldn't poke fun at you, and I guess the newspapers would crack a heap of jokes at the expense of the cop what run in a poor old cuss of a fisherman and his I-talian boy."

"You shoot your mouth off too much!" cried the sergeant, sternly, feeling that he was getting the worst of this encounter of wits. "Who are you, and where are you going?"

"My name is Gideon Turtle, and I'm going down the bay after fish, as any fool might know."

"Mighty queer hour."

"No, 'tain't!" the other rejoined, shortly. "If you're after fish, and mean business, the earlier you git on the ground after sunrise the better. The fish are on the feed early in the morning and they are hungry, but after the sun gits up and the top of the water is warm they go down into deep water so as to keep cool. Do you see, I'm going for bluefish, and I reckon I'll git some, too!"

"Is that boy your son?" the officer asked, trying to get a chance to give the old fellow a shot.

"Not much. I ain't no I-talian."

"What's your name, boy ?" the sergeant queried.

"Me no speek goot English mooch," responded the lad, with an idiotic grin.

"Paolo is his handle, but I calls him Billy for short," remarked the old man.

"Well, take care that I don't run across you some night when you've got a 'boodle' aboard, for I know you're on the 'cross,' and I'll run you in, sure. Give way, men!"

Off went the police-boat, and then to the ears of the patrol came a remark from the old fellow:

"Don't take no great shuck of a man to be a police sergeant, Billy."

CHAPTER XVI.
WHO THEY WERE.

The remark coming plainly to the ears of the police sergeant, irritated him, and he was provoked into exclaiming:

"I believe there is something crooked about that old man and boy! It don't seem reasonable to me that anybody would be going after fish at such an hour as this."

"Well, I don't know, sergeant, about that," said one of the policemen. "These old cranks who follow fishing for a living are up to all sorts of queer practices. I shouldn't be surprised if he has given it to you straight enough."

"The durned old rascal!" and the sergeant shook his fist at the fast receding boat. "I would give a trifle to get a chance to run him in."

"He was a cheeky old blackguard, too fresh entirely," remarked one of the men.

Leaving the patrol boat to go on its lonely way, we will turn our attention to the other craft.

The old man and the boy kept their eyes on the police-boat until it was swallowed up in the gloom, and then the man turned to the boy, and, in an entirely different tone of voice from the one he had used while conversing with the police official, said:

"That was a pretty good test of the completeness of my disguise. That was Sergeant Murphy, and if there is a single man on the police force of New York who ought to be acquainted with me, Tom Murphy is the party."

"But he didn't recognize you," observed the other, with a laugh.

"No, not in the slightest degree, and although he had a suspicion that there was something wrong about us, he fell into the error of thinking we were abroad on crooked work intent."

"Oh yes, there isn't any doubt about that." The speaker had dropped the Italian boy business and was using as good English as can be generally heard.

"I'm glad the incident took place, for this is the first time I have ever tried a disguise of this kind and I was not quite sure it would be as perfect as some of my others," observed the old man, but there wasn't the slightest trace of age about the speaker now.

"If I have succeeded in pulling the wool over Sergeant Tom Murphy's eyes, there isn't much danger that any one else will be able to recognize me, for Tom and I have been intimately acquainted for years and he knows me as well as though he was my own brother."

"My disguise is not bad either, that's plain," remarked the other, "for none of the officers suspected that I was anything but an Italian boy."

"Oh, you are an apt scholar, and if you keep on in the way you have begun, I've no doubt you will be a credit to the profession."

Possibly by this time the reader has made a shrewd guess at the identity of the old man and the Italian boy.

The worthy police sergeant had reason for his suspicion. The two in the boat were not what they seemed, but he was on a false scent when he suspected they were engaged in some "crooked" business, for the old man was Joe Phenix, and the boy his Decoy Detective, Kate Scott.

The quest they were on, and why they had assumed such complete disguises, the reader will soon learn.

"It ought not to take us over an hour to run down the bay," mused Phenix, as the boat glided onward. "Even with this light breeze; if we had a fair wind we could do it in half the time."

"I am not competent to judge, for you have not yet informed me as to where we are going."

"True, I had forgotten that, but I did not know myself until I saw the superintendent of police," Joe Phenix answered.

"The worthy chief was unusually mysterious about the affair. He sent word yesterday morning that he wished to see me on particular business, and when I waited upon him, he was careful to assure himself that no one could possibly overhear what passed between us, and the first question he put to me was in regard to my ability to handle a sail boat.

"When I informed him that I was considered an expert in the management of all sorts of small craft, he appeared to think it was extremely fortunate, and then he came immediately to the business in hand.

"It was an important matter too. For some months now the police authorities have been satisfied that there is in existence in New York and its vicinity an organization of desperate criminals banded together for the purpose of defying the law.

"These men are bound by the most fearful oaths to be true to each other, and death is the penalty of treachery."

"Such organizations of rascals are quite common, too, I believe," the girl remarked, eager to learn all she could in regard to the scoundrels to whose destruction she had devoted her life.

"Oh, yes, it is only natural for these men who make a living by preying upon society to league together, for in union there is strength. And then, too, when it comes to a big job it is impossible to work the trick without three or four men, for the ground cannot be covered and the details properly attended to otherwise.

"But this organization is on a far more elaborate scale, and must not be confounded with these petty bands of outlaws," Phenix remarked.

"I presume not, or else the police authorities would be easily able to cope with it."

"Exactly, but this league seems to be one of the most elaborate and dangerous that has ever come to the notice of the police department.

"It was just by accident, too, that the superintendent got a clew to it, for he hadn't any suspicion that such an organization existed, although he has been puzzled to account for some large robberies which have been committed lately. The work was performed in such an adroit manner that it has been impossible for the police to secure any clew to the perpetrators, and yet from the way in which the trick was done it was clearly the work of experts.

"Two nights ago, though, one of the best-known 'cracksmen' in the country was shot in an up-town sporting-house in a quarrel with some of his pals, and as far as the police could ascertain, the trouble arose about the division of the plunder obtained by some bold robbery.

"The wounded man was carried to the hospital, but his assailants managed to escape, and the police were unable to get any clew to them.

"In the hospital the wound was examined, and the doctor expressed the opinion that it was mortal, and that the man had not three days of life left.

"When this fact was made known to him he fell into an intense rage. The wounded man declared he had been assassinated by the gang to which he belonged because he had kicked against the power wielded by the master spirit of the organization, whom he called the Spider.

"He swore he would give the whole thing away. He did not know personally the men who had forced the quarrel upon him, except that he felt sure they were 'crooked,' and had been set on by the Spider in order to punish him for his rebellion.

"Strangers had been selected to inflict the punishment so that the victim might not suspect that the secret organization was at the bottom of the matter and out of revenge be induced to betray the secrets of the band.

"The man became so excited that the doctor in charge was compelled to interfere.

"This disclosure took place in the wee small hours of the morning, right after the man had been carried to the hospital, so it was arranged that the superintendent should be informed of the important disclosure the wounded man proposed to make, and an interview was appointed for the following afternoon, the doctor promising to brace the man up with strengthening cordials so he would be able to tell his story.

"But when the superintendent arrived at the hospital on the following afternoon, as per agreement, the man was dead.

"Is it possible?" exclaimed the disguised girl, who was listening to the recital with the utmost interest.

"The man had been poisoned," continued Phenix. "The secret organization evidently had a spy in the hospital, and when it was discovered that the victim intended to make a clean breast of it, measures were taken to effectually stop his mouth."

"And so no clew was obtained?"

"A slight one only; he was out of his head at the time of his death and raved incessantly, and from his disjointed utterances it was gathered that the criminal league had a secret haunt down the bay somewhere on the Long

Island shore, and as near as could be learned it was between Bay Ridge and Fort Hamilton.

"Before taking any steps in the matter the chief did me the honor to ask my opinion about it, and at the same time he was careful to keep entirely to himself what the doctor had disclosed to him, for as he frankly remarked to me: 'There may be some leaks right in my own office.' His idea was to set his detectives to work to examine every house in the suspected quarter, but I represented to him that such a course would certainly alarm the rascals. It is a well-known fact that the criminal class know the detectives far better than the detectives know them, so he told me that he would place the matter entirely in my hands and to go ahead in my own way. Then he asked me if I could manage a boat and suggested to get myself up in some cunning disguise and sail along the shore both by day and night.

"The neighborhood of the water had evidently been selected by the scoundrels so as to have double access to the rendezvous.

"The idea was a good one, and here we are hot on the scent. And if I deceived my old friend, Tom Murphy, with my disguise, it is not likely that the game of whom I am in search will be able to detect that I am a wolf in sheep's clothing."

"It is not likely."

"No, and if fortune favors me I will hunt this Spider Captain to his den."

09. Bernard Andrews, the master of Blithewood.

CHAPTER XVII.
THE MASTER OF BLITHEWOOD.

New York bay is truly renowned; well-informed travelers have often remarked that it was very little, if any, inferior in natural beauty to the far-famed bay of Naples.

The shores are well-wooded, and charming villas, some of them perfect palaces, are scattered here and there.

The Long Island shore is particularly attractive and there is hardly a drive in America more beautiful than the shore road which, at an elevation of a hundred feet above the water, leads from Bay Ridge to Fort Hamilton, and then continues, dropping to a lower level, to Bath and New York's famous summer breathing spot, Coney Island.

On this delightful bay view road, about halfway between Bay Ridge and Fort Hamilton, stands a massive mansion built in the Gothic style with a bewildering amount of wings and gabled roofs.

There are some ten acres of pleasure-grounds attached to the house, which stands quite a ways back from the road with an elaborate lawn in front, fringed by stately forest trees in the English park style.

The public road cuts through the grounds of the house, and that portion of the estate which lies on the bay side of the drive, slopes from the road to the water's edge, along which is built a massive stone wall.

Resting on the wall is an extensive boathouse, with room below for half-a-dozen pleasure-craft, while the upper part is utilized as a billiard and card room.

A balcony two stories high, running completely

around the boathouse afforded a pleasant promenade when the weather was suitable for such enjoyment.

At anchor in the bay, a short distance out, were two elegant yachts.

One, sloop-rigged, of about twenty five tons, and the other a steam launch of smaller dimensions.

Take it all in all, Blithewood Hall, for so this country place was named, compared favorably with anything of the kind in the neighborhood of the great Metropolis of the New World.

There were many larger places, estates which cost a deal more money, but few of them were as perfect in all their details as this *bijou* country place.

The owner of the property was a well-known man in the lower portion of great Gotham, the territory tributary to Wall Street and the stock exchange.

He was a young man, not over thirty-five, a tall, handsome, olive-faced, dark eyed, dark haired fellow, with a prepossessing face, a musical voice, and an uncommonly gentlemanly appearance.

He was called Bernard Andrews and was, comparatively speaking, a new-comer in the great Metropolis.

New York had only known him for some five years.

He had made his appearance in the guise of a financial agent of a rather obscure railroad in Texas, which amounted to very little actually, although to read its prospectus one would have been apt to imagine it was destined to be the trunk road of the world.

The position secured him admission into a certain circle of operators who were supposed to be about the sharpest men in Wall Street, though many wiseacres shook their heads and, prophet-like, predicted that the young man would soon be sheared of all his golden fleece by these keen wolves.

But Andrews, although new to the lairs of the stock exchange, soon proved to all who had the curiosity to watch his career that he had long ago cut his wisdom-teeth, and soon he convinced the wise men of Gotham that he was fully fit to wrestle with the best of them in a trial of wits, although where he managed to procure the money to back his enterprises was a mystery, until it leaked out that he was a scion of one of the old cattle-kings who by the wondrous rise of land and livestock in Texas had suddenly become enormously rich.

It was little wonder that Andrews succeeded with a million or two of dollars at his back for a "starter," to use the slang of the street.

And now after a brief five years the young man was recognized as one of the leading men in Wall Street.

Andrews was a bachelor, much to the wonder of all his acquaintances, who marveled that such a deuced handsome fellow with such a taking way with him and so much money, did not take a better-half unto himself.

It was not for want of an opportunity, for Dame Rumor, with her hundred tongues, declared there were at least a dozen of the dainty belles of the "upper crust" who would be only too glad to be wooed and won by this gay southwestern gentleman.

But although Blithewood Hall did not possess a mistress yet the establishment was kept up in first-class style.

There was a housekeeper and a butler, both most excellent managers, assisted by a full corps of well trained servants, and as there was plenty of money to grease the wheels of domestic economy, everything went like clockwork.

The young man was of a hospitable nature, and never seemed so happy as when entertaining a house full of company, and so it happened that Blithewood was rarely without visitors.

In right royal style too, the master of the domain assured his guests that his house was Liberty Hall, and they must make themselves perfectly at home.

There wasn't any regular hour for either breakfast or luncheon.

A repast was ready whenever a guest felt inclined to eat, either in the morning or at noon, but a regular cere-monious dinner was served daily at five in the afternoon, and this was the only meal when it was understood that the master of the house expected to meet all his guests at the table.

Another thing too about this hospitable mansion. The host expressly declared to each guest upon arriv-al that it must not be expected that he personally would provide amusement.

There were books in the library for those studiously inclined, a billiard-room and a bowling-alley, horses and carriages in the stables, and boats on the water—of half a dozen different patterns.

Any one who could not find means to pleasantly while away an idle hour with all these methods of enjoy-ment at command must indeed be hard to please.

At the time that we introduce the reader to this pleas-ant mansion and its inmates there were quite a number of guests enjoying the hospitality of its princely owner.

First the two dudes whose acquaintance the reader made at the beginning of our tale, Charles Van Tromp and Alexander Clinton.

This pair of inseparables, as they were commonly termed by their acquaintances from the fact that they were rarely seen apart, were Andrews' most particular friends, although they were as different in every respect from the master of Blithewood as daylight is from darkness.

Andrews was an elegant, polished fellow, but with nothing of the exquisite about him. In fact, he was a thorough-going man of the world, full of business and as sharp as a steel-trap, for all his polish and refinement.

Still he was a jovial good fellow, fond of all sorts of fun, and from the moment he made the acquaintance of the two young men, seemed to take a "fancy" to them, and it was not long before the two came to the conclusion that Bernard Andrews was about the nicest fellow that they ever had the good fortune to encounter.

Besides the young men, four more guests enjoyed the hospitality of Blithewood.

Mr. and Mrs. Dominick Grimgriskin, Miss Sidonia Grimgriskin and young Mr. Alcibiades Grimgriskin.

New-comers to the great metropolis were these Grimgriskins, and in some respects they were a rather peculiar family, worthy to be described at length, and we cannot accomplish that feat better than to relate a conversation that took place between Bernard Andrews and the two dudes on the ample veranda of the house waiting for the announcement that dinner was served.

The young men had driven down with Andrews, leaving the city at the close of business in Wall Street, about three in the afternoon.

Andrews had a stylish way of doing business. No common, vulgar horse-cars for him.

He was driven from his country-seat to his office every morning in his own carriage, a very neat affair, with a coachman in a dark livery, and drawn by a pair of high-stepping Kentucky bay horses, worth a cool thousand dollars each of anybody's money, and at the close of business the same vehicle conveyed him home.

Some of the old heads nodded their brows gravely at this display, and murmured of the pride which goes before a fall.

But these men were "croakers," who were always predicting disaster.

Others thought it was a "deuced good idea."

"Fine device to attract 'lambs,' and inspire confidence," they remarked.

Andrews had gone regularly into the stockbroker business, and although not a member of the exchange, had managed to secure quite a lucrative business.

The Grimgriskins had come by way of the Bay Ridge boat, and the host, upon their arrival, received them in person.

After seeing them to their apartments he had returned to join the young men on the veranda.

"By Jove, old fellow, that's a deuced fine girl, don't yer know!" Van Tromp had exclaimed upon Andrews' return.

"Deuced fine, by George!" drawled the other dude, "But the old fellow looks like a monkey from Central Park. Where did you pick 'em up?"

"That necessitates a tale, so I'll fire away at once," replied Andrews, seating himself.

10. Mr. Dominick Grimgriskin.

CHAPTER XVIII.
THE GRIMGRISKINS.

"In the first place," began Andrews, "perhaps it is as well to introduce that elderly, dried-up gentleman, whom you irreverently compare to a monkey, with the remark that he is worth about five millions of dollars."

"What?" exclaimed the pair of dudes in utter amazement.

Both of the gilded youths had a fair claim to rank with the millionaires of Gotham, but even in great New York, five million men are not common.

"His name is Grimgriskin, Dominick Grimgriskin, and he hails from Bradford, Pennsylvania."

"Yas, yas, we were up there once, wasn't we, Alex," Van Tromp remarked. "A friend of ours thought he had a good thing in an oil well up there, and wanted us to take a flyer with him, so we went up and examined the property, don't you know, but the place was altogether too nasty, perfectly beastly, you know, everything smelt of the horrid oil, and it really made us quite ill, so we got away as soon as possible."

"Well, Grimgriskin can thank that bad smelling oil for every dollar that he has," Andrews remarked. "Ten years ago he was keeping a little country store in what is now the city of Bradford. At that time the place didn't amount to anything, the oil discovery not having been made.

"In the course of his trade a neighboring farmer got into his debt. The man owned about a couple of hundred acres of the poorest and meanest land that ever a poor devil undertook to make a living out of, one of those miserable farms that like the ancient monster slowly squeezes the life out of anybody who is unfortunate enough to have anything to do with It.

"At last, unable to extricate himself from his difficulties, the farmer, for a paltry sum, three or four hundred dollars, I believe, just about enough to take himself and family to the cheap lands of the far West, made over the farm to Grimgriskin. He reluctantly took it on a sort of speculation, expecting to be able to strike some greenhorn with it, and so get his own money out of it, with a few extra dollars for his trouble and risk.

"On that barren farm great oil discoveries were made, and one morning the old man awoke to find himself rich.

"His head was not turned by his sudden prosperity either, but he remained the same careful skinflint as in the days of yore when he traded groceries for eggs, watered his sugar and bought potatoes with the largest half-bushel measure that was ever seen.

"As fast as the money came in he invested it in real estate, and having the luck to come in on the ground floor, every dollar he invested returned him from a hundred to a thousand.

"He is now one of the great moguls of the oil region, for he has been wise enough never to dabble in anything but oil, which he knows all about, and real estate in his own locality, in which he is equally well posted.

"He is, too, one of the largest stockholders in the biggest oil concern in the country, a monopoly which is to other monopolies as an elephant is to a rat."

"It's deuced funny that a mere nobody should be so uncommonly lucky," remarked Van Tromp, with all the contempt that the scions of the old New York families feel for these creatures of a day.

"You have hit him exactly, he is a nobody," replied

Andrews. "A little, mean, grasping fellow with a soul no bigger than that of a flea, and for all his enormous wealth he counts his pennies as carefully as when his living depended upon his getting the odd cent in every transaction.

"I've done considerable business for him in the last year, and I think the old fellow has taken a fancy to me; at any rate he says I'm the squarest business man he has ever had any dealings with and that I shall have all his business in future."

"But how about the rest of the family, particularly that lovely girl?" Clinton asked. "She's the old man's daughter, I suppose, although I can't say that I detect any resemblance."

"Yes, she's his daughter, and a perfectly splendid girl; as different from the old folks as can well be imagined, for the old woman, Mrs. Grimgriskin, is as odd in her way as the old man is in his.

"Her name is Sally, a fact of which she is utterly ashamed, for she has the highest and most ambitious kind of notions, and the joke of the thing is that she always had them, even when she was pinching along as the wife of a country store keeper.

"She always believed she was destined for great things, and when the windfall came, like many another good wife she cried, triumphantly, 'I told you so!'

"But with all her high ideas she is just as mean and stingy as the old man.

"As an evidence of the kind of woman she is, the names she bestowed upon her children can be cited.

"The girl, who is the oldest, is called Sidonia, while the young man struggles under the weight of Alcibiades."

"A mean-looking customer he is, too," Van Tromp remarked.

116

"You are quite right about that, and he is just as mean and contemptible as he looks," Andrews observed. "He is a fellow utterly without principle. He would steal in a minute, I verily believe, if the booty was large enough and he wasn't afraid of being caught, for he is as cowardly as a rabbit. There isn't really any more manhood about him than a five year-old boy. Not the slightest bit of backbone. He's like an eel; when you want to put your hand on him, you'll find he isn't there."

"A delightful family to encounter!" Van Tromp exclaimed, with a grimace. "Why on earth did you invite us here to meet such rabble?"

"Good heavens! Do you suppose I wanted to shoulder the entire burden of entertaining them?" Andrews cried, in comic dismay. "Aren't you two my most particular friends? Haven't you often protested your willingness to do anything to oblige me, and how can you render me a greater service than to help me when invaded by this ruthless horde, who have descended upon me as the old-time barbarians flocked to Rome?

"Besides, you'll have some fun; all of the three are odd characters, and you'll really enjoy their peculiarities after you get used to them.

"One caution, though, don't lend Alcibiades any money, because the chances are about a hundred to one that you will never see it again if you do.

"The young cub is of age and is in receipt of a regular allowance from his father, which is paid at stated periods, and as he makes a point of honor to spend the money on the day he gets it, the rest of the time he sponges upon credulous acquaintances."

"The old gentleman will not foot the bills, then?" remarked Van Tromp.

"Oh, no, there isn't the slightest use of his doing it.

He's tried it twenty times and found that it didn't do the least good. The more he paid, the more there was to pay. It is a sort of disease with the young man; he does not seem to be able to help it. He hasn't any backbone, as I told you.

"His intent is good enough; he'll borrow fifty from you with the firm idea of repaying the loan the moment he gets hold of his money, but when that time arrives, he finds there is something he wants, so he lets your fifty go till the next time, and when that comes it is just the same."

"Nice sort of a fellow!" Van Tromp exclaimed.

"Oh, awfully nice," remarked Clinton.

"He's an inveterate gambler, too," continued Andrews, "and is never so happy as when he has the cards in his hands. But he is about the worst player at any game you can mention that I ever met, and he generally has frightful bad luck, too. But it doesn't matter much though. Even if the cards run in his favor, he never knows enough to play them to advantage."

"He'd be a deuced good fellow to gamble with—a man might make a good thing of it," Van Tromp suggested.

"Yes, if he had any money to back his game, but he is seldom in funds and there would be neither fun nor profit in winning his worthless I. O. U.'s."

"Of course the old man wouldn't pony up," said Clinton.

"Not a red; he will not even pay Alcibiades's legitimate debts, such as tailor's, hatter's, and boot-maker's bills. If the creditors come to him, he tells them sharply that his son is of age and he is not responsible for his debts, and that if anybody is fool enough to trust Alcibiades, he can't help it."

"Cold consolation, but I should think the creditors would make it warm for the young rascal." Clinton observed.

"What good would it do?" Andrews asked. "The old man has plenty of money to waste on lawyers if not on his son, and neither the mother nor daughter will quietly submit to the scapegrace being left in jail."

"Oh, they have a better opinion of him than the old man, eh?" questioned Van Tromp.

"Yes, he is his mother's idol. She thinks his faults are only venial ones, common to all young men, and that with time he will outgrow them," Andrews replied. "And even Sidonia, who is a girl without the least bit of nonsense about her, looks with a lenient eye upon his follies, and really believes there is a deal of latent good in the unlicked cub."

"Miss Sidonia, then, is the jewel of the family," Van Tromp remarked.

"You are right there; she is a jewel beyond price. Nature does some odd things sometimes, and how it happened that such a sweet tempered, honest, thoroughly good girl, should come of such a breed is a mystery."

"Hallo! hallo!" exclaimed Clinton. "By Jove! Deah boy, you speak as if you felt a personal interest in the lady, don't you know?"

"You have hit the mark exactly," Andrews replied. "Miss Sidonia has no more devoted admirer than your humble servant."

At this point dinner was announced.

11. Mrs. Dominick Grimgriskin.

CHAPTER XIX.
ALCIBIADES PROPOSES A LITTLE GAME.

Dinner at Blithewood was an extremely elaborate affair. When rallied by his friends upon his rather extravagant bill of fare, Andrews was wont to remark, quietly, that it was all the fault of his cook, and that if a man was idiot enough to engage a French "chef," he must expect to be ruined by the efforts of the "artist" to maintain his reputation.

But for all that, Andrews was proud of the name he had gained for giving as good a dinner as could be had within a hundred miles of New York. And that is saying a good deal, when it is considered that the modern Babylon has of late years become the chosen home of the great millionaires of America, and that almost every one of these money-kings pride themselves upon the style in which they live, no matter how poor or lowly their origin.

The enemies of the young man, for Andrews had plenty as every man must expect who climbs high above the shoulders of his competitors in the great battle of life—sneeringly remarked that there was a great deal of policy in the manner in which the daring speculator carried sail.

A good dinner has sometimes a wonderful influence upon a man, and Andrews' detractors asserted that some of the best speculations in which he had been engaged had their origin in an after-dinner siesta. That is when his pigeons—Andrews was compared to a hawk sometimes—properly mellowed by the influence of a good dinner, washed down by generous wine, which at the young man's table flowed as freely as so much water, were ready to take a roseate view of almost anything.

Andrews exerted himself to the utmost to make the affair a success, for as his guests had not had time to become familiar, there was the natural awkward feeling common to new acquaintanceship.

By the time the banquet was ended, for the meal was furnished in such style that it really deserved to be so designated, all of the guests had got on excellent terms with each other.

The two dudes were thorough gentlemen, in spite of their idiotic ways, and no fools otherwise. Before the dinner was over they discovered that the account Andrews had given of the Grimgriskin family was correct in every particular.

The old man was a miserly old bunks, who thought himself to be one of the wisest and smartest men in Christendom, and was by no means bashful in letting people know his opinion of himself.

The madam, ignorant and pompous, made herself ridiculous by the airs she displayed.

Alcibiades was a lout of the first water, a mean-looking rascal, although dressed like a lord, who ate like a hog, and drank twice as much wine as was good for him. In fact, if it had not been for a warning administered openly by the pompous mother, without apparently any thought of how ill-bred such a thing was, the young man would have become so drunk as to be incapable of rising from the table.

But the daughter—ah! She was a jewel of a girl, a lady in every respect, who seemed to be mortally ashamed of the coarse behavior of her relatives.

Andrews, in his description, had only done her simple justice, so both of the young men decided.

Really, neither of the two thought that due weight

had been given to her many charms.

She was a blonde, about the medium height, with true golden hair, the loveliest dark-blue eyes that were ever seen in a mortal's head, features as regular as though formed by a sculptor's cunning hand, and a complexion so perfect that it needed not the aids to beauty in the shape of cosmetics, so common to the toilet table of the beauty of to-day.

Her voice, too, was perfect music, wonderful contrast to the squeaky tones of the old man, the harsh voice of the mamma, who invariably spoke in a high key as though she was yelling at the hired man down at the barn a hundred yards away, or the base, clownish utterances of the dull-witted Alcibiades.

Grapes grow not from thistles, yet from the mean, sordid Grimgriskin race this perfect girl had sprung.

It seemed like a miracle, yet nature, as if in sheer sport, is continually doing such work.

After dinner the party adjourned to the parlor, where a couple of hours were spent in conversation. Then as old Grimgriskin, who had been asleep in an easy-chair for the better part of the time, announced that he felt tired and should retire to bed, the ladies decided to follow his example.

Alcibiades declared, however—despite his mother's somewhat urgent suggestion that as he didn't look well he had better go to bed—that he never slept any all night if he went to bed early.

So the father, mother and daughter departed, leaving the son behind.

After they were gone Andrews suggested, as there was a brilliant moon and the night was extremely balmy, it would be a good idea to go down to the boat-house and enjoy a cigar on the balcony.

Both of the dudes and Master Alcibiades thought the idea a capital one, and so the four proceeded to the boat-house.

It was the first time that the guests had visited Blithewood, therefore they all examined the boat-house with a great deal of curiosity.

"Upon my word, deah boy, you have the most perfect place of the kind that I have ever seen," Van Tromp remarked, after the party had finished the inspection, lit their cigars and seated themselves upon the balcony. The glorious view of the moonlit bay with its vast expanse of water, and Staten Island with its myriad of lights, right before their eyes, the broad Atlantic ocean to the left and New York's great Metropolis on the right, flanked by Brooklyn and Jersey City.

"It is really a superb place, don't you know!" chimed in the other dude. "It beats all the show places that I have ever seen, and you've always kept so deuced quiet about it, too—invited us down to your 'little box,' just as if you had some little six-by-nine shanty, not big enough inside to swing a good-sized cat."

"It's a very tidy little ranch," observed Alcibiades, in his rude, rough way, affecting the free and breezy manner popularly supposed to be common to the large-limbed, big-hearted sons of the boundless West, "but you just ought to see the old man's shebang at Tarport, that's just outside of Bradford, you know. Well, I don't want to boast, but if that don't knock the socks off of anything that you can show round these diggings I don't want a red cent."

The dudes elevated their eyebrows slightly as they listened to this boast, but they were too polite to express the doubt they felt in regard to the matter, for they were certain the speaker was a colossal liar.

"You never saw the old man's place at Tarport, I reckon, Andrews," the young man continued, addressing the host in the most familiar manner.

"No, I don't think I ever had the pleasure," Andrews replied, "but from the well-known taste of your father I've no doubt his mansion and grounds are something out of the common."

The New Yorkers looked significantly at each other.

Although there wasn't anything in the speaker's voice or manner to betray it, yet they understood he was "chaffing" the boaster.

But Alcibiades was not keen-witted enough to perceive this, and took the speech in good faith.

"Oh, the old man knows a thing or two!" the young man exclaimed. "If he didn't, I reckon he would be scratching a poor man's head about this time, instead of being worth twenty-five or thirty millions of dollars."

"Not much danger of his ever going to the poor house, eh?" Van Tromp remarked.

"Not much! You can bet your bottom dollar on that. And besides dad's pile, the old woman is well-fixed too. I reckon she could scare up a million or two if she were put to her trumps.

"You see, her dad left her a farm which turned out to be right in the heart of the oil region, and she was smart enough to hold on to it.

"And my sister too is worth a couple of million. She was a great pet of my father's only brother. His name was Sidney, and if sis had been a boy she would have been named after him. As it was, marm came as near to it as she could.

"Well, when uncle kicked the bucket he left sis all he had. It wasn't counted to be any great shakes at the time, about fifty acres of mighty mean land, but it is right in the heart of Bradford now, and Siddie rakes in a big income from it.

"I'm the only one of the gang that isn't well-heeled. Just think, gents, all the old man is willing to allow me is a miserable four thousand dollars a year, and what is that to a cove with my expensive habits? But the old bloke will peg out one of these days and then I'll have my whack without any one to say me nay," declared the young reprobate, in the coarsest manner.

"I've no doubt you'll make the money fly," Andrews remarked.

"Oh, you can just bet I will! I'll show the boys a thing or two in the way of putting on style. But I say, Andrews, you've got a nice quiet place here for a little game," and the speaker glanced into the cozy room within.

"What do you say to flipping the pasteboards for an hour or two just to pass away time?"

"Well, I seldom play; cards are not much in my way," the host replied.

"Oho! You're afraid that I will skin you, I reckon!" Alcibiades exclaimed, with a loud and bantering laugh. "And you're jolly well right about that too, for I'm a boss when it comes to poker. I'll bet you fifty you don't dare to play!"

12. young Mr. Alcibiades Grimgriskin.

CHAPTER XX.
HIGH PLAY.

The two dudes surveyed the host with considerable attention; they were curious to see how he would act under the circumstances.

The coarse manner in which the banter had been given was enough to excite the angry passion of even a man gifted with saint-like patience.

Both of the New Yorkers were counted to be expert players.

Born with silver spoons in their mouths, they had become members of prominent clubs just as soon as they were old enough to be eligible, and as it is thought to be the "proper caper," in the fast clubs of the metropolis for the younger members to indulge in a little quiet gambling, as a natural consequence both of them had got into the habit of playing more or less.

They did not gamble for the sake of the money, but because they were convinced it was the proper thing for young men of their position to do, and it helped to pass away time, which otherwise might hang heavy on their hands.

Then, too, both of the young men really had more money than they knew what to do with, and the loss of a few hundred dollars now and then did not annoy them in the least.

Although a "social game, just for amusement," and for a trifle of money, "merely to make it interesting," is permitted in quite a number of the prominent clubs of Gotham, yet in few of them is there any high play allowed.

If the players are anxious to win or lose thousands,

they must select some other place to enjoy their game than in the club building.

And so it happened that both Van Tromp and Clinton were very good card-players, for since they had arrived at the dignity of being clubites, they had handled the pasteboards every week more or less. Then, too, both of them had a natural talent in that direction.

But they were not gamblers, and would never have dreamed of encountering professional players in professional rooms.

In regard to Andrews' abilities in this line they knew absolutely nothing.

The speculator was a member of a couple of the most prominent clubs, but they had never seen him handle a card, and were inclined to believe that he neither knew nor cared much for anything in that line.

Andrews took the cigar from his mouth and flipped the ashes from the end with his thumb and second finger, with an air of great deliberation.

Then he looked in a dreamy sort of way, half closing his eyes, out upon the moonlit waters and said:

"You are willing to bet me fifty that I don't dare to play you a game of poker?"

"That was my horn that you heard a-blowing, and here is the solid stuff to back up what I said!" Alcibiades exclaimed, drawing forth from an inside pocket as he spoke a thick roll of bills and flourishing them defiantly in the air.

"Well, I don't see as I can make fifty dollars in any easier way than by covering your bet," Andrews remarked, languidly, and as if he didn't take the least interest in the proceeding.

"But are you in earnest in this matter, or are you only executing that clever strategic movement, native to the soil of the New World, and which is popularly called 'bluffing'?"

"Money talks and here's my fifty," and Alcibiades put two twenties and a ten in Van Tromp's hand. Now then, put up your sugar and come up to the scratch if you mean business!"

"I really will have to take that fifty since you press me so hard," and in the same cool, careless way that had characterized his actions since the young man began to banter him, Andrews drew out his pocket book and selecting from the bills it contained—and the book held a goodly number—a fifty-dollar note, placed it in Van Tromp's hand on top of Alcibiades's wager.

"There's your money covered, the bet is made, and now I'm your man as soon as you like," he continued, rising as he spoke.

The rest followed his example.

"Hang me if I don't believe that you are going to collar that fifty!" exclaimed the hopeful scion of the Grimgriskin line, annoyed at the loss of his foolish wager and yet delighted that he had forced Andrews into a game.

Like many another man of like caliber, Alcibiades flattered himself that he was a "card-sharper," and being satisfied that the host would prove to be a pigeon worth the plucking he had deliberately planned to draw him into gambling so he would be able to fleece him.

Oh, sacred hospitality how thou art sometimes insulted!

"Yes, yes, as you elegantly and tersely put it, I'm going to 'collar' this fifty sure, whether I succeed in getting any more or not," Andrews remarked, leading the way into a snug apartment fitted up for a smoking-room at the New York end of the boat-house.

Andrews lit the gas drew down the curtains, at the same time requesting his guests to help themselves to chairs.

There was a square table in the center of the apartment which was exactly the thing required for the game.

"Egad, I forgot the cards!" exclaimed Andrews, suddenly. "We can't very well play without the pasteboards. I must have some up at the house though."

"I've got half a dozen packs in my pocket," young Grimgriskin remarked, in a rather sheepish way, and then from his coat-tail pocket he drew out a neatly done-up package.

"You see, I thought you might not have a stock on hand down here and so I laid in a supply in the city," he explained.

The dudes looked at each other. If they had not been previously warned by Andrews in regard to the peculiarities of the young man, they most certainly would have believed that by mistake they had fallen in with some regular card-sharper who went about with the painted pictures in his pocket seeking whom he might devour.

"They are all square, gents, I give you my word of honor on that," Alcibiades added, earnestly.

"Certainly, of course," Andrews remarked, in his easy way.

"I spoke, you see, because I didn't know but what you might think I was trying to put up some sort of a game on you—trying to ring in a cold deal—marked cards or something of that sort," young Grimgriskin explained, in a lame sort of way.

"My dear fellow, I am sure I should never have even dreamed of such a thing!" the host replied. "Only a low, miserable, thieving rascal would attempt such a trick as that. Among gentlemen an act of that kind would be an impossibility."

131

Alcibiades looked a little dubious at this.

In his experience he had discovered that the "gentlemen" whom he had been accustomed to associate with, would not only jump at a chance to perform so skillful an operation, but if they succeeded, would afterward boast of it as if they had accomplished a meritorious act.

"Well, I didn't know," the young man observed. "Of course I wouldn't do such a thing, but I thought, maybe, that some of you might be a little suspicious."

"Oh, no!" exclaimed Andrews.

"Certainly not," said Van Tromp.

"My dear sir, we wouldn't be guilty of thinking of such a thing for the world," Clinton hastened to remark.

But as the two dudes spoke each had caught the eye of the other and from the peculiar expression therein judged that their opinion in regard to the hope of the Grimgriskin line was exactly the same, and the words they uttered did not in the least express it.

Both believed the young man to be a rascal of the meanest degree who would not hesitate at any trick to serve his end, if there was a prospect of doing it without being detected.

Alcibiades had laid the package upon the table and Andrews opened the wrapper and took out the cards.

"I don't know much about cards," the host remarked, as he removed the individual wrappers from a couple of the packs and pushed them toward the two dudes.

"Here, you gentlemen are experts in this sort of thing, I believe, aren't these the regular articles?"

They were the common "star-backed" steamboat cards, and were all right, as far as the dudes could see, and they said so.

"Well, here's for you, then!" and Andrews took up one of the packs and commenced to shuffle the cards.

"Van Tromp, have the kindness to hand that hundred over to me. It's mine, I believe."

"All right!" Alcibiades exclaimed, "but I'll skin you out of it, and a few thousand to boot, before you are an hour older."

"Oh, it's to be thousands, eh?" said the host.

"You bet! That's the kind of man I am! No two-penny game for me. Fix the ante at a hundred—"

"And the limit?" Andrews asked.

"No limit at all till you're bu'sted!" Alcibiades cried.

"Well, well, you are going in wholesale! Excuse the question, but are you financially situated to stand such a racket?" the host inquired.

"You can bet high on that!" Alcibiades replied, triumphantly. "The old man came down with a thousand to-day, my quarterly allowance, then the old woman tipped me a couple of thousand more to square off some urgent creditors whom I pretended were after me, and, in addition, I struck my beautiful, but idiotic sister, for five thousand to invest in a paying speculation. I reckon that a game of poker with such a man as I am to manipulate the cards is about as good a speculation as a fellow can scare up nowadays.

"So, you see, I am well-heeled, and you can skin me out of eight thousand dollars, if you can play poker better than I can."

"You are just trying to scare us, I guess," Andrews said, with a laugh, "but we are going for you for all we know; so get your money ready, gentlemen, and we'll cut for deal."

133

CHAPTER XXI.
A MAGNANIMOUS OFFER.

Young Grimgriskin cut first, and he triumphantly displayed the king of spades.

"How is that for high?" he exclaimed. "I'll bet five to one that king captures the deal."

"I'll have to take you up on that," Andrews said. "I can't really allow a Westerner to frighten us New Yorkers clear out of our boots. How will you have it, in hundreds?"

"No, thousands! I'm in for big play to-night, I want you to understand!" Alcibiades exclaimed, boastfully.

"Put up your money," was Andrews's quiet rejoinder.

The young man counted out five thousand dollars and placed it on the table, Andrews laid two five hundred dollar notes on the top of the pile.

"I think, my dear Grimgriskin, that you were rather rash in making that bet," the host observed. "The odds are not warranted by the state of affairs. There are three of us yet to cut, and there are seven cards in the pack that will either tie or beat your king."

"Oh, you're one of the calculating gamblers, I see!" observed Alcibiades, with a sneer.

"Yes, I generally try to use my wits to the best advantage in any enterprise in which I may become engaged, card-playing not excepted."

"I've always noticed that the fellows who are so smart in calculating are generally the ones who come out at the little end of the horn," Alcibiades replied. "I never knew any gambler who played according to a system who didn't go broke at the end."

"My dear boy, I'm not posted in regard to that sort of thing," Andrews remarked. "My acquaintance with gamblers and their ways is extremely limited. But whether in card playing or anything else, I think that calculation and science will beat bluff and dumb-luck in the long run.

"But come, cut gentlemen, Grimgriskin is anxious to rake in my thousand."

Van Tromp cut next, and displayed a ten-spot.

"Aha!" cried the millionaire's son, in high delight, "you'll have to do a heap better than that to beat me!"

"By Jove! My deah fellow, you are giving us as much talk as a boy over a game of marbles!" exclaimed Van Tromp, nettled by the boastful ways of the other.

Clinton cut and displayed a queen.

A whistle escaped from the lips of Alcibiades. "Hang me if that wasn't a close shave!" he cried.

But the grin of exultation upon his face died away when Andrews tried his fortune and the king of diamonds greeted his eyes.

"A tie!" the dudes exclaimed, in a breath. "But the money's mine, anyhow!" Grimgriskin asserted.

"Eh?" chorused the three in a breath.

"I said the money is mine, anyhow!" Alcibiades repeated, getting red in the face and showing evident signs of anger. "And so it is, too; I win the bet!"

"How do you make that out?" asked Andrews, an amazed look upon his face.

"Yas, by Jove! I don't understand!" Van Tromp declared.

"Neither do I," Clinton protested.

"Why, you bet that you could beat my king, and you ain't done it; that king don't beat mine; he only ties it, that's all," Alcibiades responded, sulkily.

The dudes looked at each other in surprise, not

unmixed with disgust at this preposterous idea.

But Andrews laid back in his chair and laughed heartily.

"Oh, no, my dear Grimgriskin; to use the language dear to the heart of the sporting-man, that cock won't fight. You can't get out of it in that way. You offered to bet five to one that your king would capture the deal; those were your exact words; I am willing to leave it to these gentlemen who have no interest in the matter."

"Most certainly!" Van Tromp exclaimed, promptly.

"Exact words, deah boy!" chimed in the other.

"Well, I didn't intend it that way; that wasn't what I meant!" Alcibiades protested.

"Of course it is impossible for anyone to know what you meant outside of what you said," Andrews remarked, quietly. "As the matter now stands the money is in doubt; you have not lost, neither have I won. It is a tie and we must cut again and the highest card takes both deal and money."

The small soul of young Grimgriskin by this time had become alarmed. If he had not been heated by the wine, of which he had partaken so copiously at dinner, he never would have thought of making any such rash bet, and now he was in agony to find some way to get out of the matter, since his impudent claim to the stakes was not going to be allowed.

He thought he had a sure thing or else he would not have made the wager, but now that it was apparent his opponent had just as good a chance to win as himself, he was dreadful anxious to get out of the hole into which his usual recklessness had brought him.

"Oh, well, as there is a misunderstanding about the matter, suppose we call the thing a draw and let each man take his money," Alcibiades suggested, with an air of great frankness, striving to make it appear that he was anxious to do the square thing.

"But there isn't any misunderstanding," Andrews interposed.

"Decidedly not," remarked Van Tromp, who enjoyed the discomfiture of the "cad," as he mentally styled the son of oildom.

"Everything is as plain as can be, deah boy!" added the other dude, delighted at the chance to catch the boaster on the hip.

"But I'll tell you what I'll do, as you seem to think you have got yourself into a scrape," the host remarked. "The chances now are even; you are as likely to win as I, and I stand as good a chance as you. I will put up dollar for dollar with you and since we are going in for big things to night, let's make the stake eight or ten thousand a side. That will be worth cutting a card for. What do you say?"

At this liberal offer the gambler's frenzy seized upon young Grimgriskin.

It was a stupendous chance; at one blow he could clutch a small fortune if the blind goddess deigned to smile upon him, and why should she not?

"All right; I'm your man; but seven thousand odd is all I've got."

"We'll make the stakes seven thousand five hundred apiece then. How will that suit?" asked Andrews, producing his money and beginning to count it out upon the table.

"First-rate!" and Grimgriskin added bills to the pile upon the table until the sum of the wager was made up.

"This is a pretty big thing," he added, as he gazed upon the money with a longing look. "I reckon that it ain't often, even in New York, that fifteen thousand dollars depends upon the turn of a card."

"Not often, I presume, but then we're all high fly-ers here to-night, true-blue sports, and no mistake," observed the host, lightly, his easy, good-humored manner a strange contrast to the feverish anxiety which had seized upon young Grimgriskin, whose face was flushed, and whose hands trembled as he reached for the cards.

"Go ahead; take the first cut, and if you don't strike an ace, then may Mercury, the god of thieves and gamblers, have mercy upon you!" exclaimed Andrews, jovially.

Alcibiades' hand fairly shook as he cut the cards, and it was all he could do to repress a hollow groan when a miserable little five-spot met his eyes.

To his mind it was a million to one that he would lose now.

"Curse the infernal luck!" he cried. "It serves me right, though, for putting such a pot of money on a single event."

"I haven't won it yet," the host observed. "There are fours and threes and twos in the pack."

"I'd be willing to bet a million that you will skin me!" Grimgriskin cried, angrily.

"The chances are in my favor, of course; I will admit that, but there is no telling who is Governor until after election."

And with the words Andrews cut the cards and displayed a six-spot.

The stakes were his, but by a very close shave indeed.

"I knew you would win when I saw that cursed five-spot," Alcibiades observed, gloomily, his brows contracted with anger, as he watched his antagonist gather up the money.

"Say! Have you any liquor here? My throat is parched!" And Grimgriskin sunk back in his chair and glared around him in a manner which plainly showed it would delight him greatly to have been able to pick a quarrel with somebody.

"Oh, yes; what will you have—champagne or brandy?" and Andrews, rising, unlocked a closet at one end of the room.

"Brandy! Something to put some life in me after this infernal run of ill-luck!" Grimgriskin cried, fiercely.

"Will you try something, gentlemen?" the host asked, addressing the other two.

"If you had a little soda now, some brandy-and-soda wouldn't go badly," Van Tromp remarked.

"Oh, no, not at all. It would be decidedly the proper caper!" Clinton observed.

"The soda is on hand!"

And Andrews drew a little table to the side of the one in the center apartment and placed the glasses and fluids upon it.

Alcibiades took a huge horn of brandy, while the other three indulged in a modest "brandy-and-soda" apiece.

"Good-by to my fun to night," young Grimgriskin cried, "for I am about cleaned out. No poker for me unless you gentlemen will be willing to accept my I. O. U.'s."

"Certainly, why not?" Andrews replied. "Of course you are a stranger to these gentlemen, but I will back your I. O. U.'s with my name, and that will be the same as cash."

CHAPTER XXII.
ANDREWS PLAYS A BOLD GAME.

"Will you really now?" exclaimed the young man, amazed at this generous offer, the more so because it was entirely unexpected.

"Certainly, to a reasonable amount of course, say ten thousand dollars. I know you are perfectly good for it."

"Oh, yes, certainly, and if I ain't the old man is!" young Grimgriskin exclaimed, all his natural swagger and bounce returning now he saw there was a chance for him to take part in the game, backed by funds ample enough to enable him to play boldly.

Like many another would-be fast young man, Alcibiades imagined that he had a natural genius for card playing.

In fact, he believed he was a card-sharp of the first water, and felt perfectly satisfied of his ability to "get away," as he commonly expressed it, with the smartest gambler in the land.

One would have thought that after a man had tried for fifty or sixty times to accomplish this feat and had been ingloriously unsuccessful, the truth would be finally beaten into him and he would come to the conclusion he was not so skillful as he had believed himself to be.

But Grimgriskin was one of those thick-headed dolts whose self-esteem was so strong as to preclude his admitting the truth.

It was all luck every time—the cards had run against him—all the bystanders said they had never witnessed any such run of bad luck in their lives, and all the time they were laughing in their sleeves at the credulity of the "pigeon" who was being so handsomely plucked by the "hawks."

In fact, Grimgriskin had visited Blithewood for the express purpose of "skinning" the host of the mansion.

He did not know a great deal about Andrews, but as far as he had seen he appeared to be a jovial, easy going fellow, a sharp business man, but such men are often extremely ignorant as far as games of chance are concerned.

Andrews had plenty of money, and if he could be induced to play, Alcibiades felt sure he would be able to win a goodly sum from him.

True, he had made a pretty bad beginning, for it was no joke to lose nearly eight thousand dollars on a single bet, but that was just because luck happened to favor his opponent. When it came to a regular game where skill was needed, there wasn't any doubt in his mind in regard to the outcome.

Then, too, he realized that he had been careless and hasty in making the bet, and he inwardly resolved that he would not be caught napping a second time.

In spite of this good resolution, though, he helped himself in a liberal manner to the brandy, although he had already taken far more liquor than was good for him.

Andrews laughed at the young man's speech. "I tell you what it is, gentlemen, it's a deuced handy thing to have a father worth twenty or thirty millions upon whom you can draw at sight when you happen to get a little short of cash."

"You can just bet it is!" Alcibiades declared. And then they all laughed, although the others felt perfectly sure that there wasn't a grain of truth in the statement.

"Here, I'll get my I. O. U.'s ready," Alcibiades continued. "I'll draw them out and leave the sum blank, then fill'em in as I need them. Got any paper? I've a stylograph pen here."

Andrews opened the table drawer and passed some sheets of note-paper over to young Grimgriskin, who immediately proceeded to tear the sheets into the proper sized pieces.

"All you need to do is to write the amount on the face in figures and then, when the game is ended, if luck goes against you, you can give your I. O. U. for whatever amount you may have lost," the host suggested.

"That's so, that's business, every time, ain't it?" exclaimed the young man, taking another glass of brandy.

"I think it is about the ticket, and now for fun!"

Saying which, Andrews proceeded to deal the cards.

We will not weary the reader with the dry details of the scientific game, so purely American, known as draw-poker.

Suffice to say that the game continued from the time the party sat down until about four o'clock in the morning—continued through the long, long night until the cold gray light of the morning began to line the eastern skies.

And never did Dame Fortune show herself to be a more capricious jade than on this occasion, for she veered about like a weather-cock.

For the first couple of hours Van Tromp won largely and everybody else lost, then his luck deserted him and perched upon Clinton's banner, and that young gentleman's pale and watery eyes assumed a saucer-like expression when at the close of a game he gazed upon a pile of bills and I. O. U.'s which represented about thirty thousand dollars.

"By Jove, boys, I don't know but what we ought to stop!" he exclaimed, trembling with excitement. "It really seems like robbery for me to win your money in this wholesale way."

"Oh, yes, of course, draw out now when you have skinned us of our last dollar!" Alcibiades snarled, in a terrible bad humor and very much the worse for the liquor which he had drank so freely. "But you won't do it, and I want you to understand that, too! I, for one, won't stand any such infernal nonsense! I want a chance to win some of my money back, and I'm going to have it too!"

And the young man glared at Clinton in such a ferocious way that the other became really alarmed lest he should be forced into a personal encounter with the son of oildom.

"Oh, that is all right, Alcibiades," Andrews hastened to interpose. "Our good friend here hasn't the least idea of doing anything dishonorable. He only thinks of stopping out of mercy to our depleted wallets! But, old fellow, you might as well go ahead and clean us out completely since you have got your hand in."

"Certainly, just as you please, anything to oblige, you know."

And at it again they went.

But the slight pause seemed to have afforded the fickle goddess an opportunity to change her mind, for from that time forth she smiled no more upon the young dude.

And Andrews became as lucky as he had previously been unlucky.

Pot after pot—as the stake in the delightful game of poker is called—fell to his share, while the blind goddess frowned so persistently upon the unlucky Grimgriskin that in nearly every deal he was compelled to throw up his cards and "pass," not having anything worth risking any money upon.

At half past three Clinton made a brief mental calculation, and as a result announced that he believed he had got enough.

"Ten thousand dollars, don't you know, is a pretty large sum for a fellow to get rid of in one sitting," he remarked, just a trifle soberly. "And, by Jove! it is really more than I can afford, for it will make me as short as the deuce for a time, so you will have to excuse me."

"All right, but you understand that I hold myself ready to give you your revenge at any time," Andrews remarked.

Clinton nodded, but in his heart of hearts he said to himself that he hoped to be shot if any one ever caught him playing poker for more than a twenty five-cent ante hereafter.

"By George, I'm out seventeen thousand!" Van Tromp exclaimed, abruptly. He had just made the discovery, and it astounded him.

"I'll try one more hand though."

Grimgriskin had suffered less than the rest for he had only lost eight thousand in I. O. U.'s.

The cards were dealt.

With an oath the Westerner threw his down; nothing worth risking money on as usual.

Van Tromp ventured five hundred dollars upon two pair only to be beaten by "three of a kind" in Andrews's hand.

"That settles me," the New Yorker remarked.

"Keep on—keep on!" Alcibiades shouted. "Luck must turn some time, and I reckon I ought to stand a chance to win something now."

One more hand ended the game though.

Alcibiades got a pair of queens and was lucky

enough to catch another in the draw, and so he "went in" for all he was worth.

Andrews stood "pat;" that is, he was content with his original hand and did not want any cards, although Grimgriskin drew three.

This ought to have been a warning to Alcibiades that his opponent had a hand of unusual strength, but he was too rash to heed it.

He believed that fortune was about to smile upon him at last, and so he ventured rashly— desperately.

He bet to the limit fixed upon the I. O. U.'s.

Andrews "saw" him and went ten thousand dollars better.

Alcibiades was in despair. To "call" his antagonist he must put up ten thousand, and his last dollar was on the board.

He groaned aloud.

"This is a cursed shame!" he cried. "I know that I can skin you this time, for you are only bluffing; you don't hold the cards to beat my hand!"

"My money says I do," Andrews replied, with a quiet smile.

"And that is where you have the advantage. Oh, if I only had ten thousand more! Ah!" and the young man gave a quick, convulsive gasp.

He seemed to hesitate; 'twas only for a moment though. Then abruptly he pulled a memorandum-book from an inner pocket in his vest, and from it produced a slip of paper, evidently a bank-check, and the rest who were watching him noticed that his hand trembled as he placed the paper on the table.

"Here's a check of the old man's in my favor for ten thousand dollars; if you'll accept it as cash, I'll 'call' you."

"Certainly! Endorse it, that's just as good as gold, and it may be the turning-point in your luck," Andrews answered, as cool as an iceberg.

As eagerly as drowning men grasp at straws. Alcibiades wrote his name on the back of the check and threw it upon the money already "up."

CHAPTER XXIII.
THE FISHERMAN.

"There's your ten thousand and I call you; what have you got? Can you beat three queens?" And nervously Grimgriskin displayed the cards upon the table.

"Old fellow, I am really sorry for you, for I hate to clean a man out, but your three queens are not good. Here are four tens with an ace high."

Andrews laid down the cards one by one, and Alcibiades sunk back in his chair with a hollow groan.

"Take a drop of brandy, old chappie," suggested Van Tromp, really feeling sorry for young Grimgriskin's distress. Although at the same time he despised him, for it was only too plain that he wasn't anything but a vulgar cad with none of the manliness of a true gentleman about him.

Clinton, equally as ready as his friend to tender assistance, although he felt fully as great a contempt for the fellow, hastened to pour out a glass of brandy and tendered it to Alcibiades.

Grimgriskin drained it at a draught, and the stimulant seemed to put new life into him, although the principal effect of the liquor was to completely intoxicate him.

But even in this state his low cunning did not desert him.

"Oh, it's all right, boys," he said, with a thickened tongue, "but, I tell you, it hurts a man to lose as I have lost to-night. I'm about twenty-eight thousand dollars out, and the old man would give me rats if he knew that I had used that check of his, so, gents, I want you all to pledge me your words of honor that you won't let on to anybody about it."

147

"Certainly not!" Van Tromp replied, promptly.

"Of course all the the particulars of this little affair are to be kept secret," Clinton remarked. "It is all confidential, and none of us must reveal the details."

"Decidedly not!" Andrews exclaimed. "It would be a black eye for all of us if it should get out that we have been playing so recklessly. A little quiet game is all right, but we have been going at it in regular gambler style to-night, and it would undoubtedly cause a great deal of talk if the particulars should become known.

"Then, gentlemen, just consider what a tit-bit it would be for the reporters and what a fine account would be fixed up for the newspapers, with some attractive head-line like 'Gambling in high-life,' to call every one's attention to it."

The dudes fairly shuddered; above all things in this world they dreaded the ubiquitous newspaper-man with his ready pencil and his unlimited "gall," to use the vernacular.

"Oh, we mustn't any of us breathe a word of this night's fun," Van Tromp remarked, and with all his *sang-froid* he couldn't help making a grimace when he so characterized the performance which had cost the three losers so heavily.

"Not a word," Clinton chorused.

"The old man would make it hot for me, you bet your life!" Alcibiades exclaimed.

"It is understood that we are all to keep our own counsel," the host remarked. "And of course you understand, gentlemen, I hold myself ready to give you all your revenge at any time that it may please you to demand it."

"Oh, I'll go for you again—I ain't satisfied by a jug-ful!" Alcibiades cried; "I want you to understand that I don't take a back seat when it comes to poker playing for any man in the world."

The two friends nodded, but did not speak. They were not generally supposed to be possessed of any extra amount of common sense, but they were not fools enough to want any more of the "amusement" for which they had paid so heavily.

"It was all luck to-night," young Grimgriskin continued. "You had an awful run of luck, and that is all there is to it. The next time I go for you I'll bet a farm that you don't come out ahead!"

"Very likely not; there's no telling about that sort of thing," Andrews answered, picking up his winnings and stowing them away in his pockets as carelessly as though they were so much waste paper, with the exception of old Grimgriskin's check for ten thousand dollars.

This he folded up carefully and placed in his pocketbook.

Alcibiades watched the check disappear with eager, hungry eyes.

"See here, old fellow!" he exclaimed. "It was a mighty foolish thing for me to part with that check, for I believe the old man would take my scalp if he found it out, so you'll do me a great favor if you'll just keep that—don't part with it, and I'll redeem it."

"Oh, that's all right; don't trouble yourself about that. I'll lock it up in my safe, and you can have it at any time," the host replied.

"And as for the I. O. U.'s, I'll square them off as soon as I make a raise out of the old woman or sis."

"Don't worry yourself; any time will do," Andrews replied, as if the matter was not of the slightest concern to him. "Suit yourself and you will suit me."

Andrews looked at his watch.

"By Jove, gentlemen, it is after four o'clock!" he

exclaimed, in surprise. "Why, I wouldn't have believed it. The time has passed so quickly that I did not believe it was yet two.

"Well, let's take a parting drink, gentlemen, and then we'll adjourn to our beds.

"Luckily I've a day off, for it was my intention to remain at home and entertain my visitors, although it is something rather out of my line, but still, as there are ladies in the case, this time I am obliged to depart from my usual rule.

"You need not hurry yourselves about getting up, gentlemen; this is Liberty Hall here, you know, and you can have breakfast whenever you wish."

Andrews filled out a liberal allowance of brandy and then pushed the decanter toward the dudes, but before they could help themselves Alcibiades seized it, exclaiming:

"Youth before beauty, you know!" and he filled his glass to the very brim.

The young men laughed, for Grimgriskin was too much under the influence of liquor for them to take offense at his insolence.

When the glasses were filled—this was the first time that the host had drank anything since the game began—Andrews proposed a toast.

"Here's wishing you better luck next time, gentlemen, and no worse luck for myself."

The toast drank, all rose, and then the discovery was made that young Grimgriskin had taken so much liquor as to be unable to stand, and if Clinton, who was next to him, had not promptly hastened to his support he would have fallen headlong.

"Hallo, hallo, old fellow, you are considerably under the weather!" Andrews exclaimed, coming at once to the rescue and supporting Alcibiades on the other side.

"Yes, the brandy has got into my legs. Never affects my head though, I've got too much brains for that!" boasted the young man.

"Well, that is rather odd," the host admitted.

"It's always the way with me—infernal pair of legs, always disgrace me!" muttered Alcibiades, who, despite his boast, was extremely thick of utterance and beginning to talk in the incoherent fashion common to the devotees of King Alcohol.

"The air here is foul for the room is close," said Andrews. "Let us go outside; the balmy breeze of the morning will be apt to freshen us up a bit."

"Yesh, let's go outside and go a-fishing!" exclaimed young Grimgriskin, as Andrews and Clinton assisted him to the piazza.

In fact the two had absolutely to carry him there, for Alcibiades' legs were not the least bit of use to him; he could neither walk nor stand.

By this time the eastern skies were streaked with rays of rosy light, heralding the coming of the sun-god, and the breeze that swept in through the Narrows, as the entrance to New York bay is termed, came straight from the bosom of old ocean and was laden with balmy, health-giving ozone.

After the party got outside, Alcibiades, after the fashion of some drunken men, began to get disagreeable and noisy.

"Let's go a-fishing!" he howled. "Let's all go a-fishing; I'm the boss fisherman from Kala-mozoo, yip, yip, yow, yow!" and he yelled at the top of his lungs and would have executed a war dance if he had retained any control over his legs.

Andrews was annoyed. The public road was between the boat-house and the mansion, and the early birds, in the shape of milkmen, bakers, grocery clerks and butcher-boys in their wagons, were beginning to pass along. The master of Blithewood would gladly have given a good round sum rather than have the report become current that he and his guests had been indulging in an all-night spree.

"Hold your tongue! Don't act like a fool!" he exclaimed. "Don't you see the wagons on the road?—and there's some men in a boat below, too!" he exclaimed.

"Let's go a-fishing with them, old fel'!" Alcibiades cried. "I'll stand the expense! What's the odds as long as you're happy?"

An idea flashed upon Andrews. He had taken a quick survey of the boat, and saw from the lines and basket of bait exposed upon the deck that it was a fishing craft.

If he could arrange the matter with the people on board—there were only two on the craft; a weather-beaten old man and a tawny-faced kid—it would be an excellent plan to sail down the bay for a few hours and thus give young Grimgriskin an opportunity to "sober up."

Not for a great deal would he have been willing that the peerless Sidonia should know that her scapegrace of a brother had got drunk in his company.

And so he at once hailed the fisherman in the boat:

"Hello, don't you want some passengers?"

152

CHAPTER XXIV.
PHENIX'S IDEA.

And now we must return to the two in the sail-boat, in order that they may march up abreast of the time when they were accosted by the owner of Blithewood from the boathouse, for, as the reader has doubtless guessed, the two in the boat were the great detective and his new ally.

The girl had not had an opportunity to relate to Phenix the particulars of the strange adventure through which she had passed.

She had been warned by letter to meet him at a certain place at a certain hour, and a disguise suggested.

Through her ignorance of the way—for it is not an easy matter for a stranger unacquainted with the water-side to go directly to any particular point after nightfall—she was some ten minutes late in reaching the dock from whence the start was to be made.

And at first she was really in doubt whether to address the grim and grizzled old man who was sitting on the string-piece of the pier, smoking a short pipe when she approached, for he was as unlike the man whom she expected to see as could possibly be.

But Phenix, being posted in regard to her disguise, recognized the girl at once.

"You are late," he said, speaking in his natural voice, so that she might know who he was.

She explained that she had considerable difficulty in finding her way.

Then they embarked, and for the first half-hour or so the veteran was busy in instructing her how she could aid him in sailing the boat.

153

Then they encountered the police patrol, and with what happened after that the reader is already acquainted.

The girl became so interested in the recital by the detective of the difficult case which he had undertaken that not until he had finished did she attempt to speak of her own strange adventures.

And to this her companion directly led the way.

"By the by, you became mixed up in a strange affair last night," he observed. "I happened to be in the office of the superintendent of police when the particulars were received.

"I recognized your name at once and from the location of the house, I perceived that it was not a stranger by the same name.

"I am free to confess, though, that I am sorry the thing occurred, for in our business we cannot be too careful in keeping out of the gaze of the public.

"You perceive I have different ideas on the subject from the average man in our line, who delights to conspicuously display himself. The kind who is never so happy as when surrounded by a gaping crowd and he hears the whisper passed from one to another, 'That's him—that's the great detective!'

"In reality, such men are of little use. To catch the first-class rascal, the sleuth-hound of justice should be as cunning as the fox creeping upon its prey, and cannot be too careful in keeping in the background until the time arrives to spring, panther-like, upon the criminal."

"There isn't the least doubt but that you have the true idea," she remarked, thoughtfully.

"To the criminal, dreading detection, the thought must be terrible that some unseen foe is hovering near, and gradually drawing closer and closer, but who will never reveal himself until the final spring is made."

"It has been the theory of all the greatest and most successful thief-catchers, since the world began, that the more mystery with which a detective surrounds his operations, the better he will succeed in not only capturing criminals, but in preventing crime," Phenix remarked.

"It certainly seems reasonable, but my adventure with the ruffians who attempted to enter my window—there were two of them, for I saw them distinctly, although only one was captured—is nothing to what happened to me earlier in the evening."

"After you parted with me on the bridge?"

"Yes, the events began not ten minutes later."

"That is odd; tell me the particulars."

"It sounds like a romance, but it is actual truth, and if I were to attempt to make up a startling story, I am sure I should never be able to think of anything one-half as strange or as improbable."

"There is an old saying, you know, that truth is stranger than fiction," the detective observed.

"In this case it most certainly is."

And then Kate proceeded to relate the strange adventures which had befallen her after leaving the bridge and while proceeding to the house of her friends in lower Brooklyn.

She described everything that had occurred as minutely as possible, from the time she was attacked by the ruffians in passing the blind alley until she escaped from the old barn, situated on the outskirts of the city, somewhere near Canarsie.

The detective listened with the utmost attention.

"This is indeed a marvelous story," he observed, when Kate had finished her recital.

"And does it not seem as if the hand of Providence was in it?" she asked. "And, in attempting to make me his prey, has not this scoundrel rendered himself vulnerable to an attack?"

"Most assuredly," the detective replied, immediately. "Strange how fate sometimes arranges matters in this life.

"If I had not chanced to be put upon the trail of this outlaw band, and happened to meet you upon the bridge, the knowledge which you have gained would not have been of much use. But as it is, I believe you were in the stronghold of the very man of whom I am in search."

"Yes, that is what I thought when I listened to your story of the Spider Captain," she remarked.

"There is hardly a doubt of it, unless, indeed, there exist two bands of desperate ruffians, formed on the same model, and that is not likely. How did the ruffians term their leader—did they give him any title?"

"I do not remember to have heard him called anything but the captain and the boss."

"It's a hundred to one that he is our game!" the sleuth-hound exclaimed, decidedly.

"The location of the house and the peculiar way in which they conducted themselves seems conclusive, and this attack upon you, was not that made by some of the members of this same band, think you?"

"Oh, yes, I am sure of it," the girl answered, readily. "The ruffian that I wounded—"

"William Crockey, but known better to his pals and the police as Stingy Bill," said Phenix.

"Yes, well, he is one of the men who were in the cellar, and who drove me in the wagon to the old barn. It was his revolver that I took."

"And then used it upon himself. That was turning the tables upon the rascal with a vengeance!"

"Yes, it was strange, wasn't it?"

"Altogether, as I before remarked, it is as strange an affair as I ever had anything to do with," Phenix observed, thoughtfully.

"I do not think there is any doubt that this Tappan, as he calls himself—that is not his true name of course—is the Spider Captain, the rascal we seek.

"The puzzle now is to find out what he calls himself in the world—to discover what part he is playing."

"Yes, I suppose that will be difficult, unless we can trace him through this captured ruffian," she remarked.

"That, of course, is the first move, but I do not think that much information can be gained from him, for as long as the gang sticks to him he will not be apt to betray his pals.

"And then is is possible that he could not betray his leader, even if he so wished. This Spider Captain may be shrewd enough to so arrange his plan as to keep his identity concealed from all of the rascals of the band, excepting his lieutenants, through whom he communicates with the rank and file."

"Do you think this Stingy Bill is one of the principal men?"

"No, I do not," the detective replied, after a moment's thought. "I know him well enough by reputation, although I never happened to have any business dealings with him.

"He is a desperate fellow, but a mere tool with no head to plan any fine work."

"The other seemed to be a far superior man."

"Four Kings?" Phenix asked.

"Yes, that is the name."

"He is a different kind of a fellow altogether, and rates as one of the few first-class rascals in the country.

"For some years now the two have traveled together, and it is very likely that Four Kings is in the confidence of this master-rascal for he is of the right stamp."

"The moment I recognized that the man whom I was obliged to shoot was the same one whose revolver I had made free with in the cellar, I suspected that my escape had been discovered. I believe this scoundrel of a captain had made up his mind to kill me at all hazards, thinking that with the knowledge I had acquired I might prove dangerous."

"You are right beyond a doubt, and his thought was correct too, for with the clews we have it will be a wonder if we do not hunt him down.

"Our game is now to cruise up and down from Fort Hamilton to Gowanus, and keep our eyes open. I feel sure that the rascals have a way of reaching their haunt by means of the water, and sooner or later we'll run into them."

"But the story that this man told of my sister's death, do you think it is the truth?" Kate asked, anxiously.

"It sounds probable enough, and yet it may not be true. We will soon learn."

By this time the two were off the Narrows, then they "came about" and headed up by the Long Island shore.

CHAPTER XXV.
ON THE BOAT.

"Hey? What do you say?" asked the fisherman, who seemed to be rather hard of hearing.

"I say, don't you want some passengers on board of your craft?" Andrews repeated. "My friends and I feel as if a little trip on the water would do us good."

"Waal, I dunno 'bout that," replied the old man, who of course was the detective in disguise. "We're after fish, and I dunno as I kin spare the time."

"Oh, I'll make it worth your while. I'll give you five dollars for the use of your boat for about four hours, and I doubt if you can make as much as that by fishing."

"Waal, thar's an old saying that a bird in the hand is worth two in the bush, so I reckon I'll rake in that little five dollars of yourn, seeing as how you seem to have plenty of money to throw away," the old man observed, with a grin.

Then, with a dexterous movement, he brought the boat up alongside of the landing float.

"Come along, gentlemen," said the host. "A trip down the bay will freshen us up," and he led the way to the landing stage, the two dudes following, supporting between them young Grimgriskin, howling:

" 'A life on the ocean wave,

A home on the rolling deep.' "

"For Heaven's sake, stop your noise!" Andrews exclaimed, who did not relish this unseemly behavior.

"Wait until we get out on the water, and then you can sing to your heart's content."

"All right, old fel'! Wish I may die if I howl any more, but I want you to understand that I am at the top of the heap when it comes to singing.

159

"Sis thinks she is some pumpkins when she dips into her high flown opera trash, but she can't hold a candle to me, for I'm the sweet singer of oildom, I am, and don't you forget it!"

Andrews hurried Alcibiades on board of the craft as soon as possible, the young men assisting to the best of their ability, and away they went.

"Now, skipper," said the host, "run straight down the bay, and when you have gone far enough I will tell you."

"All right, sir."

The boat was what was called cat-rigged, having only a single sail and no jib.

Acting on a whispered suggestion from Andrews, the two young men took Alcibiades to the bow of the boat, while the host remained with the old man in the stern, the Italian boy being curled up in the middle of the craft.

With the coming of the morning the wind had freshened so that there was now a good breeze. As it was blowing straight down the bay, the boat, which was like a singed cat, being far better than it looked, glided through the water at a good rate of speed.

All of the party, with the exception of Andrews, were affected by the liquor they had drank, now that they had come from the close room into the open air, and too they began to feel the loss of sleep.

The easy motion of the boat as it glided as gracefully as a swan through the water, was conducive to slumber, and within twenty minutes after starting, the two dudes and young Grimgriskin were fast asleep, stretched out at full length upon the bare boards.

But the host was seemingly a man of iron, for he did not show the slightest trace that he had been up all night, nor of the exciting events through which he had passed, but looked as fresh as though he had just arisen from his bed after a night of health-giving slumber.

The detective had scanned his unexpected passengers closely, although not apparently taking any particular notice of them.

Of course he had recognized the two dudes the moment he had set eyes upon them, and was delighted at this piece of good fortune which had given him a chance to play the spy upon them.

Neither Andrews nor young Grimgriskin were known to him, and he was glad of an opportunity to examine them at his leisure, for he had not forgotten the information that the girl had given him in regard to the two dudes.

From what she had overheard, she thought there was a probability they knew something of the mystery which began in the heart of the Catskills.

Phenix was perfectly certain that neither one of the young men was likely to prove to be the party who had decoyed the girl.

If the unknown Henry Tappan and the Spider Captain were one and the same, as seemed more than probable, it was likely that he was masquerading in good society under some false appellation and might be an acquaintance of the young men.

In the circle to which the two dudes belonged an adventurer of the Spider Captain's stamp would be able to secure pigeons well worth the plucking.

So the sleuth-hound felt interested in all the associates of the dudes.

At the first glance this keen-eyed observer detected that the gentleman who had hailed him was no common man.

There was an air of superiority about him which would have impressed a far less shrewd observer than the veteran thief-taker, yet there was nothing to suggest anything wrong.

As for Grimgriskin, Phenix dismissed him as a fool at the first glance.

There wasn't anything about Alcibiades to suggest that he had the brains or the nerve to successfully play the *rôle* of a commander of a desperate band of outlaws.

The detective was thirsting for information, and as the character he had assumed was that of a talkative old man, he began operations the moment the boat got out into the stream.

"That friend of yourn has been h'isting a little benzine, I reckon," he remarked.

"Yes, he's naturally weak headed and it doesn't take much liquor to affect him," Andrews replied.

"'Pears to me it's rather early in the mornin' fur to go to h'isting," the seeker after knowledge remarked, innocently, and he looked in the face of the broker with a smile that was childlike and bland.

"Yes; it is rather early."

"P'raps you bin at it all night?" the other suggested, with a grin, just as if the idea had but now presented itself to him.

"Very likely."

"Didn't fetch any of the benzine aboard with you, I suppose," and the fisherman wiped the back of his hand across his mouth in a very significant way.

"There's plenty aboard, but stowed away in such a manner that you can't very well get at it," and Andrews nodded to where young Grimgriskin had stretched himself out.

"That cuss is no better nor a hog," the boatman observed. "What's the use of a man's wasting good licker by swilling it down by the bucketful. Say, do you live up in the big house thar?" and he pointed to Blithewood, standing out prominently from among the trees.

"Yes, that is my place."

"I reckon you've got about as nice a shanty thar as thar is 'round?" the fisherman remarked, surveying the estate with a critical eye.

"It is generally considered to be as fine a place as there is along the shore."

"No finer as far as I kin see, and I'd go my bottom dollar on it, too. Say, are you one of the Vanderbilts?"

"Oh, no; not quite as well off as all that."

"What might your name be?"

"Andrews; Bernard Andrews."

"Are you a trader?"

"Well, yes, in a certain sense I am. I do business in Wall Street."

"I see, I see. You're one of them Wall Street fellows. Waal, Wall Street is as good as a goldmine, I reckon, to a man who knows the ins and outs of it."

Andrews contented himself with nodding his head.

"Heap of money made thar, and a heap lost, too, I reckon."

Another nod by Andrews.

"And your friends—-are they in Wall Street, too?" the boatman continued. "Don't look as if they had it in 'em to wrastle with the bulls and b'ars that I've hearn tell on in that air quarter. No offense, you know, but thar ain't one of the three what looks as if he knew enough to go in when it rains."

"No, they are not in business at all. They are all gentlemen of independent fortunes."

"I reckon that air is a pretty lucky thing for them, for if they had to wrastle for their hash without anybody to help 'em, they would be apt to come out of the little end of the horn, unless appearances are dreadfully unsart'in," the fisherman remarked, with the air of a prophet.

"Oh, they are smart fellows enough in their way. If they had to come right down to hard work the chances are that in time they would be able to hold their own. You can't always judge by a man's appearance in this world, you know," Andrews answered.

"Right you air; no mistake 'bout that. Now take this hyer boat; she don't look as if she was worth over ten dollars, but I'm giving it to you as straight as a string when I say that a hundred of no man's money couldn't buy her!"

"She certainly is doing well now."

"Oh, she's a bully boat, but she's an odd fish, like myself, I reckon. My name is Turtle— Gideon Turtle— but all the boys call me Gid Turtle for short, and that is the reason why I call my boat the Sea Turtle."

"That's an odd name."

"You bet! But, as I said, I'm an odd fish. Say, that's a nice house next to yourn, in among the trees, but it looks awful lonesome—some of those ducks live there?" and he nodded to the young men forward.

"Oh, no, that house is deserted; no one lives there, and the folks hereabouts say that it is haunted," Andrews replied.

CHAPTER XXVI.
AN UNEXPECTED OFFER.

The house to which the boatman referred was an old fashioned, gloomy-looking pile, situated a few hundred yards down the road from Blithewood.

It was a massive building, built in the old Gothic style, with many wings and curiously constructed peaked roofs.

It was surrounded by a regular thicket of trees, so that only the peaked roofs of the house were visible.

"Haunted! You don't say so!" the boatman exclaimed, and with open mouth he strained his eyes to examine the marvel.

"Yes, so I have heard, but I do not take any stock in such stories," Andrews replied, carelessly.

"All old houses deserted and left to go to rack and ruin are always declared to be haunted, but as I have never encountered any ghosts yet in my travels, I give no credence to hobgoblin stories."

"Nobody lives thar?" the disguised man asked.

The sleuth-hound was not merely assuming an interest in this matter.

The moment he heard of the haunted house, the thought immediately suggested to him that this story was a cunning device, put into operation by the lawless gang who had seized upon the old house for a head quarters, to keep inquisitive people from examining the premises too closely.

"No; and it has been deserted for years, I understand."

"Waal, that 'ere is mighty strange, now, for it seems to be a right nice house, and all it needs is a leetle fixin' up."

"The story goes that a couple of murders were committed there some years ago—nearly ten years back, I believe.

"A son murdered his father and also mortally wounded his sister who interfered to save the old man.

"He fled to escape the punishment due to his crimes and nothing has ever been heard of him since.

"The estate, which was a large and valuable one, fell into the hands of the lawyers, and they have been fighting over it ever since, so the house and grounds have gone to ruin."

"Nobody but the ghosts to live in the old house, eh?" questioned the fisherman, apparently taking a deep interest in the tale.

"Well, as I have told you, I don't take any stock in ghost-stories, but the people in the neighborhood who have known all about the old house for years, say there isn't money enough in the world to induce them to pass a night within its walls."

"The ghosts walk, hey?" asked the boatman.

"So they say."

"What do they look like—did anybody ever see 'em?"

"Oh, yes. There's hardly a person in the neighborhood who hasn't a story to tell about the ghosts, and there's scarcely one of them, man or woman, who is willing to pass by the old house anywhere around midnight."

"What do the ghosts look like—did you ever hear tell?"

"Oh, yes. First, there's the ghost of the old gentleman, with his snow-white hair and beard, all clotted with blood, which flows from a ghastly wound in his temple where his murderous son struck him, and then the sister, all clad in white, but with frightful blood-stains upon the otherwise spotless robes, wanders up and down, wringing her hands and mourning bitterly."

"Sakes alive!" the boatman exclaimed, "I reckon a couple of ghosts like that would be 'bout enough to scare a man into fits."

"Yes, it wouldn't be pleasant to encounter the pair on a dark night."

"Pleasant!" the other ejaculated. "Waal, I reckon it would be the north side of pleasant to run across two sich critters."

"As far as I am concerned I think the stories are all bosh," Andrews remarked, with a slight expression of contempt in his voice, "but there isn't any one in the neighborhood who agrees with me. Why, I don't believe there's a man on my place who would be willing to risk a visit to the 'haunted house' as every body calls it, after midnight, if even a hundred dollars were offered as a reward."

"A hundred dollars wouldn't do a man no good if he was going to git the life scared right out of him," the old man remarked.

"Yes, that's the way they all look at it."

By this time the boat had passed through the narrows and the open waters of the lower bay were reached.

There was a good breeze, very little sea, and the boat sped onward like a sea-bird.

The Italian boy, happening to move a little, attracted Andrews's attention, and he surveyed him with evident interest.

The boy was lying with his back to the gentleman, so he only had a partial view of the youth's face.

"Is that your son?" he asked.

"Oh, no; he's no kid of mine. He's a I-talian boy."

"Ah, yes; I see," the gentleman remarked, in a careless way, but all the time he was studying the face of the boy intently.

"I noticed he was dark-complexioned, but thought he was tanned."

"No, he's one of them I-talians. He run away from his folks 'cos they didn't treat him well, and while fooling around the docks he kinder struck up an acquaintance with me. You see, boss, I ain't so young as I used to be, and he helps me considerable.

"I'm all alone in the world, with neither chick nor child and nary a relation that I knows on, so I wasn't sorry when the boy said he'd like to come along with me."

"I should think it was a very good idea, indeed. What's his name?"

"Waal, I call him Billy, 'cos it's an easy name to handle, but his right name is Paolo something or other. He spits it out as easy as rolling off a log, but I'm darned if I could ever git my tongue 'round it. It's one of those cussed I-talian names, a regular jaw-breaker, you know, and about as long as a man's arm."

"He seems to be a bright fellow enough, to judge from his face," Andrews observed.

"Oh, he's jest as 'cute as they make 'em, as spry as a grasshopper, and as bright as a new dollar."

"Does he speak good English?"

"How?" asked the fisherman, evidently not understanding the question.

"Does he speak English—speak so you can understand what he says?" Andrews explained.

"Oh, you mean does he talk good United States?"

"Yes, that is it."

"Waal, pretty good. You kin always make out what he is a-trying to git at."

"I have a vacancy in my household for just such a boy as that," the other remarked, "but I suppose you wouldn't like to part with him."

The sleuth hound for a moment was puzzled by this unexpected development and hardly knew what to think of it.

It was evidently a whim on the part of the gentleman. He had taken a fancy to the boy.

Now, would it not be a good idea to seize upon the chance to domicile his spy right in the neighborhood of the haunted house to whose story he had listened with the utmost interest?

He thought he could easily solve the mystery of the old mansion.

There was not the least doubt in his mind that the house was haunted, but not by spectres from another world.

The thief taker was a sad skeptic in regard to ghosts.

He had lived some time in this bustling world—had passed through strange adventures—yet had never encountered a ghost, nor met any man of sense who had, so it was not strange he was incredulous.

His explanation of the mystery was simple; the old house was the head-quarters of the outlaw band of whom he was in search.

They had taken advantage of the dread with which the mansion was regarded by the dwellers in the neighborhood, and had probably done a little in the ghost line themselves, so as to add to the terror.

No one in the vicinity would be apt to come near the house, particularly and if any belated wayfarer should happen to see dark figures flitting about in the neighborhood, he would most certainly imagine the ghosts had appeared for his particular benefit.

Then, too, if the spy was in the house, she would be able to pick up some information in regard to the two dudes.

Perhaps this very man who made the offer was the one whom the trackers sought.

This was a wild idea, of course, and one that had not a particle of evidence to sustain it, but, sometimes, these fanciful imaginings come near the truth, and for such a sober, practical fellow, Joe Phenix gave considerable heed to them.

"Waaal, I s'pose I should kinder miss the little cuss," the boatman replied, slowly, "but then I ain't the kind of man to stand in anybody's way, and if the boy kin better himself I ain't a-going to lift a finger to stop it. I s'pose there won't be any objections for me to come and see him once in a while?"

"Oh, no, not at all. I'll give the youngster eight dollars a month and his board, and he can come right ashore with me on our return. Wake him up and see how he likes it."

This was done and the boy appeared delighted at the chance, and so the matter was arranged.

Some four hours the party spent on the water, and this afforded time for Alcibiades to sleep off the effects of the liquor, so, when the party returned, he was able to take care of himself.

The boy landed with the rest and the old man sailed away, waving his hand in salutation.

CHAPTER XXVII.
A BUSINESS CONSULTATION.

The trip had wonderfully refreshed all of the party, and when they reached the house none of them betrayed any signs that they had been dissipating all night long.

The Italian boy was turned over to the butler, with instructions to see him fittingly attired and comfortably bestowed, and then, as they all protested that they were almost starved, breakfast was immediately and vigorously attacked.

None of the other inmates of the mansion had yet made their appearance, with the exception of Andrews's confidential man of business, a portly, well-preserved, middle-aged gentleman, whose looks immediately manifested competence.

He was a Hebrew man, by name Abraham Goodchild.

A meek and prepossessing name, and yet many of the men who had happened to have business dealings with this soft-voiced financier declared vehemently that the name did not indicate the character of its owner at all. In fact, instead of being a good child, he was a hard-hearted, merciless skinflint.

But then business men do talk roughly about one another sometimes, particularly the fellows who do not succeed in getting the good end of every bargain.

As far as the laws of trade went the genial Abraham lived up to them, and so it was not easy for his enemies to drive him from the marts where the cunning speculators amuse themselves by cheating each other and call it business. But, it was well known that he was utterly unscrupulous and any one who had dealings with him must be on the lookout for sharp practice or else he would be likely to suffer.

Personally, though, the fat, jolly fellow seemed to be one of the nicest men in the world, and a better companion with whom to while away a social hour could not be readily found, even in so big a city as great New York.

But it was a noteworthy fact that the men who endorsed him as a jolly, good fellow were not men who had business dealings with him.

The "street"—by which comprehensive term the denizens of the Stock Exchange and its environs are known—shrugged its shoulders and looked wise when it was reported that the gentleman had joined his fortunes to those of the bold southwestern speculator.

There was hardly but one opinion about the matter: it was the old story.

The financier had the experience and the southwesterner the capital, and in the course of a year or two the position of the parties would be reversed—Goodchild would have the money and Andrews the experience.

In spite of these oracular sayings, however, the two seemed to get along very well together, and the chronic grumblers, men who never had a good word for anybody, accounted for it by declaring it was their belief that in this particular instance the fellow had met his master, the Westerner being fully as colossal a rascal as the financier.

In this life evil tongues are forever wagging.

But to return to our tale.

It was quite a jolly breakfast party, and after the meal was over Andrews excused himself on the plea of having some particular business to which attention must be given, as he did not intend to go to New York as usual.

As he smilingly expressed it:

"I'm going to take a couple of days off and devote myself solely to the amusement of my guests. It is something that I do not often do, so you may consider yourselves fortunate."

"I reckon if a certain young girl wasn't here that you wouldn't trouble yourself much," Alcibiades remarked, in his coarse way.

"I suppose I must plead guilty to the soft impeachment," the host replied, pleasantly.

"It's a man's first duty to attend to the comfort of the ladies."

"Particularly if they are young and good-looking," observed Alcibiades, with one of his disagreeable leers.

"That goes without saying, to use the French expression," returned Andrews, and he and the man of business then departed.

The host led the way to a little snuggery, half library and half smoking-room, which was situated on the ground floor in one of the wings of the mansion.

This was Andrews's favorite retreat.

There were three windows in the room, two in the front looking out upon the lawn and commanding a view of the street and the bay beyond, while from the one in the end of the room an outlook of the road leading to the city could be had for fully a mile.

The lower parts of the windows were protected by curiously contrived screens so arranged that while an ample view could be had from the interior of the room of all that passed without, it was impossible for any one on the outside to see into the room.

Andrews sat down in the luxurious embrace of a comfortable easy-chair, told Goodchild to help himself to another, drew out his cigar-case, selected a "weed," and passed it to the other, remarking as he did so:

"Try a cigar? There isn't anything in the world, in my opinion, that will settle a man's breakfast like a good cigar."

"Dot is so," observed Goodchild, who spoke with a decided accent, and he helped himself to a cigar.

"I understood you to intimate last night that you had some particular business to discuss," Andrews said, tendering the burning match to ignite the other cigar.

"Yes, and I told you, mine friend, dot there vas no time to be lost," the other replied, a shade upon his face.

"Last night we might have done somet'ing, but now, mine gootness! You cannot fight a battle mitout preparations."

"What kind of a battle is it to be, and how do you know I am not prepared?" Andrews asked, puffing away at his cigar in a perfectly placid manner.

"Mine gootness! I know how de bank-account stands," the man exclaimed. "We cannot do anyt'ing mitout der money. I put up der last dollar yesterday; you know we are short on der market, and if there is anodder drop to-day it vill be all up mit us."

"Yes, *if!* But what makes you think that prices will go down? There was a reaction just at the close of the market yesterday, and about all the wise heads predicted that there would be a general advance all along the line today."

"So there would be—there isn't the slightest doubt about dot, if der market was let alone!" the Jew rejoined, in quite an excited state.

"But I vas up-town mit der boys last night and I came across der mans who knows how der cat jumps. He vas an old friend of mine—he knew how I stood and he hated to see me smashed.

"Der 'street' is to be 'milked.' There is a large party

who have bought for a rise; we are not alone in der boat.

"A drop of three points this morning vill clean us all out; der gang will be bu'sted.

"Very likely," Andrews observed, just as calmly as ever, although he knew the full extent of the danger.

"Then, when we are cleaned out, der prices vill go up again, so as to encourage der outsiders to come in."

"Give them a chance to walk up to the captain's office and settle, eh?"

"Dot is so."

"How much money will carry us through?"

"Oh, it is not much, but der way things are now on der street, a dollar is as big as a cartwheel."

"How much money? Do you know the figures?"

"Oh, yes; t'irty t'ousand dollars vill see us through."

"Thirty thousand, eh?"

"Dot is der sum, and not a penny less vill do!" the financier exclaimed, decidedly.

"Then if we succeeded in raising thirty thousand, we would be able not only to tide over this crisis, but make a big stake when the reaction takes place?"

"Oxactly! Dot is der truth! In der first place values are to be depressed so as to freeze out der weak kneed lambs, milk dem of der moneys which they have been foolish enough to put up, and then, when der odder gang rush in to buy short, thinking dot everyt'ing is going to de eternal smash, the screws are to be put on, der figure lifted, and der new gang will be bu'sted as bad as der old one."

"A very nice little scheme—a double-edged knife, in fact, warranted to cut both ways."

"Oh, mine gootness, Mister Andrews, do not joke about der matter—it is nothing to laugh at!" the Goodchild exclaimed, really distressed. "It may be dot it is all right to you, but it is all wrong to me. I have about all my eggs in dot basket and I likes not to see them go to smash."

"Tranquilize yourself, gentle Abraham, we are not bu'sted yet."

And then Andrews produced his pocket book, which was a large and exceedingly bulky one at present, and drew from it a goodly pile of bills, together with the checks he had received from the young men in payment of their gambling debts.

"See how much there is there all together, bills and checks," he said, tossing the precious tokens of wealth carelessly into the man's lap.

Goodchild's eyes fairly bulged out from their sockets at this unexpected display, and he fell at once to work to count the money.

"How much?" asked the host, as his confidential man of business finished the task.

"Forty-seven thousand and fifty-one dollars to a cent," was the answer.

"That check for ten thousand I do not wish to use, so we won't count that, but deducting it we have thirty-seven thousand to the good."

13. Abraham Goodchild.

CHAPTER XXVIII.
THE SECRET CONFIDANT.

"Wonderful, wonderful!" muttered the financier, as he stroked the pile with his fingers, as though he could hardly believe the evidence of his own eyes.

"I vill give you mine word, as I am an honest man, I thought you were bu'sted and der jig vas up."

"Oh, no, not quite so bad as that," Andrews replied, in his easy, careless way, just as if he had a million or two of dollars at his back. "I am a firm believer in the old Scotch proverb, 'Never stretch out your hand further than you can easily draw it back.'"

"Dot is a good idea—dot is a grand idea, but we can not always carry it out in dis world," remarked Goodchild, reflectively.

"Well, we must live up to it as nearly as possible. I was on the lookout for just such a trick as this, and held part of my funds in reserve, so instead of being forced to the wall by this movement I stand a good chance of making forty or fifty thousand dollars."

"Oh, yes, there isn't the least doubt about dot. You vill do it as easy as turn your hand over," Goodchild asserted. "Oh! you have taken a weight from mine mind. I thought it would be all up with us, and Mister Andrews, I had so much faith in your operations dot in dis matter I followed your lead and put all my little saving into der t'ing."

"Is there enough money there to cover you also?"

"Oh, yes."

"Use it then, and put on a bold front. Don't let anybody suspect that we were afraid of getting squeezed."

"Oh, mine gootness, no!"

"The checks are all endorsed, ready for use."

"I will be off then."

Goodchild stowed the money away carefully in his capacious wallet, and with a parting salutation withdrew.

The door closed with a spring lock, so that it was impossible for any one to open it from the outside without using a key.

The master of the house evidently did not mean to be intruded upon without warning.

Hardly had the door closed with its sharp snap behind the portly figure of his man of business, when a section of one of the book cases in the room swung out clear from the wall of which it seemed a part, disclosing a secret stairway, dark as a pocket, leading to the lower regions.

In the passageway stood a tall, mature-looking man with iron-gray hair and a short beard of the same hue.

He was neatly attired in a dark business-suit, and looked like a sort of an upper servant, for he was evidently not a gentleman.

This person was known as Michael Jones, and he occupied the position of secretary and agent to Andrews.

Mr. Jones had a little room in one of the wings on the second floor, although he was seldom at Blithewood, for his duties in attending to Mr. Andrews's western business took him away most of the time.

He was a very quiet man, this Mr. Jones, and was not regarded with much favor by the rest of the servants.

In fact, he had such a peculiar, ghost-like way of moving around the house, making his appearance when least expected, that the servants got the idea he was a sort of a spy upon them, and so they were always on their good behavior when the secretary was around.

"Hallo! Are you there, Mike?" Andrews asked, turning toward the secret door, his quick ears detecting the slight whir made by the bookcase as it moved, otherwise noiselessly, through the air.

"Yes, I'm here."

The secretary advanced into the room and helped himself to the chair from which Goodchild had just risen, first taking the precaution, however, to carefully shut the secret door; and when the bookcase was replaced it would have been a shrewd guesser indeed who could have suspected there was a secret door behind it.

"Did you hear what passed between our man and myself?" Andrews asked.

"Yes, I was just going to enter the room when you and he came in, so I kept back and waited.

"He's a smart fellow, but for all that he pretty near got his fingers pinched this time. If you hadn't been lucky enough to have made that big raise, where would he have been?"

"Among the missing, gone where the woodbine twineth, and you can bet all your wealth on that too," Andrews replied.

"He never would have stayed to face his creditors in the world, but instead he would have gathered all the funds he could get his hands upon and skipped to parts unknown.

"In the new cities of the far West there is always room for a man like Goodchild to make a strike."

"And they call that business," grumbled the secretary. "Hang me! If it don't seem as if the most of the business men are as big rascals in their way as the poor devils who are 'doing time' up the river."

"They are not like Caesar's wife, above suspicion,

and between you and me and the bedpost, I am getting a little tired of this life that I am leading. It's mighty risky, and a man never knows exactly how he is standing. It's like walking over a slumbering volcano which may burst forth at any moment and hurl destruction around," Andrews remarked, thoughtfully.

"That's so," replied the secretary, "but you are in so deep that I don't exactly see how you are going to get out. But, I say, how on earth did you make that haul? Where did you strike so big a boodle?

"I thought the whole thing was going to smash when Goodchild spun his yarn about how the big spiders in Wall Street intended to skin all you little ones.

"I knew you had about reached low-tide mark, for it was only yesterday when I spoke to you about some little bills that ought to be settled, you said you had less than a hundred dollars in your pocket."

"It was the truth too," Andrews observed. "But I managed to make a raise of a couple of thousand dollars in town."

"Out of this old Grimgriskin?"

"He's the man."

"You must have played your cards pretty well, for if I'm any judge of human nature the old fellow is about as sharp a skinflint as a man would run across in a long day's journey."

"You are right there, but I have been studying him for some time, and, to use the slang, I think I have got him down fine.

"He is one of the suspicious men who would have instantly taken the alarm if I had proposed to him to go into anything requiring him to put up any funds.

"I played him as skillfully as an angler does a big fish."

I never even hinted if I knew of any good speculations, but at the same time caused the fact to become known to him that I had managed to do pretty well for some parties who had sufficient confidence to trust me with their money. So, at last, after pondering some time over the matter, the old man came to the conclusion that he would try a 'flyer.'

"When he mentioned the matter to me, I played offish for a while, and said I really didn't know of anything good just now, the market was dull—there was too much money seeking investment, and all the usual jargon of the street.

"And at last—any one who knows the man would hardly believe it—he brought me two thousand dollars and insisted upon my using it as I thought best.

"He had confidence that I could make a 'turn' with it to his advantage, and, Mike, although I was as hungry for that money as a starving man is for food, for I knew I had got in too deep, and that a little depression of prices would clean me out, yet I really made him press me before I would consent to take it."

"It came in just in the nick of time; but where did you get the rest?" Mr. Jones asked.

"I made the 'turn' last night, or, to speak more correctly, last night and this morning combined, for we commenced the wrestle about ten last night and wound up at daybreak."

"Aha, I begin to comprehend; you made your guests pay for their entertainment," observed the secretary, with a chuckle.

"Exactly, that was the little game I played, and I think you admit that I played it for all it was worth," Andrews remarked, complacently.

"The two dudes and young Grimgriskin I presume were the victims?"

"Yes, and the joke of the thing is that my bold Alcibiades took me for a greenhorn."

"You don't say so?"

"Fact! As sure as you are sitting there, he played me for a sucker.

"My idea, of course, when I invited the dudes here was to ease them of a little of their surplus wealth, if the trick could possibly be worked.

"I knew they were in the habit of playing at their clubs, although not for any great sums, a thousand or two at a sitting being the outside, and I calculated that if I managed the affair shrewdly I could get them interested in a quiet game, and before it ended I could make them pay dearly for their fun.

"On young Grimgriskin I did not count, because, as a general rule, the young donkey never has any money and his I. O. U.'s are not worth the paper on which they are written. But this time he came prepared for slaughter."

"Oh, he did?" and the secretary rubbed his hands gleefully together and chuckled as he thought how woefully the son of oildom had been disappointed in his calculation.

"Yes, came with money in one pocket and a pack of marked cards in another."

"Well, well, that was cutting it rather fat!"

"Oh, yes, but I tumbled to the trick immediately. The marked cards were the old style, all played-out; the dealer knew his customer was a greenhorn and so he stuck him with unsalable tools."

CHAPTER XXIX.
A DEEP PLOT.

"Ho, ho, ho!" laughed the secretary, "well, now, that is what I call a joke."

"Yes, and a mighty expensive one it was for him too before he got through," the other observed. "I saw what he was up to right at the beginning. He had provided himself with the marked cards and deliberately set out to fleece me.

"Of course he took me for a greenhorn, and never for an instant dreamed I was an expert in handling the pasteboards.

"He felt so sure he could fleece me that he tried to banter me into a game by offering to bet me that I dared not play with him."

"Oh, he was just hot for it, wasn't he?"

"He thought he had a sure thing, you know; with the marked cards he imagined he would have everything his own way."

"Well, how was it that you flaxed him?" asked the other, deeply interested in the recital.

"In the easiest manner possible.

"In the first place, he had been drinking freely so his head wasn't in a good condition. Then, as I told you the marked cards were the old style, difficult and complex, and such a man as this lout would require about six months' constant practice to be able to use them to advantage.

"Now my whole idea in getting the party down to the boat-house was to inveigle them into a game, and though I did not expect to get any money out of Alcibiades, yet I had concocted a little scheme by means of which I could make his I. O. U.'s valuable.

"So, when he proposed to play, it exactly answered my purpose, as I was prepared for just such a thing.

"I had a marked pack of cards in my pocket too, but the modern article; star-backs, just the same in appearance as his pack, and the private marks upon them much the same also, but much simpler and with just changes enough to bother a man who was not completely acquainted with the secret characters."

"I see, I see!" chuckled the secretary.

"It was the easiest thing in the world for me to substitute one pack for the other and the idiot never had the slightest suspicion. And, I knew I must make hay while the sun shone as it was not likely I would ever get a chance at the two dudes again, I went in for a big stake.

"I caught one man for ten thousand and the other for seventeen."

The secretary gave utterance to a prolonged whistle.

"That was a master-stroke!" he exclaimed, in admiration.

"And not only that, but Alcibiades, in order to make a big strike out of me, had raised eight thousand and some odd dollars and I scooped that in also," remarked Andrews, with a quiet smile.

"I give you my word that this is the biggest deal that I ever heard of!" the other exclaimed.

"Yes, but I haven't got through yet; these spoils that I have told you of are all cash. In addition I have young Grimgriskin's I. O. U. acknowledgments for as many thousands more and a check for ten thousand drawn by the old man in his favor."

"Well, you did skin him completely!"

"Yes, the contemptible scoundrel! And it really did me good, for now I have the mean rascal completely under my thumb."

"But I don't exactly understand why you should care to have him there," the secretary observed.

"Because unless I have him completely in my power he might be apt to make me trouble," Andrews replied.

"I have laid out a certain game to play and if I am successful, there's an end to all risks in the future.

"I'm in for a big stake, and I mean to win it if I can."

"What's the game now?"

"This girl, Sidonia Grimgriskin, is an heiress in her own right to a couple of million dollars. She is just the kind of girl to suit me, and if I can get her I will be able to cry quits with the world.

"No more risk—no more desperate adventures, but a life of ease and luxury. I can go into politics backed by a million, run for President, maybe, one of these days. Who knows?"

"Durn me if you ain't got the head for it!" the other exclaimed, emphatically.

"Everything is possible to a man with brains and courage, if he has capital at his back."

"That's true enough—the only obstacle I see is the girl herself," the secretary observed, thoughtfully. "How do you stand with her? These women are such durned peculiar cattle that there's no telling how to take 'em sometimes."

"She likes me well enough; has not exactly fallen in love with me, but I fancy she thinks more of me than of any other man whom she has ever met. If circumstances arise so that it would seem to her to be the proper thing to wed me, I do not think she would object, and at this point Alcibiades's gambling debts to me come in."

"You're too deep for me," the other remarked. "I'm over my head and shall have to swim out."

"It's as plain as the nose on your face when you get the hang of the matter," Andrews replied.

"In a day or two this miserable cur will come whimpering to me about the notes. He knew when he gave them that there wasn't any chance for him to pay them, or at least not for years.

"I shall suggest that if he made a clean breast of it to his sister she might be able to help him out; let fall a covert suggestion that if she came to me about the notes I would only be too glad to find some way by means of which they could be paid, and without letting the old folks know anything about it.

"The rascal is deadly afraid of the news coming to his father's ears that he has been gambling, for the old man has sworn he will have nothing to do with him if he persists in playing cards."

"I think I begin to see your game," the secretary observed. "You will help the young fellow out of the scrape, and so earn the gratitude of the girl."

"That is about the size of it. The I. O. U.'s, mind you, will all be in my hands.

"I get short of cash, you understand, and I part with a few of them to a banker friend, who kindly accommodates me with a loan, I indorsing the paper. Of course it will be easy for me to give up those which I hold to the girl, but rather difficult to get at the ones which I have parted with until the period of their redemption comes.

"The friend is a broker, a hard man to do business with, and care must he exercised not to allow him to suspect that the paper is anything but gilt-edged, and all right, and regular."

"Oh, yes, I understand the old dodge. It is very convenient sometimes to have these 'friends' in the background who will do just as you require. But suppose this don't fetch the girl? It ought to, I know," he hastened to add, "but these women are so deuced uncertain."

"Oh, I have yet another string to my bow," Andrews replied, with a meaning smile and a peculiar light shining in his dark eyes.

"At the last moment in the card game, when it came to the final *coup*, the young scoundrel had exhausted his resources and produced a check drawn by his father to his order for ten thousand dollars. But he said that while he would like to risk it upon the hand he held, yet in case he lost he did not want the check to be presented, for he had promised the old man not to use it except for actual necessities. So he asked me would I agree, if I won the pot, to hold the check for him until he could get a chance to redeem it?"

"I see, I see," and the secretary laid his forefinger alongside of his nose, and then winked in a knowing way.

"It was fishy, of course; I understood that the moment the bit of paper made its appearance, and it made me determined to get it into my hands, for it would be a weapon which would to me be invaluable."

"I bet you!" cried the other, with decided emphasis.

"I agreed immediately; anything to oblige my dear friend, Alcibiades," and Andrews laughed in a way that was anything but amusing.

"I knew that the game was in my hands as surely as though the faces of the cards were exposed instead of the backs.

"When the show of cards came of course I raked the pile, and here is the forged check," the host displayed the bit of paper as he spoke. "My esteemed friend put himself in a hole!

"I told him I would hold on to the check until he could redeem it, but I'm afraid I shall be so much in want of money that I will be obliged to raise some on it.

"It goes into the hands of a third party—an innocent holder for value. My same financier friend it will be again, who is a believer in the old law, an eye for an eye, a tooth for a tooth, and not at all the kind of man to compromise a felony, unless subjected to a powerful pressure."

"Beautiful!" and the secretary rubbed his bands in glee. "It is as fine as silk! To save her brother from the State Prison the lady will undoubtedly consent."

"Yes, for I shall have to almost ruin myself to work the trick, and she surely will be willing to reward my sacrifice," and Andrews laughed again.

"But I say, about this Italian boy," said the secretary, abruptly, as if the thought had just occurred to him. "I heard a couple of the servants talking about the beggar. What is your idea in bringing him into the house?"

"Mike, the moment my eyes fell upon that boy, when I encountered him in the boat, a cold chill ran all over me!" the master of Blithewood exclaimed, his tone low and earnest.

"I felt that in some mysterious way he boded danger to me. I am a slave to my presentiments, and in this case I acted promptly."

CHAPTER XXX.
A CROSS-EXAMINATION.

The secretary nodded his head.

"I can understand a feeling of that kind, but in this case I don't really see what harm the boy could possibly do you."

"Neither do I, yet in my heart of hearts, the moment I caught sight of the face of this Italian boy, something whispered that he was fated to prove dangerous to me," Andrews remarked slowly and reflectively.

"It is one of those odd things which cannot be explained. There wasn't the slightest reason in the world why I should take the least notice of the boy.

"Italian lads are common enough. I see probably fifty a day on the average, every time I go to the city, and do not remember ever seeing one whose face produced enough impression upon me to warrant a second glance."

"But this one did, eh?"

"Mike, the moment I looked upon him, a sudden cold chill ran all over me. You know the old superstition that when a man experiences a sudden and peculiar chill, it is produced by some one walking over his grave?"

"Oh, yes, but that's all nonsense!" exclaimed the other, who was evidently of a practical nature and not at all given to such fancies.

"Perhaps it is, but some of the wisest and most successful men that the world has ever known believed in just such superstition," the other replied, slowly.

"That may be, but I don't take any stock in the game."

"We are not all constituted alike in this and what seems natural and reasonable to one man will not so appear to his neighbor.

"Take the gift of genius, for instance. Here and there comes a child into the world who, without the least training, is able to perform feats that are impossible tasks to another, apparently equal to the first in every way.

"So it is with these strange presentiments. Some men are born with natures so sensitive that, as the mercury in the thermometer records to heat and cold, an evil influence makes an immediate impression upon them."

"Oh, you're getting too deep for me now; I'm over my head again," the secretary remarked.

"I suppose you think that sort of thing is all imagination, eh?" the master of the mansion remarked, with a quiet smile, apparently not in the least annoyed by the unbelief of the other.

"Well, yes, to put it plainly, I think that is about the size of it."

"Of course in a matter of this kind it is impossible for a man to offer much proof outside of his own experiences, and the world at large is apt to think that such evidence is not as reliable as it might be."

"That is natural enough, isn't it?"

"Yes, but then we might as well deny that certain men have genius for particular things."

"People don't believe unless the thing is proved," replied the other, in his abrupt, blunt way.

"The possession of the faculty of which I speak is not so easily made manifest to the world at large as many other peculiar gifts which might be mentioned, but the men so favored by nature are positive enough on the point.

"Now I am as certain that I possess this gift as I am that I am in this room this very minute.

"A hundred times at least in the course of my career

I have escaped serious peril by being timely warned by these peculiar presentiments.

"A face captures my eyes and immediately something whispers to me that I must be on my guard, for the owner of the face is a foe."

"And it has turned out afterward that there was something in it?" the secretory asked, incredulously.

"Yes, and in not a solitary instance has the presentiment failed to come true."

The other shook his head dubiously; he did not know what to make of this positive statement.

"Well, all I've got to say is that it beats my time; I've heard of such things, but I never took the least bit of stock in them."

"I've no doubt that you thought the fellows who made such claims were a little cracked in the upper story," Andrews suggested.

"Honestly, I reckoned their heads wasn't screwed on exactly right, and in this matter the idea of your being troubled by this beggarly Italian boy seems absurd.

"What possible hurt can the rascal do you?"

"That is just exactly what I have got to find out. I can imagine, though, a scheme in which he might be able to play an extremely prominent part.

"The fellow is a shrewd rascal, I can detect that from his eyes, although otherwise he appears to be rather stupid.

"Would not such a smart rat be just the one to play the part of a spy?"

"Oh, yes, he would do well enough for that, but it seems to me that if you suspected any thing of the kind you have made a great mistake in taking the young scoundrel into your service," the secretary remarked, reflectively.

"Not at all. How could I watch the fellow better than by having him right under my eyes?" Andrews replied.

The other stared; such an idea had never occurred to him.

"Well, governor, you just take the cake, you do!" he exclaimed, in admiration. "This is about the shrewdest dodge I ever heard of!"

"The idea is a good one, I think myself. If he is a spy I will find it out before he has been in the house a week."

"And then?" and a dark look came over the face of the secretary as he put the question.

"I think I shall be able to find some way to deal with him."

A simple sentence, and yet there was a world of fearful meaning in it as delivered by the speaker.

"Have you had any talk with the boy yet?"

"No, but I ordered John to bring him here after having him properly dressed, and it is about time he made his appearance."

Hardly had the words left the lips of the speaker when a whistle sounded from the speaking-tube which connected the room with the servants' quarters.

"There's John and the boy now, I guess; see!" remarked Andrews.

The secretary went to the speaking-tube and asked what was wanted.

As the master of the mansion had anticipated, it was the butler who desired to inform his master that the boy was in readiness to wait upon him.

"Send him in," commanded Andrews.

"Shall I remain?" the secretary asked.

"Oh, yes, I want you to inspect the fellow and pass judgment upon him. Just see what you make of him, and after the inspection is over we will compare notes."

Five minutes later the butler introduced the Italian boy, and then directly retired.

The lad's measure had been taken and a messenger dispatched to the city, who had returned with a full suit of common dark clothes, in which the boy was now arrayed, and he looked quite respectable, although, despite his new clothes, there was a wild, brigand-like air about him, caused, no doubt, by his bold expression, his keen black eyes and the crispy ebon-hued curls which adorned his head.

He had come into the room, twirling his new cap between his fingers, evidently abashed by the situation.

Andrews reclined in the easy chair, puffed away at his cigar, and regarded the boy with a languid sort of curiosity.

The secretary, on the contrary, fastened his eyes upon the lad with a hawk-like glance.

"Well, they have dressed you up like a gentleman," the master remarked.

"Si, signor," replied the boy, with a grin.

"Do you like to wear good clothes?"

"Si, signor," again he responded, and the grin increased.

"Like good things to eat, too?"

"Si, si," and the boy pressed both hands upon his stomach, and the grin widened until he exposed every tooth he had in his head.

"Did my people give you a good breakfast, as I ordered?"

"Si, si, nice-a breakfast-a."

"We will not starve you to death while you remain here."

"Oh, no, no, no starve-a!"

"What is your name?"

"Billa," and the boy grinned again as though he had given utterance to a good joke.

"No, no, I don't mean that one; I don't mean the name that the old fisherman gave you, but your own."

"Si, si, Paolo."

"That name is fully as easy to remember and pronounce as the other, so we'll have no more of the Billy, if you please," Andrews observed. "What is your last name?"

"Gismondi."

"And from what part of Italy do you come?"

"Za citee of Naples."

"You cannot speak very good English, I suppose?"

"No speck mooch English," replied the boy, shaking his head.

"You understand it pretty well though?"

"Si, signor, me-a understand ze English varra goot."

"You'll get along all right then; just do what you are told, keep your eyes open, look sharp, and you'll have a good place here. That's all."

Andrews rung his bell. The butler made his appearance, and the youth departed.

"What do you think of him?" the master asked quietly, after the door closed behind the two.

"His face seems familiar," replied the secretary, as if puzzled.

"It ought to seem so, for it is Kate Scott disguised!"

CHAPTER XXXI.
THE NEW MAN.

"The deuce you say!" the secretary cried, in utter surprise

"It is the girl!" Andrews, exclaimed, positively. "There isn't the least doubt about it, so you see my presentiment was not a false warning.

"If it had not been for the feeling that took possession of me the moment my eyes fell upon the face of this supposed Italian boy, I should not be as well situated as I am to cope with this foe, the most dangerous by far that has ever menaced me."

"It's a mighty bold game," the secretary remarked, with a grave face and an ugly look in his eyes.

"Yes, if it was anyone else, one would hardly think she would muster up courage enough to try such a desperate adventure, but what puzzles me is how the deuce she struck at me so directly. By what lucky chance did she come so near to the trail? Have we been careless and neglected to cover up our traces as we ought to have done?"

"Oh, no, we have been just as careful as usual. It's nothing but a piece of luck, that's all. Some of these women seem to have the fiend's own luck sometimes," the secretary replied.

"You know my opinion about women pretty well, by this time, I reckon," he continued. "And if you remember I advised you not to pay any attention to this woman. I was afraid we would get into a snarl if we bothered our heads about her."

"And I was equally afraid we would get into a snarl if we did not. I tell you, Mike, this girl has the perseverance and pluck of a bloodhound," Andrews rejoined.

"If we had allowed her to go on, unmolested, she would have certainly got us dead to rights in the long run.

"I foresaw from the beginning that she was likely to prove the most dangerous foe that ever struck in on our track, and that was the reason why I was so anxious to silence her."

"We've got the best of it now, anyway," the secretary suggested.

"Oh, yes, a most decided advantage," and a dark smile came over the face of the speaker.

"We know her, and she cannot be certain about us. At the worst she can only suspect, and it may be possible that she does not know how hot is the scent she has struck.

"It may be that she only has an inkling that the secret which she seeks is located somewhere in this neighborhood, and jumped at the chance which I offered her in order to get an opportunity to examine this locality at her leisure."

"I shouldn't be surprised if you have hit off the right thing," the secretary remarked, after deliberating about the matter for a moment.

"And now do you see how wise I was to put faith in the secret, incomprehensible instinct which warned me that danger threatened?"

"Oh, I give up beat in regard to that. I wouldn't believe it if I didn't know it was so, but then there's a great many wonderful things in the world—things which a man can't understand at all, and it ain't of much use for a fellow to bother his head about them."

"That's solid chunks of wisdom, Mike," Andrews observed. "Accept the world as it is, make the best of it, and don't worry your head about things you can neither understand or alter.

"Now, as far as this girl is concerned, I think we have got the dead wood on her in the worst kind of a way.

"She has thrust her head into the lion's mouth. I think it is probable that she does not know it, but she will make the discovery when the teeth close upon her," and Andrews laid back in his chair and laughed as if he had given utterance to a pleasant jest.

"How soon will that little operation take place?" the secretary asked.

"What is your idea about it?"

"The quicker the better," the secretary replied, with savage accent, and he clinched his muscular hands as though he was longing to perform the job there and then.

"That is my opinion; the girl is dangerous, and I shall not rest quiet until she is placed in a situation where she will not be able to do any mischief," Andrews remarked slowly, and with an air of deep reflection.

"There's only one thing to be done," the other observed, with a dark look upon his countenance.

"Oh, yes, there isn't the least doubt about that, and there mustn't be any slip up in the proceedings this time."

And then the two men put their heads together and engaged in a whispered conversation, the purport of which the reader will know anon.

And now leaving the two to their dark meditations, we will turn our attention to an incident, apparently hardly worth the detailing, yet which has an important bearing upon our tale.

A huge black man, of immense strength, had charge of the horses in the really elegant stables attached to the mansion.

Pericles Johnson, he was called, and, like the majority of mankind, he was not fond of doing any work that he could avoid.

He was a well paid fellow, for he was a glib tongued chap, and was popularly supposed to be a first-class man in regard to horses.

Thirty dollars a month he got, and for some time he had been on the lookout for an assistant to aid him in his arduous duties.

He had complained to his master, alleging that the work was too much for one man, but that gentleman thought differently.

All the satisfaction he could get was that his employer would be willing to board a man if he, the hostler, would pay him.

So Pericles, acting on the principle that half a loaf was better than no bread, had done his best to pick up some cheap man upon whose shoulders he would be able to put the greater part of his work.

This was not so easy a matter as he had anticipated, for all the men who applied for work set a fair value upon their labor, and were not disposed to work for their board and a trifle of money.

But on the morning that the interview occurred between Andrews and his confidential agent, the particulars of which we have just detailed, an applicant made his appearance at the stables who seemed likely to come up to the ideas of Mr. Pericles Johnson.

He was an Irishman of forty-five or fifty, a powerfully-built, muscular fellow, plainly capable of a deal of work yet, in spite of his age.

The clothes he wore were old, and from their texture and cut had evidently never been fashioned in the "land of the free and home of the brave."

The man was a new importation, clearly, and one whose lines had not been cast in pleasant places since crossing the stormy brine.

He had a rather intelligent face, although it was disfigured by a short stubby beard of reddish gray.

The first word he spoke betrayed his nationality.

"Arrah, now, boss, do yees be afther wanting a dacent man to help around the stables?" he asked, and he took off his well-worn hat and bowed respectfully.

The deference of the man tickled the vanity of the hostler, and he fairly swelled with importance as he answered:

"Well, I doesn't exactly know 'bout dat, mister. What kin you do? Does yer know anything 'bout hosses?"

"Hosses is it?" and a broad smile came over the face of the man, while he winked in a knowing manner. "Shure, ye might look the country over, big as it is, and not find a man who knows more about hosses than meself."

"Dat's a pretty big brag, fust thing, you know, mister," Mister Johnson observed, with the air of an oracle.

"Upon me word, sur. I'm the b'ye that can make it good, if you'll only be kind enough for to give me the least bit of a try."

"Well, Cap, I dunno as we want a man as big as youse is. Now if youse was a right smart chap of a boy—"

"What's the differ, anyhow?" exclaimed the old Irishman, eagerly. "Shure, I'm able for a b'ye's work, any day in the week."

"Oh, yes indeedy, dar ain't any doubt 'bout dat, but is you willing to take de wages dat a boy would git?" the hostler inquired, shrewdly.

"How can the likes of me tell till I hear what they are?" responded the Irishman.

"Well, Cap, you see de way de matter is, de boss ain't willing for to git any more help, 'cos he's like all de big-bugs and wants to git all he kin for his money, so all he's willing for to do is to find de fodder, and de wages has got to come out of *my* pocket."

"Oh, did any mortal ever hear the likes of that!" exclaimed the old man, in mingled horror and indignation.

"De boss will feed yer—and we lives on de fat of de land here, too, I wants you to understand —youse kin sleep in de hayloft with plenty of blankets and buffalo-robes fur to keep you warm in de winter-time, and I'll give you four dollars a month."

"That's a poor cry for an able-bodied man like meself, but I'll take it, please the pigs, for it may lead to something better."

And so the bargain was concluded, much to Johnson's delight, particularly when, after a test of the Irishman's abilities, he found that his helper was a handy man about the stable.

After the cleaning up was performed the hostler went to the mansion for orders, and the new man improved the opportunity to take a look at the loft above. A window in it commanded a view of the house, and the Irishman, taking up a position by it, drew a pair of opera-glasses from his pocket.

"Oh, this will do nicely," he muttered, with none of his recent brogue.

201

CHAPTER XXXII.
SIDONIA'S RESOLVE.

A week had elapsed since the Grimgriskin family had entered the portals of Blithewood as the guests of its master.

And during that time Andrews had played his cards in the most admirable manner.

He had managed by means of a lucky coup in the stock market to land old Grimgriskin a winner to the tune of over ten thousand dollars, and as a natural result the great oil king became possessed of the idea that the young man was a genius. And when his better-half had suggested that if they did not look out there might be danger of a love affair between their host and their beautiful daughter, the old man had looked wise and remarked that in his opinion Sidonia might do a great deal worse than to become the mistress of Blithewood.

Andrews had not neglected to conciliate the old lady, but had devoted himself to her fully as much as to the daughter.

He treated her with the utmost deference, listened to her extravagant stories with the greatest interest imaginable, and flattered her in such a delicate manner that it quite won the heart of the shrewd, yet unsophisticated matron.

Then, too, Andrews made a great impression upon her by the respectful manner in which he conducted himself toward her uncouth cub of a son.

He spoke of and treated Alcibiades as though he thought him to be one of the finest young men in the land.

If he had been a prince and the heir to a kingdom,

the cunning adventurer could not have treated him with more respect.

Mrs. Grimgriskin at first did not know exactly what to make of this, for she had generally been accustomed to hearing some unpleasant truths in regard to her rascal of a son from almost every one who came in contact with him, but Andrews spoke in the lightest possible manner of his "peculiarities."

All young men were a little wild, so he asserted. It was only natural; with age would come soberness, and, in fact, it was a well-known thing that all the great men whom the world has delighted to honor had more or less mischief in them when callow youths.

By such specious pleading as this the wily flatterer made a deep impression upon the mother and daughter, who were both too weak where Alcibiades was concerned.

At the end of the week, Andrews felt perfectly sure that as far as the father and mother were concerned there would not be any objection to his suit.

As for the lady herself, he did not feel so sure, but she was a quiet, odd kind of a girl, not one of those who wear their heart upon their sleeve that all the world may run and read.

He felt certain that he was not disagreeable to her. Nay, more, if he was any judge of womankind—and he flattered himself that he was—the girl's actions plainly indicated that she liked him. But whether the liking was strong enough to induce her to give a favorable answer when he put the all important question was something that could only be settled by actual trial.

He felt sure enough of his ground to go ahead upon the first favorable opportunity, though.

One obstacle only could he discern in the way.

Three members of the Grimgriskin family were favorably inclined, but the fourth, the one who by rights ought to be his warmest ally, he doubted.

He felt certain that Alcibiades was not inclined to be friendly.

That individual had been in the sulks ever since the night when he went for wool and succeeded in getting shorn.

He avoided everybody and generally conducted himself as though he considered himself a much-abused individual.

Both the mother and sister had taken the alarm and endeavored to discover what was the trouble, but for a time Alcibiades was as close as an oyster.

For a week he resisted all the persuasions of his mother, and the blandishments of his sister, but at last, in an incautious moment, he had succumbed to the influence of Andrews's good liquor, and before he hardly knew what he was doing, confided his troubles to Sidonia.

She was amazed, for Alcibiades confessed to her that he had lost a terrible amount of money at play, and the master of Blithewood held his I. O. U.'s for an amount that he could never hope to pay.

He was deep enough in his cups to be honest, though, for once in his life, and he bluntly revealed to the astonished and disgusted girl that he had entrapped his host into playing, intending to "skin him"—such was the terse expression he used—of every dollar he could be induced to venture.

"But he will not press you for payment of the debt?" she exclaimed, hardly knowing what to say.

"No, I suppose not," he snarled, "but it will have to be paid some time, and then it is a debt of honor, you know, and a feller is expected to pay that sort of thing, even if it takes the last shirt from his back.

"Besides, suppose dad or marm should hear of it?" he continued. "These cursed things do leak out once in awhile, wouldn't my cake be all dough?

"Hang me if I believe the old man would ever consent to look me in the face again."

A bright idea occurred to the girl as she meditated over the situation, and the idea was of such a nature that the bare thought brought a burning blush to her face.

She cast a quick glance at Alcibiades to see if he noticed her agitation, for she was certain she must be blushing furiously, her face being as hot as fire.

But Alcibiades had reached that point of maudlin intoxication when all acuteness has vanished.

"Suppose," she said, hesitatingly, "suppose I see about the matter?"

"Great Scott!" he cried, startled by the idea, "you don't mean to say that you would be willing to take up the I. O. U.'s? Why, Sid, it will cost you a small fortune!"

"Well, I have money enough," she replied, the color still in her cheeks, for her agitation was too intense to permit it to subside.

"Since I came into my property I have never been able to spend even one half of my interest, to say nothing of the principal."

"But it's a colossal sum—a fortune!" he repeated.

"I did not say I would pay it, you foolish boy!" she replied, lightly. "I merely said I would see Mr. Andrews about it."

"Yes, but of course I know what you intend to do," he observed.

"You'll have to pay it of course. Andrews is no fool for all his smooth ways and devilish politeness. I picked him out for a pigeon, but, hang me, if he didn't turn out to be the worst kind of a hawk.

"He's no fool," he repeated. "He won't give up securities calling for thousands and thousands of dollars without getting his money."

"It will not do any harm for me to see him, so make yourself comfortable on the lounge and I will have a talk with him immediately," she remarked, rising and taking a look at herself in the glass in order to see that she was in proper trim to visit the man whom she knew to be her devoted admirer.

Alcibiades extended himself upon the lounge. "I know, of course, that you're going to pony up the rhino, for that is the only way you can get those infernal bits of papers, and I must say, Sid, you are just the dearest old gal that ever walked in shoe-leather."

"Wait till I get the I. O. U.'s before you praise me," she remarked.

"But keep it dark, Sid, for heaven's sake!" he exclaimed abruptly, sitting bolt upright on the lounge in his excitement. "Don't breathe a word of it to a soul, or it will be my ruin! If you have any love for your poor, unfortunate wretch of a brother, keep it dark."

"Don't fear! I will be as silent as the grave."

"And, Sid, if you do get those cursed papers, don't examine them—that is, only enough to be sure that they are all right."

"Certainly not!"

"My signature is at the bottom of all of them, with the exception of one, father's check for my quarterly allowance, and it's on the back of that."

His face was white as he uttered the lie, but his

tongue never faltered.

"That's the important one," he continued. "Be sure you get that, for dad would be ready to kill me if he knew I gambled his check away."

"I will be careful."

"And the moment you get the cursed things into your hands be sure and burn them up. Don't let a soul see them, if you don't want to drive me into a lunatic asylum. There are thirteen of them altogether."

"Do not be alarmed. I will be careful."

And then the girl departed upon her mission. She went with heightened color and a rapidly beating heart.

Why?

Because this was to be the touchstone to test the love of Bernard Andrews.

By his behavior in this important matter she believed she could tell whether it was wise to entrust all her future life into his keeping.

If he proved to be current gold, then herself and fortune she would gladly give to him.

If he was but dross, why, it would be a narrow escape for her.

CHAPTER XXXIII.
ALCIBIADES TAKES A STAND.

Anxious as was Alcibiades to learn the result of his sister's quest, yet he had drank so much liquor that he could not keep awake, and in ten minutes after Sidonia quitted the apartment he was fast asleep.

Just a short half-hour was the girl absent, and when she returned there was a look of triumph upon her face, which was flushed with excitement.

"Poor boy," she observed, gazing compassionately upon the sleeper, who looked anything but interesting, sprawled out upon the lounge with his mouth open.

"I suppose he must have worried terribly over this matter," she continued, "but thank Heaven, it is all over now."

At this moment Alcibiades opened his eyes and stared around him with a vacant look.

Young Grimgriskin was one of those men so constituted that it only required a small quantity of liquor to upset him, and, as a general rule, he recovered as speedily as he was overcome.

"Hallo! Have you got back, sis?" he said, rising to a sitting position, and looking questioningly at the girl.

"Yes," and she sunk into an easy-chair, while a smile of satisfaction played over her features.

"Well, by your grinning, I reckon you have fixed the thing up all right," the young hopeful remarked.

Strange anomaly that such loutish brutes as this worthless wretch should be able to command the love and services of sympathizing and sacrificing women.

Sometimes it seems as if the more worthless the object, the greater the love and devotion inspired in the breast of womankind.

"Yes, I have succeeded."

"Bully for you!" cried Alcibiades, rubbing his hands together gleefully.

"Oh, yes, there wasn't the least trouble about the matter," and a peculiar expression appeared upon her face as she spoke.

"Sis, you are the boss girl, and no mistake!" the young man exclaimed, exultingly.

"Ah! You don't know what a weight you have taken off my mind.

"I s'pose you'll hardly believe it, sis, but I've not been able to either eat or sleep during the past week."

"I have noticed that you seemed to be worried about something," Sidonia replied.

She could not with truth say that she had noticed that there was aught amiss in regard to his eating and sleeping, although she had fancied he had been indulging more freely than usual in strong drink, and both herself and mother had repeatedly cautioned him to he careful, admonitions which had not produced the slightest effect upon him.

"I have been worrying over the infernal thing ever since it occurred!" he declared.

"I feel as if I had grown ten years older in these few days."

"Make your mind easy now for everything is all right," she remarked.

"And the cursed things are destroyed?" he asked, anxiously.

"Yes, every one!"

"Thirteen of them?"

"Yes, thirteen. Mr. Andrews counted them into my hand, and I held them while he lit the match and only let go when the flames began to scorch my fingers."

"Sid, you are just the gayest girl that's going!" Alcibiades cried. "And you can just bet I shan't forget this little affair. I'll make it all right with you one of these days.

"You're sure you saw the paper with my name on the back? It was a note of the old man's payable to my order and endorsed by me."

"Yes, I noticed it."

"Did you observe the amount?" Alcibiades asked, carelessly, and yet with a certain amount of trepidation which he could not entirely conceal, despite his efforts so to do.

"No, I was only too anxious to destroy the horrid things to examine them particularly."

"It doesn't matter." the young man replied, a great weight taken from his mind.

"But I say, Sid, don't ever let on to anybody, either marm or dad, and dad particularly, that you know anything about that check, 'cos it might make a heap of trouble for me.

"As long as it is destroyed it is all right."

If the girl had been a better business woman than she was and had taken time to reflect upon the matter she would have been perplexed to guess why the young man was so anxious for the harmless check to be destroyed.

"This has cost you a pile of money, Sid, but I s'pose he didn't exact the full amount, did he?" Alcibiades continued.

Again the blush crept up in the face of the girl, and a faint smile illuminated her features as she said:

"It did not cost me a penny, Alcibiades. When I told Mr. Andrews of the nature of my errand, he promptly said the papers were at my command, and when I hinted at payment he replied that he would scorn to accept money. The papers were at my service, he never intended to claim the amount called for by them. You had the gambling fever strong upon you and he thought a severe lesson might do you good."

"Curse his impudence!" muttered the now independent Alcibiades between his teeth.

"And the best thing I could do was to apply a match to the compromising documents soon as possible."

"Which you immediately did?"

"Yes."

"Well, Andrews is a bigger fool than I thought!" the young man exclaimed, coarsely. "Catch me throwing away a fortune in that style. The man is an idiot!"

"You mustn't speak in that way, Alcibiades, of the gentleman who is to be my husband," replied the girl, with a smile and a blush.

"What?" and the other started to his feet.

"I presume Mr. Andrews perceived by my face that I was deeply impressed by his noble conduct, and he thought the opportunity a fitting one to declare his sentiments," the girl explained.

"And you accept him?"

"Yes; and I feel sure I have made a wise choice," Sidonia observed, slowly, for she perceived by the expression upon her brother's face that he did not approve of the match.

"Wise, fiddlesticks!" Alcibiades cried, in a passion, for with his usual inconsistency he chose to feel aggrieved because he had not been consulted in regard to the matter, and had immediately come to the conclusion to do all he could to break up the arrangement.

"See here, Sidonia, this fellow has pulled the wool over our eyes in the finest kind of style. Blessed if I don't think he roped me into that game of poker just to be able to skin me so as to get a chance at you.

"I guess I'll have to see him and give him a bit of my mind in regard to this riffle.

"He can't fool me; I'm no soft-headed gal!" And Alcibiades marched toward the door.

Sidonia was naturally mild, still she had a temper when roused.

"You had better mind your own business!" she exclaimed, indignantly. "I am not half so soft-headed as you are!"

"Don't get huffy, sis, you can't help it, you know, for you were born that way," and with this decidedly cool remark Alcibiades departed.

"It serves me right for trying to do anything for him!" the girl exclaimed, in disgust. "But he will not make much by going to Mr. Andrews, for, unless I am greatly mistaken, he is fully able to attend to his own affairs, and Alcibiades will be sent away with a flea in his ear."

Alcibiades, like all men of his stamp, had a great idea of his own importance, and now that the papers were destroyed he felt fully equal to the task of expressing to Andrews his disapproval of his suit.

"Thought I needed a lesson, did he? Confound his impudence!" the young man muttered, as he proceeded in search of Andrews.

"I believe upon my soul that he was jest a-trying to rope me into a game so as to be able to skin me.

"I'll bet a hat that it was all a game on his part to get me into a fix just so he could play the grand gentleman for Sid's benefit.

"I don't s'pose that my speaking will do much good, but if I'm ugly I can make trouble, and as Andrews seems to be so well fixed as not to care two pins for money—catch me burning up I O. U.'s calling for thousands of dollars—maybe he'll be inclined to come down and let me have six or eight thousand 'chucks.'

"He can spare the money well enough, for he must have won pretty close to forty thousand dollars that night."

From these utterances it will be seen that Alcibiades was proceeding on a well-defined plan, and in his overweening vanity he fancied he was smart enough to cope with such a man as Bernard Andrews.

After his interview with Sidonia the host had retreated to his snuggery on the first floor of the mansion, and thither Alcibiades sought him.

"Hullo, Alcibiades, old fellow, come in!" Andrews exclaimed heartily when, in answer to the young man's knock, he opened the door and the applicant for admission stood revealed.

From the sulky expression upon the face of young Grimgriskin, for Alcibiades had tried to look as ugly and insolent as possible, Andrews immediately guessed that his visitor had not come in a friendly mood and so was warned to prepare for war.

Alcibiades marched into the room, helped himself to the most comfortable chair in the apartment, sat down and proceeded at once to business.

"See here, Andrews, what have you been saying to my sister?" he exclaimed.

CHAPTER XXXIV.
AN EASY VICTORY.

Andrews laughed, sat down, took out his cigar-case, helped himself to a weed and proffered the case to Alcibiades just as if the other had approached him in the friendliest manner possible.

"Have a smoke, old fellow?" he asked.

"No, I didn't come here for any fun," young Grimgriskin snarled. "And I want you to understand that I don't like the way things are going at all!"

"Don't you? Well now, that is really too bad," and the host lit his cigar and proceeded to smoke with the air of a man at perfect peace with himself and all the world.

Alcibiades was enraged; it was plain from the manner of the other that he cared but little for his opinion.

"Yes, and I must say I think there has been really indecent haste in this business, and I want you to understand that, as one of the principal members of the family, I most decidedly object to the arrangement."

"A union between your sister and myself doesn't meet your views, then?" Andrews asked, puffing out great clouds of smoke.

"No, it does not; the whole thing is too sudden—"

"I'm a little too previous, eh?"

"Yes, that expresses the idea exactly."

"And this is your opinion?"

"It is!" snarled young Grimgriskin, defiantly.

"By the way, did your sister tell you about the destruction of the I. O. U.'s?" Andrews asked, abruptly

"Yes, she did," responded Alcibiades, with the air of a man who has suffered a grievous wrong.

"That was a mighty smart trick of yours, too; I s'pose

you think I ain't up to it, but I am. I tell you when you tackle me you ain't got a fool gal to deal with. I've got the biggest kind of a head for all such games; I wasn't born yesterday, and don't you forget it!"

"Oh, you think I have been playing a little game, eh?" and Andrews as he put the question laid back in his chair and fairly laughed in the face of the angry Alcibiades, as much as to say, "What are you going to do about it?"

"Why, I know it," young Grimgriskin cried, "it's as plain as the nose on your face! You can fool Sidonia all right, for she's a big fool like all women, but you can't pull the wool over my eyes!

"You let go of my I. O. U.'s because you had a bigger thing. It was throwing a minnow to catch a whale. What's a few thousand dollars when you were playing for an heiress with a couple of millions?"

"As you justly observe, what is it? Nothing at all, and I made the trick, too, old fellow; your I. O. U.'s I gave to the flames, but I have secured your sister's consent to marry me, and that was richly worth the sacrifice."

"But you ain't married to her yet!" the other cried, exasperated by the coolness of his host.

"Right again! I am not married to her yet, but as I have her word there isn't much doubt that the ceremony will soon take place."

"Not if I can prevent it!" Alcibiades exclaimed, savagely.

"What! Are you against me? Why, I thought you were a friend, and after my letting you off on the I. O. U.'s, too!" cried Andrews, in a way that plainly revealed even to the obtuse son of oildom that the other was "chaffing" him.

215

"You'll have to do a deuced sight more than that for me before you can count me in on your side!" Grimgriskin declared, so much enraged by the coolness of Andrews as to lead him to expose the game he desired to play.

"Oh, I must buy your consent?"

"Well, I reckon I will have something to say about matters, and if you are wise you will 'square' me!"

"Now you are dipping into the vulgate, and to give you your answer in terms that you cannot misunderstand, allow me to say I am not that kind of a hairpin!" Andrews replied.

"You may be able to bulldoze your mother and sister, but you cannot scare me for a cent," and the contemptuous manner in which the host spoke showed how lightly he regarded the young man's threat.

"Oh, you want war, then, do you?" and Alcibiades rose to his feet and glared at the other.

"War between you and a man like myself?" Andrews cried. "Go hang yourself to the first tree for a fool! If you dare to attempt to interfere with me, I'll crush you as though you were only a worm in my path!"

"You will?" and the young man grew red with anger. He had not anticipated any such display of spirit on the part of his host, whom he had set down in his own mind for a milksop.

"I will, most decidedly."

"We will see!" cried Alcibiades, threateningly, and he laid his hand on the door knob.

"By the way, before you depart, I want to know about this check of yours?" exclaimed Andrews abruptly.

"Check!" responded the other, amazed.

"Yes, that one for ten thousand dollars, made by your father to your order and endorsed by you to me.

When can I look for the money?"

Alcibiades stared, and his legs began to tremble. Could it be possible that he was in a trap?

"Why—why, the check is burned. Sidonia told me she saw it destroyed," he stammered, his voice trembling and uncertain.

"Nothing of the kind: she mistook some one of the I. O. U.'s for it, if she said so," Andrews replied, pitilessly.

"That check has been out of my hands for three days. I was short of money, and I raised a loan upon it from a financier friend. I told him not to attempt to cash it, but to hold the paper and I would redeem it."

Alcibiades staggered against the door, and but for its support most certainly would have fallen.

"What's the matter with you? Are you going to faint, man? That check is all right, isn't it? Nothing crooked about it, is there? For if there is, Heaven help you! This financier is like a wild beast when any one attempts to trick him.

"If there is anything wrong about the check and he finds it out, he'll put you in the State Prison as sure as you're a living man!"

A hollow groan came from Alcibiades's lips, and he sunk down upon his knees.

"For Heaven's sake, spare me!" he stammered, with thickened utterance.

"Spare you, old fellow? Why, I wouldn't hurt a hair of your head for the world!" Andrews cried, in the most jovial manner.

"Aren't you going to be my brother-in-law, and do you think I would do anything to cause you any trouble?"

The miserable young man tottered slowly to his feet. He fully understood now the nature of the trap into which he had fallen.

"Of course I know that you are my friend," he said, with whitened lips. "I know you wouldn't do anything to hurt me for Sidonia's sake."

"Certainly not!"

"For Heaven's sake, though, get that check back in your own hands as soon as you can."

"Oh, don't be alarmed about that. The man is the soul of discretion, and he will not attempt to use the check until I tell him that it is impossible for me to take it back."

"Get it back, though—get it back!" pleaded Alcibiades, groveling like a whipped cur.

"That will be all right, don't you worry, and, Alcibiades, I think you are wrong to oppose my union with your sister, for within four and-twenty hours after I am married to Sidonia, I will place that check in your hands."

"Oh, will you, though?" cried the other, eagerly.

"I will, as sure as I stand here, so do all you can to hurry the match forward."

"You can depend upon me. I'll do my level best!" cried Alcibiades, a weight lifted from his mind.

"Did you tell Sidonia that you did not think a union between us would be advisable?"

"Yeh—yes," was the reluctant reply.

"Better tell her now, as soon as you can, that you have changed your mind, and you think it is a good thing," Andrews observed.

"Oh, you can depend upon me!"

"Go ahead then, and don't worry about the check. It you keep faith with me you are all right."

Somewhat relieved in his mind by this assurance, young Grimgriskin retreated from the apartment. He sought his sister told her that after a talk with Andrews he had come to the conclusion that she couldn't pick out a better man.

Alcibiades was a thorough cur, and having once felt the lash of the master's whip was not anxious to provoke a second chastisement.

Hardly had Andrews' door closed behind the young man when he left, before Mr. Michael Jones made his appearance from the secret passageway.

"Well, you settled him, all right, captain," the secretary observed, with a chuckle.

"Oh, yes, he was inclined to be ugly, but when he found that I had the ring in his nose he weakened," Andrews replied, grimly.

"It seems to me that the outlook is mighty good," Jones remarked.

"Yes, everything is altogether lovely. I have secured the heiress, and the moment she is mine with her two millions I think I can bid good-by to this life of adventure with all its desperate risks."

"You bet!" the secretary exclaimed, decidedly. "The moment that stroke is made you mustn't be fool enough to take any more chances."

"Oh, trust me to carry sail cautiously. I think the best thing we can do, Mike, is to go abroad, a wedding-trip for me, you know, and we'll stay away for five or six years until all danger is past."

"But this girl, Kate Scott—this spy, right in your house? What is to be done with her?" the other asked, his voice growing low and his face dark.

"This night will settle her. I have arranged a plan so that she will disappear and the keenest sleuth hound will not be able to connect us with the affair. Listen while I unfold the particulars."

And then the two men put their heads together.

CHAPTER XXXV.
ENTRAPPED.

Kate's sojourn at the Blithewood mansion in the guise of an Italian boy had not profited her in the least, for not a single discovery of the slightest importance had she made.

True there was the old haunted house near by, with its ghostly traditions, and the thought had occurred to her that within this old and deserted mansion the Spider Captain and his secret band might have their head-quarters.

A couple of secret inspections, though, after night-fall, had not resulted in any discoveries and after five days she was on the point of abandoning the pursuit in this quarter in order to turn her attention to some other, when she received a message from Joe Phenix—conveyed to her by a scissors-grinder who came into the yard to sharpen the cutlery of the establishment—the purport of which was that she was to stick to her post at all hazards.

From this message it was evident that the veteran detective was on the alert and believed they were on the right track.

Kate, with all her natural shrewdness, was at fault, for there wasn't anything wrong about the house or any of its inmates, as far as she could see.

She resolved to double her exertions, so that not a suspicious circumstance should escape her.

For a sleeping apartment the supposed Italian boy had been given a little garret room in the left wing of the building, and as there was a stout bolt upon the door, Kate felt secure.

It was on the night of the seventh day of her sojourn under the roof of Blithewood that, after sitting in the kitchen with the other servants and listening to their idle gossip until after ten, Kate went up to her little apartment feeling decidedly discouraged.

As a measure of precaution, the Decoy Detective did not remove her disguise when she retired to rest. Phenix had warned her that she must always keep herself ready for action, as she was liable to be called upon at any hour, day or night.

The garret room and its furniture requires but little description.

It was an apartment about nine feet by ten; a dormer window afforded light, and the only furniture in the room was a small iron bedstead with an extremely hard mattress, a scanty amount of bed-clothes, and a broken-backed chair.

In the opinion of the servants, any sort of an apartment was good enough for the vagabond Italian boy.

Kate bolted the door securely, put out the small hand-lamp with which she had been supplied, and after an earnest prayer—a supplication to unmask and punish the villain who had so cruelly wronged her innocent sister—retired to rest.

But not to sleep, for she was strangely nervous.

She seemed to hear all sorts of strange noises to-night. I say "seemed," for the girl was sure it wasn't anything but imagination.

Her room being away from all the rest of the occupied apartments, at the very top of the house, and no one else sleeping on the same floor, it was always as quiet as a tomb. This was with the exception of the shrill cries of the wild, free denizens of the shrubs and trees without came in through the window.

221

And on this night in question, after Kate had reclined upon the bed, the chorus without of the nocturnal insects rose freely on the air.

But there were other noises which appeared to be nearer at hand and which the girl could not help paying attention to, although she felt tolerably certain that her imagination had magnified something out of nothing.

There was a slight breeze, and the old timbers of the stately mansion creaked as the wind played around its corners.

Strange fancies were in the girl's mind.

She was working in the dark, for she had not the slightest conception of the plans of the veteran detective under whose directions she was proceeding.

And with a natural impatience she chafed at being thus kept in ignorance.

"If he had only confided in me so that I would be able to understand why it is necessary I should remain here," she muttered, as she turned restlessly on the hard bed.

Many times since she had received Joe Phenix's message, so mysteriously conveyed to her, had she uttered the sentence. Now, having nothing else to do but to think and ponder over the matter, she was decidedly inclined to blame the detective for not allowing her to understand the game.

"If I could only see him I am sure I could convince him that it would be a great advantage to allow me to understand the programme. I know I could work to better advantage if I knew what I was doing.

"Yes, yes, I'm sure of it."

Twenty times at least she expressed this idea, slightly varying the words, and at last, after nearly two hours had elapsed, she began to feel that slumber was beginning to weigh down her eyelids.

And glad enough was she when she became conscious of this fact, for she felt strangely restless and excited. If she had been a believer in presentiments she would have imagined that some terrible danger threatened her, but as she had not the least faith in anything of the kind, she strove to dismiss the idea.

And then, just as her senses reeled in the misty border land which exists between wakefulness and sleep, a strange idea came to her.

She thought that the veteran detective had climbed to the top of the great oak tree which grew so near the house that its branches brushed against her window and bending over so as to bring his face almost against the glass, whispered:

"Don't worry, my girl, everything is going on all right. I am playing the deepest kind of a game, and it is absolutely necessary that you should not know what I am up to, for the slightest false move on your part would ruin everything.

"The part you are playing is a very import ant one indeed.

"You are the bait, my girl, to attract the prey I seek. You will lure them into the trap which I have set and then I will capture all of them at one fell swoop.

"Of course you are risking your life, but don't be afraid, the trap is as perfect a one as the wit of man ever planned, and I shall not fail to make the haul.

"They will attempt to kill you and I will nab them."

In these strange sorts of dreams all probability of course flies to the winds.

Naturally, it was an utter impossibility for a muscularly-built man like the detective to cling to a slender branch, not over half the size of his arm, and whisper through the glass of a rightly-shut casement.

And then too, after he had delivered his message, he disappeared as mysteriously as he had appeared.

No prosaic descending of the tree, but he simply let go his hold of the branch and vanished.

And then the girl thought that she grumbled a little to herself, saying:

"You might as well let me know just what I am doing if I am risking my life as you say."

But this discontent was of short duration for a new event drove it from her mind.

From without the entry she heard the stairs creak under the weight of footsteps ascending them.

The noise came as clear and distinct to her ears as though she was standing at the head of the staircase.

There seemed to be a regular army ascending, for she could distinctly hear the measured tread of many footsteps.

"Ah, well, it doesn't matter to me," she said. "They can't get in here anyway."

The footsteps came nearer and nearer, and at last they all halted just outside of her door.

"They can't get in—they can't get in!" she kept repeating to herself, and she thought she laughed merrily when she reflected what a strong bolt there was upon the door.

And then she heard the men without try the door, and to her horror it yielded to their touch and opened as easily as though the iron bolt were but a wedge of putty.

Now she realized that she was in the embraces of that grim and horrid, yet not tangible monster known as the nightmare.

She strove to wake herself, for now she understood she was fast in slumber's chain, but the effort caused her terrible suffering.

Her tongue clove to the roof of her mouth when she attempted to speak, and she felt as though she would suffocate before she could relieve herself of the dread incubus.

But she felt that if she could only utter a sound the monster would vanish into thin air.

As she struggled, fighting this phantom of the imagination, there came a sudden interruption.

From an intangible foe she came suddenly upon a real one.

Rude hands were laid roughly upon her; a spoonful of some strange-tasting liquid was forced into her mouth.

Waking to reality she attempted to prevent herself from swallowing the decoction, but her assailant was on his guard against this action.

The moment he squirted the fluid into her mouth, he compressed her nostrils so that she was obliged to swallow the drug.

Wonderful was the effect it produced upon her, and almost instantaneous was the action.

She was thrown at once into a sort of trance, conscious of all that was going on around her, and yet unable to move a muscle.

Kate was as completely helpless as though clutched in the cold embrace of death itself, but her busy brain still worked steadily on.

Two men were in the apartment, a bull's-eye lantern which one of them carried revealed this fact and also disclosed their identity.

The two were the master of the mansion, Bernard Andrews, and the secretary, Michael Jones.

14. A "Bull's-Eye" lantern, also called a Dark Lantern or a Police Lantern. This example was made by the Adams & Westlake Company around 1890.

CHAPTER XXXVI.
A FIENDISH PLAN.

"The job was more easily performed than I had anticipated," remarked the secretary with a hoarse chuckle.

"Oh, I did not think there would be any trouble about the matter," Andrews replied. "When I plan anything of this kind I generally arrange it so carefully that in the execution everything goes like clock-work."

"In this case most certainly everything has worked to perfection."

"Yes, but come, we have no time to lose for midnight is near at hand."

"That was a capital idea of yours—the loosening of the screw that held the bolt socket, so that while it looked to be firm, yet the screw had so little hold of the wood that a finger's pressure would force open the door," the secretary remarked, as he advanced to the bedside.

"Yes, if the bolt had been all right we should not have been able to get into the room without making noise enough to wake this plucky girl who has so foolishly put herself in our power."

If the drug had not transformed the girl into a marble-like statue, incapable of moving, she most certainly would have given a great start when she heard these words, for they showed her that her disguise had been penetrated, and that from playing the part of a spy, she had been transformed into a victim.

Andrews held the lantern, but the hands of the secretary were not encumbered.

So, when he came up to the bedside, he stooped, and lifted the motionless form of the girl in his strong arms without any trouble.

Then, with the master of the mansion leading the way, the two quitted the apartment, the secretary carrying the girl.

When the two gained the entry without, Andrews led the way to a door at the further end of the passage from where the staircase was situated.

With a natural curiosity Kate had tried this door when she first took up her quarters in the garret, but as it was locked she concluded it was merely the door of some unused closet, as from the position in which it was situated it did not seem possible that it could be the door to a room.

But it stood open now, revealing that it led to a narrow staircase.

The girl remembered now that there was a flight of stairs in the rear of the house used by the servants, but she had no idea that they led into the garret.

Down this staircase went the two men, Andrews taking care to carefully lock the door after him.

And before leaving the apartment which had been occupied by the supposed Italian boy, he had taken pains to shoot the bolt back and restore the catch to its normal condition, so that it did not show any signs that it had been tampered with.

Straight to the cellar went the two.

The house seemed to be wrapped in slumber, and not a single sound gave evidence that there was a soul in the mansion.

In the cellar, through a secret door, so carefully masked as to defy detection, they made their way into an underground passage, a narrow way, damp and disagreeable, excavated right through the solid earth.

After this passage was traversed, and it occupied some minutes, the two entered another cellar. The secretary placed his burden upon a rude sort of table and uttered a cry of relief.

"Pretty solid gal, now, I tell you, Cap!" he exclaimed.

The voice of the man had sounded familiar to Kate before now, and she had tried to remember where she had heard it, or a voice like it, yet had not been successful in the attempt. But at this speech all of a sudden the truth flashed upon her.

The speaker was one of the ruffians from whose power she had previously escaped.

It was the notorious Four Kings.

Oh! how blind she had been, but her eyes were opened now.

Bernard Andrews, the polished gentleman, the master of Blithewood, was the Spider Captain, the man who had lured her sister away, masquerading under the name of Henry Tappan.

"Well, captain, this is the last act in the play, eh?" Four Kings remarked.

"Yes, this is to be the wind-up, and a most excellent one it will be, too," Andrews replied.

"In another hour the Spider Captain and his trusty lieutenant, Four Kings, will disappear from this world never to be seen again by mortal man.

"You are the only one of the band that knows me in my real character—the link which connects me with the gang.

"Now that I have secured the future by this wealthy marriage, it is not necessary that I should longer tread in the path of crime. It is desirable now that all who knew the Spider Captain, pals and detectives alike, should believe that he has cashed in his checks, and gone to that 'bourne from whence no traveler returns.'

"This old house and its secrets must vanish from existence.

"Under the stairs, yonder, are two bodies, dressed in the clothes that we used to wear when we met the gang, and with their faces disfigured by bullet-wounds.

"Now take your revolver and empty the contents into the body of this daring spy, and place the empty weapon under her.

"Then we will set fire to the old house; the room above is saturated with coal oil so that it will readily burn.

"Amid the ruins the bodies will be found, and no doubt the falling timbers will preserve them so that they can be easily identified.

"The story of the tragedy then will be plain to all.

"This female decoy tracked the Spider Captain to his lair, succeeded in killing the chief of the gang and his lieutenant, but lost her own life in the fight.

"Thus at one blow we destroy the sleuth-hound and at the same time gull the world into the belief that we are no more."

"Beautiful! Couldn't be finer!" and Four Kings drew out his revolver as he spoke.

"Yes, at one stroke we obliterate the past!" Andrews cried, in exultation.

"But you haven't counted Joe Phenix in!" cried a stern voice.

A cry of horror came from the lips of the two, and, turning, they beheld the detective, drawn revolver in hand, standing in the mouth of the secret doorway through which they had come.

Behind him were four armed detectives.

"Surrender! you are my prisoners!" the bloodhound cried.

But the two were game to the backbone.

With a vigorous kick Andrews sent the lantern flying into a corner of the room, while Four Kings discharged his revolver at the intruders.

But the detectives anticipated the movement and escaped the bullets by dropping to their knees, while Phenix returned the fire as fast as he could discharge his weapon, which was a self-cocker.

The lantern fell into the pile of waste stuff saturated with coal-oil in the corner of the room; there was an explosion, and in a twinkling the whole place was on fire.

By the light the forms of the Spider Captain and Four Kings, struggling in the agonies of death could be plainly seen.

Phenix's bullets had been fatal.

The chase was ended.

So rapidly the flames spread that it was as much as the detectives could do to escape from the burning building, and Phenix had his clothes scorched in rescuing Kate, whom he believed to be in a swoon.

The girl recovered, under a doctor's skillful care, from the effects of the powerful drug, but it was a week before she was really well again.

Our tale is told, for with the death of the Spider Captain ends the record.

The destruction of this bold ruffian and his secret band, for the death of Andrews and Four Kings put an end to the league of crime, was due primarily to the clew afforded by Kate Scott overhearing the chance remark made by one of the dudes to the other.

This clew Phenix followed up diligently, and the dude when brought to book acknowledged that he had once met Andrews in the Catskills masquerading under a false name, and that by accident himself and friend were witnesses of the departure of Andrews and his victim after the marriage.

The officers of the law seized upon Blithewood and all left by the dead villain.

Great was the disgust of the Grimgriskins when the truth came out.

Sidonia had a lucky escape, and her heart, caught on the bound as it were, was captured by Van Tromp, who undertook to console her in her mortification.

This was greatly to the annoyance of Clinton, who was puzzled to understand how he was going to get along without his "deah old chappie, don't you know!"

Old Grimgriskin was obliged to take up the forged note to save Alcibiades from the State Prison, and he was so much enraged that he banished the rascal to the wilds of the far West, allowing him only enough to live upon.

Phenix still continues in the man-hunting business, and at some future time we may detail some other adventures of his in company with the brightest "pal" he ever had, his Decoy Detective, Kate Scott.

THE END.

Thank you!

Please join us at the **Dark Lantern Tales** web site, where you will find more contextual history, including our regularly updated **Gilded Age Slang Glossary**.

The Joe Phenix Detective Series
Gilded Age Detective Stories
Steam-Age Crime Stories

https://darklanterntales.wordpress.com/

Glossary of Slang and Period Phrases

Bijou, a jewel, a treasure

Bull's eye lantern, also called a police lantern, or dark lantern. These were about the size of a modern small thermos bottle and had a large, "bull's eye" lens in front. Such oil lanterns had an internal shutter that allowed the light out at will or blocked it. Lanterns of this design were commonly used from the mid 1800s to the 1910s, and later. The reliability of the oil lanterns made for a slow conversion to battery-powered electric flashlights for police, watchmen, and some military uses.

Bu'sted, means "busted," and is contracted from "bursted."

Coal Oil, originally a lighting oil refined from oil shale and bituminous coal. It was patented as, "Kerosene," but the public called it coal oil. The term kerosene was later applied to a refined oil derived from petroleum.

Darbies, handcuffs

Hairpin, whimsical slang when the speaker refers to himself

Irish vernacular, it was expected of dime novel writers to provide characters with accents related to their ethnicity, country of origin, or the region of the US where they were raised. "Phwat" (what), "B'ye" (boy), and other examples are approximations of an Irish accent, at least as popularized at the time.

Just for greens, presumably equivalent to "just for grins," although there are quite a few historical uses and explanations.

Leg bail, gave leg bail, ran for it, escaped

Papers, pasteboards, can refer to sets of playing cards

Pony up the rhino, means pay up the money. "Pony up" is slang still used today, of course, and "rhino" is an old term for money, apparently dating to the 17th century and still used in the 19th century.

Prussic Acid, Hydrocyanic acid, a strong poison.

Speaking-tube, an acoustic intercom system that routed metal tubing through a building or a ship. Each end would often be plugged with a stopper that contained a whistle. Someone who wished to talk could remove the plug at their end, put their mouth to the tube and blow, alerting someone at the other end by sounding the whistle there. Then they could talk to each other through the tube.

Spring, like a switch or button in modern terms.

Still hunt, refers to a stealthy hunt

Acknowledgements and Gratitude:

First for my wife, **Ann Wicker**, a professional writer and editor, who has tolerated my obsession with these old stories and helped review my editing. Two close friends of ours from my years in the recording business helped by reading and reviewing stories for me. They are noted singer, songwriter, and record producer **Don Dixon**, and noted singer, songwriter, and playwright **Jim Wann**. I certainly appreciate the help from Ann, Don, and Jim!

Joe Rainone and **Bob Robinson** are two collectors and sellers who supply my habit for ancient sensational literature. I've learned a great deal from them both. Bob Robinson's web site can be found at: http://stores.imaginationradio.com/

Joe Rainone, with co-author **E. M. Sanchez-Saavedra**, created the deep reference source I rely on frequently, The Illustrated Dime Novel Price Guide. That reference book has a vast amount of information in a very readable form, and hundreds of illustrations. Visually, it is a mate to The Dime Novel Companion by J. Randolph Cox. https://www.youtube.com/watch?v=17e99w2zuqI

J. Randolph Cox, the recognized authority on all things related to Dime Novels and the popular press of the late nineteenth century, has been generous with answers to my questions over the years. When his Dime Novel Companion was published, it immediately became my first choice reference volume.

Pascal Storino, Jr., Criminal Investigator, Retired, is otherwise known as "Pat." This career detective has a fascinating website about the history of the New York Police Department at http://www.NYPDHistory.com and it is worth many visits. Pat has also been a great resource to help me understand more about the equipment and policies of the NYPD during the time of the Joe Phenix stories.

John Coulthart, artist and designer, for creating a cover design and art that captures the essence of period wood engravings while delivering modern impact. A visit to his site is well worth your time. Don't miss the Steampunk covers! http://www.johncoulthart.com/

Martin Howard, collector and recognized expert in early typewriters. Martin was generous with his time and knowledge to help me learn more about typewriters in the Beadle and Adams' era. His web site is a delight to stroll through, so take a look: http://antiquetypewriters.com/

Demian Katz of Villanova University has been a great resource and helped with advice on many topics, including how best to take pictures of original material.

Northern Illinois University Libraries, in whose worthy hands the collections of Albert Johannsen and Edward T. LeBlanc are well curated and studied.

James Harper, MLIS, Z. Smith Reynolds Library, Wake Forest University, for helping me to locate some scarce text. They have an excellent library staff!

Illustration Acknowledgements and Sources

Frontispiece: Barker, George, photographer. New York. The Bay, looking towards the Narrows. , ca. 1889. Photograph. https://www.loc.gov/item/2004681913/.

01. Brooklyn Bridge, cropped detail, Currier & Ives, ca 1883, www.loc.gov/pictures/item/2001704263/

02. Edited image, first page of Beadle's Weekly, Vol. II, No. 65, February 9, 1884, courtesy of Northern Illinois University Libraries, Nickels and Dimes from the collections of Johannsen and LeBlanc.

03. Detail, first page of Beadle's Weekly, Vol. II, No. 65, February 9, 1884, courtesy of Northern Illinois University Libraries, Nickels and Dimes from the collections of Johannsen and LeBlanc.

04. Detail, first page of Beadle's Weekly, Vol. II, No. 66, February 16, 1884, courtesy of Northern Illinois University Libraries, Nickels and Dimes from the collections of Johannsen and LeBlanc.

05. Beadle's New York Dime Library, Vol. XXXI, No. 391, April 21, 1886, collection of the editor.

06. Detail, edited, cropped, The Illustrated Police News, 1887, collection of the editor.

07. Detail, edited, cropped, The Illustrated Police News, 1887, collection of the editor.

08. Simple map of New York City area where events in *Kate Scott, The Decoy Detective* take place. Doodled by editor.

09. Detail, edited, cropped, The Illustrated Police News, 1887, collection of the editor.

10. Detail, edited, cropped, The Illustrated Police News, 1887, collection of the editor.

11. Detail, edited, cropped, The Illustrated Police News, 1887, collection of the editor.

12. Detail, edited, cropped, The Illustrated Police News, 1887, collection of the editor.

13. Detail, edited, cropped, The Illustrated Police News, 1887, collection of the editor.

14. Photo by editor of a Dark Lantern, made by Adams & Westlake Company ca 1890.

But wait!
There's More!

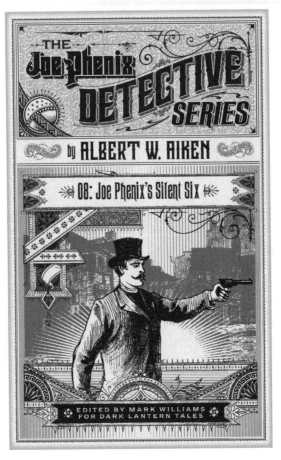

TURN THE PAGE to read the first chapters of
Joe Phenix's Silent Six;
or,
The Great Detective's Shadow Guard

Joe Phenix's Silent Six;

or,

The Great Detective's Shadow Guard

By Albert W. Aiken

Edited by Mark Williams

CHAPTER I.
A MYSTERIOUS MESSAGE.

The great hands of Trinity's ancient clock pointed to the hour of nine, and the money center of the metropolis, far-famed Wall Street, was shaking off its "downy lethargy" and preparing for the day's business.

All the "down" Broadway cars were crowded with the lords and lackeys of the commercial world, hurrying to business.

From one of the cars descended a lion-like man—a gentleman of forty, or thereabouts, tall, powerfully-built, and with that peculiar air about him which denotes the leader, born to command.

This eagle-eyed, massive-featured gentleman was the celebrated detective, Joseph Phenix, renowned far and wide as being one of the most successful man-hunters that the metropolis had ever known.

For those who have not met him, it can simply be said that Joe Phenix won his reputation while working as one of the regular bloodhounds on the city police force. Then, having accumulated a moderate fortune as the result of his endeavors, he retired from the police force and set up as a private detective. With clients in the financial sector, it was best to set up his office on Wall Street, right

241

in the heart of the money center of the metropolis.

He followed his profession now for amusement, as he had ample means to satisfy his simple wants. Among those who knew him, it was understood that he did not care to trouble himself about any small matters. But, if a big case was brought to his notice, an affair that puzzled the ordinary bloodhounds of the law, Joe Phenix would undertake the task with alacrity. As a rule, too, it was but seldom he was baffled.

On this particular morning the detective had nothing in hand. He was on his way to his office to inspect his mail, and had made up his mind that unless something turned up to engage his attention he would take a little trip to the country for a few days.

Joe Phenix's office was located in one of the huge buildings, towering heavenward, which that modern invention, the elevator, has made possible and profitable.

His assistant, Tony Western, a muscular young man of twenty-five, was in the office when Joe Phenix arrived.

"Any mail, Tony?" the great detective asked.

"Only a single letter, sir."

Joe Phenix took a seat at his desk and took a look at the envelope.

It was what is known as a "drop letter," having been posted in the city.

The detective opened the missive and a check fell out upon the desk. It was for a hundred dollars, drawn to the order of one George F. Jones and bore the signature of Russell Sage, one of the oldest and most prominent men in Wall Street.

"What does this mean?" the detective muttered to himself as he took up the check.

Then he turned the bit of paper over and saw that it bore the signature of George F. Jones on the back.

"Ah, I see! As it is indorsed, it is just as good as so much cash, but who is George F. Jones?" Then the detective read the letter, which ran as follows:

Dear Sir: Enclosed please find check for one hundred dollars. I desire to consult you upon a little business matter and send this check as a guarantee of good faith. Have the kindness to assume a disguise, so that your identity will not be suspected by any acquaintance, and meet me at the corner of Broadway and Fiftieth Street at two o'clock this afternoon.

Stand on the north-eastern corner, with a folded newspaper in your hand. I will be in a hack and will halt and address you as Mr. Jones, then you must get in.

It is necessary for me to have a private interview with you and I desire to arrange the affair in such a way that no one can suspect that there has been a meeting between us.

And at this point the letter came to an abrupt end, there being no signature.

Joe Phenix placed the letter upon the desk and then took up the check and examined it again.

Tony Western, glancing up from his newspaper, saw that his principal seemed perplexed and ventured to ask:

"Anything out of the way, sir?"

Joe Phenix had a great deal of confidence in Tony Western's judgment, for he regarded him as being one of the most promising young men in the detective business, so he requested him to inspect the letter and check.

"Just give me your opinion about this matter?" he said.

Tony Western read the letter and then examined the check.

"Well, I don't know, governor," he remarked, with

243

a dubious shake of the head. "If you were a millionaire now, worth the kidnapping, I should say that it was a little game to get at you."

"It does look like a 'plant,' for a fact!" the detective declared.

"That's so! After you were in the coach the man would work the chloroform act and then it would be, 'good-by John!'"

"Well, as I am not a millionaire, and it would not be possible to make anything by kidnapping me, I suppose that the only explanation of the mystery is that if it is a game to entrap me, it proceeds from some man who has cause to want to get square—some criminal whom I have been instrumental in placing behind the bars."

"Yes, but then it is odd that any man of that class should be willing to put up a hundred dollar check as a bait to draw you on. I am supposing, you know, that the check is good," the other observed, thoughtfully.

"Well, that matter can be quickly decided. Take the check to Russell Sage's office, ask if it is all right, and find out if they know anything about this Mr. George F. Jones," the detective said.

Tony Western departed with the check and Joe Phenix turned his attention to the morning newspaper.

In twenty minutes Tony Western returned.

"The check is all right and you can put it in the bank as soon as you like," Western announced. "Jones is a broker, doing business in New Street, a first-class man. Sage gave the check to him yesterday in payment of an account."

"Yes, I see; Jones indorsed the paper and passed it over to somebody else, and it may have gone through two or three hands before it came into the possession of the man who sent it to me," Joe Phenix observed.

"I say, governor, I have changed my mind about this matter!" Tony Western announced, abruptly. "I think this thing is all right. It isn't a 'plant,' nor a trap of any kind, but some big fish wants to consult you upon some important matter, and has adopted this queer method to make sure that no one will be able to learn anything about the affair."

"That is the inference to be drawn from his letter," Joe Phenix replied.

"Yes, and though I, at first, jumped to the conclusion that the man wasn't honest in his statement, yet, as he has planked up a hundred in solid cash, it ought to be good proof that he means business."

"Very true; if it was a foe who wanted to entrap me I doubt if any such sum of money would be risked, even if the man thought to lull me into security by so doing."

"Oh, no!" Tony Western exclaimed, decidedly. "It would be a big crook indeed to put up a hundred dollars just as a bait for a man with whom he wanted to get square."

"I believe that your surmise is right, and that the summons comes from some man of standing who has a business matter on hand of such great importance that he hesitates to arrange an interview with me in the regular way for fear that some one might discover that we are in consultation."

"That is my notion, governor!"

"I will keep the appointment!"

"Yes, and just remember that I predict that it will turn out to be a matter of importance!" the other declared.

This ended the conversation.

Joe Phenix read his newspaper, took a stroll down the street about noon time, got his lunch, then returned to the office and prepared to keep the appointment.

There was a large closet attached to the inner room—Phenix had two apartments—and this closet was well-stocked with a variety of disguises.

The one that the detective selected on this occasion was a plain dark suit, which showed evident marks of wear. When he was attired in this, with a short-haired, iron-gray wig, so made as to hide two-thirds of his forehead, he presented a good representation of a country clergyman or schoolmaster, and this was heightened by a liquid dye which Joe Phenix applied to his face and hands, giving them the tan tint common to the denizens of rural districts.

But in the side pockets of the sack coat which he wore were two articles altogether out of keeping with his peaceful aspect—a pair of revolvers of the bulldog pattern, short in barrel and carrying unusually heavy balls.

"There, I think this will do," Joe Phenix remarked after his preparations were complete.

"Oh, yes, you look like a regular hayseed. It would take a smart man to recognize that you are not a countryman. Look out that the bunco men don't pick you up!" Tony Western exclaimed with a laugh.

Joe Phenix departed by the rear door—there were two entrances to his office—descended to the street, then to Broadway and boarded an up town car.

He timed his movements so well that he arrived at Fiftieth Street at five minutes of two.

CHAPTER II.
THE MONEY KING.

Joe Phenix stood on the northeast corner, according to the directions, with a folded newspaper in his hand.

At three minutes past the hour his attention was directed to a shabby-looking hack approaching from down-town, and as it came to the cross-street the driver changed his course so as to bring the vehicle in near the curbstone.

The hackman was in keeping with the coach, a poorly-dressed old Irishman who evidently could not boast of much prosperity.

"This does not look much like the turn-out of a man of wealth and standing," the detective muttered as he noted the poverty-stricken appearance of the man and his rig.

All the doubts of the detective had returned.

He changed the newspaper to his left hand, thrust the right one into the coat pocket and took a firm grip of the revolver.

Joe Phenix had determined to go on and see just what there was in this affair.

"If it is a trap intended to catch me perhaps I may be able to give the man a lesson which he will not be likely to forget for some time," he muttered, a grim smile hovering around the corners of his resolute mouth.

As the carriage approached, the disguised detective was all prepared to see some benevolent looking gentleman—some notorious crook in an elaborate disguise, got up for the express purpose of trying a little bunco business upon him.

The hack halted by the corner.

The door opened and the face of an odd, peculiar-looking man, rather undersized in stature, appeared.

He was well along in years, fifty or thereabouts, and was dressed plainly in a neat, dark business suit. The man had a long face, which seemed unusually so because the chin was adorned with a pointed beard, sandy gray in hue, the same tint as the sparse locks of hair that came out from under his derby hat. His eyes were a restless, shifting gray, deep sunken, and overhung by bristling sandy-gray eyebrows; the general appearance of the face, with its prominent nose and high cheek-bones, strangely resembled a fox.

The detective recognized the man immediately, and he relinquished his grasp upon the revolver.

"Get in, Mr. Smith, please," said the bearded gentleman, in a sharp, peculiar way, speaking like a man accustomed to command.

The detective entered the carriage, the driver chirruped to his horses, and the vehicle proceeded on up Broadway.

After the coach got in motion the foxy-looking gentleman surveyed the disguised detective for a few minutes with the greatest interest, and then abruptly exclaimed:

"Well, sir, I must compliment you upon your disguise! It is simply perfect! I know you very well by sight, as I have often seen you in Wall Street, although I never had the pleasure of meeting you personally. But I never would have known you, and as the carriage drove up I had grave doubts. If you had not held the paper in your hand I should have believed you to be a stranger."

"To be able to assume a disguise which cannot be easily penetrated is one of the first essentials of the successful detective," the man-hunter replied.

"I presume there isn't any need of introducing my-self—you know who I am?"

"Oh, yes, although I never had any personal acquaintance with you, yet I have known you by sight for the last ten years."

"I suppose that I am pretty well known," the gentleman observed, with a shake of the head, as though he did not relish it. "The newspapers, both daily and illustrated, have done their best to make my face familiar to the public at large, and I have no doubt my personal appearance and my business matters are familiar to thousands who will never meet me, and who have no possible interest in my affairs."

"Tis the penalty of greatness," the detective remarked. "The man who climbs high challenges remarks from all. As one of the foremost business men in America, it is natural that people should take an interest in you. And I must say that if you were amazed at the completeness of my disguise, I was equally surprised when I saw you in a hack of this kind, for such a vehicle I would not have imagined a man like yourself would have chosen to ride in, Mr. Engleburt."

The detective had spoken the name of one of the greatest money-kings of the day.

Abraham Engleburt—Old Abe, as he was popularly termed in Wall Street—was a man who was supposed by people who were well-calculated to judge to be worth a good twenty millions of dollars, and all this money had been acquired by his own individual efforts.

He was no Vanderbilt, nor Astor, who had millions bequeathed him by his ancestors to start on.

All that he possessed he had made personally.

A great many men spoke harshly of him. Sometimes the cry went up that he was a man who had mounted to prosperity by trampling upon his fellows less skillful, or cunning, or more scrupulous, than himself.

The loud-mouthed talkers who meet in the halls over the beer-shops and spout wildly about the tyranny of capital, and the rising of the downtrodden toiling masses, called him a bloated monopolist, and declared that if justice was done he would ornament a lamp-post.

Still, fair-minded men were of the opinion that he was not any worse than the rest of the speculators from whose ranks he had risen, and that there wasn't one of them who would not have taken all the advantages that Old Abe was accused of taking if the opportunities came to them—or if they had been skillful enough to make the opportunities—as the gigantic speculator was accused of doing.

Philosophers, who had studied the subject, declared that it was not the man who was at fault but the system, and when the world grew older and wiser, laws would be enacted so that there could be no more Old Abe's who could rise to kingly magnificence upon the ruins of weaker men.

Old Abe was a man merely—and no worse than the average man.

These declarations seemed to be truth, for in his private life the man's character was without a stain. He was a good husband, and a good father, and though he crushed his rivals without mercy, yet it was said that he never went out of his way to injure a man who was not trying to injure him.

"Well, I will admit that this is not exactly the kind of vehicle that I usually ride in," the money-king remarked, with a glance at the dingy interior of the hack. "But there is a method in my madness. As I wrote to you in regard to this interview, I desired above all things that it should be kept strictly secret; that is why I asked you to assume a disguise. But if I had taken you in my own carriage, which, of course, is well known to a great many people, comment would have been immediately excited, for somebody would be sure to see us; then the question would immediately arise, 'Hello, who is that man riding with Engleburt? It is a stranger—what game is the old fox up to now?' for by such playful names I am sometimes called."

"Yes, no doubt that if I were noticed riding with you in your coach, it would have excited talk."

"It surely would, my dear sir, for there are plenty of men in the world who firmly believe that I lay awake nights planning and scheming how to increase my wealth, just as if I hadn't now all I could possibly take care of. Truly, my great concern at present is how to prevent losing what I have got, not to acquire more. People would believe, if they heard that I was riding with and conversing on familiar terms with a stranger, that I had some scheme on hand. And there are certain parties so anxious to learn what I am about, that they would leave no stone unturned, not only to discover who the stranger was, but also to find out what the motive of his business is with me."

"You are correct in your assumption, no doubt."

"Now the main thing about this matter is to keep our interview a profound secret. Not a soul must have the slightest suspicion that I have placed myself in communication with you, for if the fact leaked out my object would be defeated."

"In all detective matters, to keep the affair perfectly quiet is of the first importance," Joe Phenix declared.

"Yes, I fully understand it, and have acted on that idea in this instance.

"I did not sign my name to the note to you, and even took the trouble to send you a check which came into my office in the course of business, so that while you would be assured that the sender of the note was in earnest, yet it would not be possible for you even to guess who it was that wrote."

"That is true; if I had been given twenty guesses I do not think I would have named you in any one of them."

"I have been a successful man, and think one of the principal reasons why I have been successful is that I have always made it a rule to do anything I had to do as well as I could possibly do it. I never knowingly shirked any work, no matter what it was."

"That is undoubtedly one of the best rules that a man can follow."

"Well, in this case I have taken all possible pains," the money-king explained. "I went to lunch about twelve. After lunch I got into my carriage and was driven to one of the office buildings near the City Hall; told the coachman to wait for me until I came out.

"This building has two doors, as it is on a corner. I went in one door and came out through the other, jumped on a car and rode up to Chatham square, where I made a bargain with this hackman to drive me to Bloomingdale, and arranged to pick you up as we came along. Now, although I could not hope to show myself in the money district without being recognized, yet in Chatham Square no one appeared to know me, and I believe I have succeeded in getting this far without a soul suspecting who I am."

"The east side knows but little of the money center and its men," Joe Phenix observed.

"So I calculated. The point with me was to secure an interview with you, and have the matter so arranged that we could speak with perfect freedom, and without danger of any one knowing that we have been in consultation."

"Well, it seems to me that all the conditions are fulfilled," the detective replied. "Most certainly we can speak freely here. The man on the horse could not overhear our conversation if he desired to listen. On the Boulevard you are not likely to meet any one who knows you, and by leaning back you can keep out of sight, there is little danger of your being recognized."

"And now for business!" Engleburt exclaimed.

CHAPTER III.
A STRANGE STORY.

"As one of the wealthy men of New York, I am naturally selected for a victim by all sorts of people who try to get at my money by various schemes," the millionaire exclaimed.

"Twenty or thirty begging letters reach me in every mail, ranging from the church people in some country town who ask, unblushingly, for a check for a thousand or more of dollars to help them along, to the needy man or woman who craves a little assistance to keep them out of the poor-house."

"That is the common experience of all men of wealth."

"Then, there are the inventors, with all sorts of wonderful things, who only need a little aid from me to put them on the high road to fortune. I do not doubt that there might be one or two out of a hundred who really have good things, which would pay me well to go into, but it is out of my line, and I have no time to examine into the merits of the inventions. Then, lastly come the swindlers, the adventurers, the cavaliers of fortune, who think that they are smart enough to either cajole or frighten me out of some money."

"That is the penalty a man pays for being successful," the detective observed with a smile.

"I understand that, of course, and, as a rule, I am not at all worried by these applications. The letters I do not see, for I have a secretary who attends to my mail, and does not allow any of these epistles to reach me. And, if the parties try to secure a personal interview, they find they have to submit to a cross-examination before they can get at me. Not over one in a thousand succeeds in fooling the vigilant guard who keeps watch over me."

"Necessary precautions!"

"Yes, and I flattered myself that I had the matter so well arranged that it was not possible for me to be annoyed, but for the last month I have been the victim of a letter-writer who manages to reach me with his notes despite of all my precautions."

"Now your recital is beginning to become interesting," the detective observed.

"The first letter came just about a month ago. After dinner I went to my library and picked up one of the evening newspapers from the file on the table, where they are always placed for my inspection. As I unfolded the paper a letter dropped into my lap; I had drawn a rocking-chair up to the table and sat down in it. The letter was merely a sheet of note-paper folded, and was without an envelope. Thinking that it was some circular, which had been folded in with the newspaper as is often done, I opened it. You can judge of my surprise when I found that it was a letter addressed to me, and of course, under these peculiar circumstances it was natural for me to read it."

"Very natural," Joe Phenix remarked.

"It ran about in this way:

Abraham Engleburt, you have millions of dollars and I have not hundreds. Do you think that this is right? I do not. If you are a just man, and as wise as you are skillful, you will see that you ought to give me some of your millions. About fifty thousand dollars, I think, would satisfy me. If you care to make any arrangement, put a personal in this paper to-morrow addressed to Rex. All you need to say is 'Rex, I think it will be wise for me to do so.'

"A covert threat!" the detective exclaimed.

"Yes, I took it to be that."

"You paid no attention to it, of course?"

"Certainly not! All I did was to laugh at the cunning displayed by the rascal in getting his letter before me."

"It could be easily done by either getting the man who delivered the papers to put it in one of them, or else by collusion with some of the servants in the house," the detective declared.

"I threw the missive into the fire and dismissed it from my mind.

"Two nights after, sitting in the library with my wife, she opened a magazine, which had just come by mail, and a folded note fluttered out.

"Immediately I guessed that it was another communication from Rex.

"My wife opened the note, read it, then handed it to me, saying, 'What does this mean?' The note was in the same handwriting as the other, a firm, legible back-hand, evidently adopted as a disguise, and all it contained was a single line, 'Old Abe, you will be sorry if you don't "see" Rex.'"

"Brief and to the point!" Joe Phenix commented.

"Yes, I did not want to alarm my wife, so I passed it off as a joke, saying that probably some of the young brokers of the Stock Exchange were endeavoring to have some fun at my expense.

"She was deceived by my manner, and contented herself with the remark that she did not see any fun in such jokes.

"By this time I had made up my mind that it was necessary for me to take some action in the matter so I preserved the note, intending if I heard any more from Rex to put the matter into the hands of the police.

"Three days passed and then I got another message

which created a deal of commotion in my household.

"My wife and I had gone to our room, my son and daughter came in for a moment to say good-night, and I was talking to them, when a cry of alarm came from my wife.

"She had turned down the bedclothes from the pillows and to one of them a folded note was fastened by means of a miniature dagger about two inches long.

"The note said: 'Beware! See Rex or die!'"

"Extremely melo-dramatic!" said the detective, with a smile.

"I laughed at the idea; my son became enraged at the audacity of the rascal, but my wife and daughter were seriously alarmed. It seemed terrible to them that any one should be able to penetrate to my very bed-chamber and leave such a message."

"Some of the servants of your household are in league with the man," Joe Phenix remarked.

"That was the conclusion to which I came immediately, and I thought that it was high time that I tried to see if a little salt could not be put on the tail of this bold bird, so I called upon the chief of police and laid the matter before him."

"He is a good man; none better in the country, an old and experienced officer," the detective announced.

"The chief made light of the matter, and said that it was an old game. Like you, he was satisfied that some one in the house was aiding the rascal, and at least had no doubt he could succeed in trapping the parties.

"So, by his direction, I inserted a personal to Rex asking how I could communicate with him.

"The advertisement appeared that evening, and the next morning when I got up I found a note pinned to the very head-board of my bed; the sheet was not folded this time, but placed so it would catch my eyes the moment I arose.

"This note told me that I might employ all the detectives in the country, and I would not succeed in catching any one, and wound up by saying that I would soon discover I would have to choose between losing fifty thousand dollars or my life."

"The fellow was certainly playing an extremely bold game," the detective commented. "In fact, I don't think that I have ever heard of a much bolder one."

"That is exactly what the chief of police declared when I reported the matter to him," the millionaire replied. "My door, mind you, was locked and bolted. The letter was affixed to the head-board at some time during the night while I slept, which plainly showed that the man who placed it there must have been able to gain access to my room despite the fact that the door was securely fastened."

"A smart hotel thief is not troubled much by ordinary locks and bolts," Joe Phenix remarked.

"So the chief said, but he took such an interest in the case that he came in person with a couple of his keenest detectives to examine into the matter.

"As he explained to me he regarded the boast of the mysterious scoundrel in the light of a personal challenge to him, and he was going to try and see if he could not convince Master Rex that he was not so smart as he imagined."

"A very natural feeling."

"But after the detectives made a thorough examination of my room they declared they were puzzled to guess how the man gained admittance in the dead hours of the night. The lock could have been opened by means of a false key, but as there wasn't any transom over the door, nor any signs that a hole had been bored, and the keyhole was so situated that it would be almost impossible for any one to reach the bolt by poking a wire through it—the usual way a hotel thief gets at the bolts, as the chief told me—it was a mystery to them how the entrance had been accomplished."

"If the affair puzzled the chief it showed that the man Rex is a master of his profession."

"The detectives agreed on one thing though, and that was, that some of the inmates of the house were concerned in the affair."

"No doubt about that!" Joe Phenix declared in a tone of conviction.

"So the chief proceeded to have each and every servant in the house shadowed, and in order to carry out this scheme in the most complete manner he introduced a couple of detectives into the house, a man and woman. I keep eight or ten servants so it was an easy matter to find some pretense for engaging a couple more."

"The chief was working on the old lines," Joe Phenix observed in his quiet way. "Such a proceeding is usually successful where the game is a common, every-day rascal, but with such a man as I take this Rex to be, I should not suppose it would work."

"It did not, sir!" Engleburt exclaimed. "And the third day after the detectives entered the house, as I took down my hat in the hall, a letter dropped out, written by the rascal, in which he fairly laughed at the precautions which had been taken—and he gave a full account too of all that had been done, spoke of the two detectives in the house in the disguise of servants, and said that he would give me one month to find out how foolish the attempt was to discover him by employing a lot of dull-witted bloodhounds."

"Rather sarcastic," Joe Phenix remarked. "Still, his being able to tell you just exactly how you were playing the game showed that he had a decided advantage over the men who were trying to catch him."

"When I showed the letter to the chief of police it made him angry, and he swore he would not leave any stone unturned to catch the rascal.

"Two weeks have gone by and the detectives have not succeeded in getting the slightest clew, but every third or fourth day I get a letter from the scoundrel, all of them coming to me in the most mysterious manner; the writer jeered at the detective's want of success, and in the last he asked me how many years did I suppose it would be before the officers succeeded in getting a clew.

"Now, I will frankly admit, Mr. Phenix, that I am getting a little alarmed!" the money-king declared. "I begin to believe that this mysterious individual could do me a mortal injury if he felt disposed, and I made up my mind that as the chief of police and his detectives seemed unable to do anything I would seek for other aid.

"Your name occurred to me—your reputation as an expert man-catcher is great, and so I resolved to put myself in communication with you, and to arrange the affair in such a way that it would not be possible for any one to know that I had consulted you.

"I have succeeded in getting the best of some pretty smart men in my time and I did not relish the idea of being beaten by this mysterious, unknown scoundrel."

CHAPTER IV.
A NOVEL SCHEME.

"You have acted wisely, Mr. Engleburt," Joe Phenix remarked. "And if you have not succeeded in this instance, in baffling this party who designs to make you a prey, then he must be more than man."

"This is my idea. I have not spoken of making an arrangement with you to a single soul!" the money-king declared. "But before I applied to the chief of police I discussed the matter with my family, and although none of the servants were present, yet as we did not use any particular precaution against eavesdroppers it is probable that the conversation was overheard."

"Oh, yes, hardly a doubt in regard to that, and as the parties were thus put upon their guard—I assume that there is a couple or more in your household who are concerned in this plot—they were able to detect the police spies when they came disguised as servants."

"That is the explanation the chief of police gave in regard to the matter."

"Well, didn't the detectives succeed in finding anybody in the house against whom suspicion might be directed?" Joe Phenix asked, thoughtfully.

"No; the men did their best, the chief said, but were not able to hit upon a clew."

"You pay me quite a compliment by thinking I can do better than the regular detectives," the man-hunter remarked with a quiet smile.

"Well, the trouble with them is that they have been hampered from the start!" Engleburt declared. "I agree with you that there is probably more than one in this scheme, and, in fact, I have come to the belief that there is a regular gang at the bottom of the matter, and as they possess the advantage of knowing the detectives, while the detectives do not know them, it is not possible for the spies to get any clews."

"I see your idea; I will have the advantage of starting in without the scamps suspecting that I have taken a hand in the game."

"Exactly! And now, Mr. Phenix, let me explain to you my ideas about this matter: I am a man who, as a rule, decides what action to take in any matter that may arise without consulting with any one, but when this affair occurred, as it was something entirely novel to me I thought best to consult the chief of police, but as it appears that the schemers are too much for the regular men, some other plan must be tried.

"I put on my thinking cap, so to speak, and went to work, to study the thing out just as if it was a puzzle which had occurred to me in the regular course of business.

"The conclusion to which I came was that this attempt to get fifty thousand dollars of my money was not a common-place scheme, got up by everyday rascals, but that some men of more than ordinary ability had banded themselves together, and that the only way to defeat their plans was for me to organize a band, who would be equally as secret in working as this criminal league."

"The idea is a good one," Joe Phenix observed, with an approving nod of his massive head.

"It is fighting fire with fire!" the money-king declared.

"The failure of the regular detectives, although I presume they are as skillful man-hunters as can be found anywhere, satisfies me that some extraordinary means must be adopted if I desire to checkmate the ingenious rascals; the idea of the secret band came to me, a sort of silent body-guard, ever on the watch—ever ready to defend me from danger, and yet acting in such a way that no one will suspect it has been all arranged beforehand, that their principal business is to protect me."

"It is an ingenious scheme," said Joe Phenix, "and if it is properly carried out I have no doubt it will succeed, not only in beating the game of the men who are striking at you from the dark, but in bringing them to justice."

"That is my calculation. I am satisfied that the ordinary detectives in this case will not be able to do anything, but I believe a man like yourself, Mr. Phenix, with your vast experience and the knowledge of human nature that you must possess, would be able to find six agents, men and women as your judgment dictates, who could be depended upon to carry out any orders given them by you."

"I think the scheme can be carried out," the detective observed. "And if I use proper care in selecting the parties I do not doubt that I can get six agents who will do splendid work."

"That is my idea!" exclaimed the millionaire, rubbing his hands briskly together. I have a suspicion, you know, that these regular bloodhounds get into ruts, just the same as men do in other lines, and so fail to do as good work as they might."

"I do not doubt that there is a great deal of truth in the supposition," Joe Phenix remarked.

"Your secret and silent six will be as fresh people, not hampered by any old-time ideas as to how the work must be done, and they should be able to accomplish important results."

"The main advantage which they will possess is that they will work in the dark, and so be covered by the mantel of secrecy.

"By the way, have any of these mysterious letters ever

come to your office down-town?" the detective asked.

"No, not one."

"You received them all at your residence, then?"

"Yes."

"From that, one would be apt to conclude that no one in your office had anything to do with the matter."

"Yes, that was what the detectives said."

"Are any of the inmates of your mansion also at the office?"

"Yes, my son, his valet, who being a handy fellow and a man of considerable education also serves as a confidential man of business as my secretary, Mr. Somerdyke."

"These persons, being above suspicion, I suppose the detectives did not trouble their heads about them," Joe Phenix, observed carelessly.

"Oh, yes, they did!" the money-king exclaimed. "For the chief of police suggested at the beginning that somebody like Somerdyke, my son's valet, men who would not be apt to be suspected, might be concerned in the affair. The chief asked if I wanted to really get at the heart of the mystery, no matter who was hurt by the investigation, and I replied that I certainly did. I said to him, if it is my own son who is at the bottom of this villainous thing I want him discovered and punished."

"That was plain enough."

"Yes, and on that basis they went into the matter. Every soul in my house was shadowed. In fact I have an idea that neither my wife nor daughter were exempt."

"And the shadowing was fruitless of results?"

"Yes, not a single suspicious thing was discovered by the shadowers in connection with any of the people who dwelt beneath my roof."

"Well, under the circumstances, that was not strange," the detective remarked. "It is plain from the letters which you received that the members of the gang knew the bloodhounds had been placed upon their track. It would be a very strange fact indeed if they did not take care to be upon their guard."

"Yes, that is true, and that is, probably, the reason why the detectives failed."

"But your agents, working in secret, ought to be able to do better."

"I think they will."

"Now, while we have been conversing, the outline of a plan has come into my mind," Joe Phenix continued, after pausing for a few moments. "It will not be an easy thing for me to get just the kind of agents I require for a scheme of this kind, but they are in existence and can be got, only it will take time.

"The question of expense, you know, does not enter into this calculation at all!" the money-king declared. "You are free to go ahead, no matter how great the cost! I am fighting for fifty thousand dollars, and I would rather spend a hundred thousand than allow these rascals to have the satisfaction of triumphing over me. I am not afraid to speak so plainly to a man like yourself, Mr. Phenix, for I know you can be trusted."

The detective bowed at the compliment.

"I feel sure, sir, that no matter whether I succeed or fail in this enterprise, you will not have cause to regret your confidence," Joe Phenix remarked.

"Now, the agents I want can be got, but, as I said it will take some time to find them. I shall not wait though until I secure the whole six before I commence operations."

"Certainly not! As soon as you engage the first one let him, or her, as the case may be, begin, and the sooner the better!"

"Another point. I must arrange matters so that some of the agents can enter your service and I may desire to have one or two of them in your office."

"I will do exactly as you say about the matter, so form your plans freely, and rely upon it that I will aid you to the best of my ability."

"These agents must enter your service in such a natural manner that no one will be able to guess that they are not what they appear to be."

"Of course! Otherwise they will not be able to be of any service."

"Do you read the Morning Chronicle?"

"Yes."

"In the future, look in the personal column each morning and whenever you see an advertisement which reads, 'I am ready!' direct a letter to the address which follows, and ask the question, 'What can you do?' Give your address in such a way that the answer will be sure to come to you without being seen by anybody else."

"Yes, I understand. I can arrange that matter easily enough."

"Then, when the answer reaches you, and in it the writer will state what he can do, you must make a place for that party, but be careful to do it in such a natural manner that no one will suspect that there is anything out of the way about the proceeding."

"Yes, yes, I see."

"Perhaps on some occasion it will be as well to advertise for a party, so as to divert suspicion. When the applicants come you will know the right one from the frequent use of the words 'I am ready.'"

"I understand, and, so far, I must say the scheme seems to be an excellent one."

"I think it would be well, too, that you do not speak

to the spies in regard to their work, but treat them exactly as though you had no suspicion that they are anything but what they pretend to be."

"That is a good idea, I think," the millionaire observed, after reflecting upon the matter for a moment. "I might address the secret agent in a familiar manner at some time when I imagined there was no one near, and yet there might be a spy on the watch."

"That is exactly what I want to guard against," the detective remarked,

"You fully comprehend that there isn't any question of expense in this matter," Engleburt observed. "You are to go ahead, regardless of the cost. I will have five thousand dollars placed to your credit in the First National Bank, you are at liberty to draw on it as freely as you like, and if that is not enough I will make it ten thousand."

"I think the five will be ample."

"It is not a question with me of money, but it now has become a personal matter," the money-king declared. "If a gang of mysterious, unknown scoundrels can bulldoze a man of my standing with impunity, then the times, indeed, are out of joint!"

"I think I can trap them," Joe Phenix said, in his quiet way.

Then the pair arranged a method by means of which they could secretly communicate with each other, and as the carriage had arrived at the Bloomingdale Hospital, the pair got out. The millionaire paid the driver and he departed.

CHAPTER V.
THE BUNCO MEN.

The money-king and the detective walked up the boulevard until the hack disappeared in the distance.

"Here comes an omnibus!" Engleburt exclaimed. "I will take that down-town, and you can go in the next. I think we have managed this matter so that it will be impossible tor any one to know that there has been a meeting between us."

"No doubt about that, and if we are as successful in the rest of the scheme, we will trap our birds."

Then the two parted, Joe Phenix kept on up the Boulevard, while the money-king halted to await the approach of the omnibus.

After Engleburt departed, the detective came to the conclusion that he would go through one of the cross streets, and take the Elevated Road, as he could save time by so doing.

This course he pursued, and soon was on his way down-town.

During the ride he meditated upon the situation.

"Six good people," he murmured, "and they must be extra good to do the work. I know a dozen spies and stool-pigeons, but there is hardly one of them that would fill the bill in a case like this, for I need fresh tools that have not been used to the business.

"Engleburt is right, I think, in believing that there is a regularly organized band, and if I get some of my agents into his house and office, there is a chance that the gang, not suspecting that they are spies, may make a proposition to some of them to join the band, and so give me a clew.

"Because none of the letters have come to the office, the inference is drawn that no one there has anything to do with the matter, but is it correct to look at it in that light?

"Is it not more likely that the letters were only sent to the house so that no suspicion might be directed to the men in the office?

"That seems to me more probable than the other surmise, and on that theory I will work.

"The main thing is to secure the proper agents, and I do not doubt I shall have trouble about that, but I will be able to accomplish it in time."

The detective had some people in his mind, all of whom he thought would make good agents, but he was not sure that he could place his hands on them immediately.

Joe Phenix got off at the Cortland Street Station, and as he descended to the street the attention of two young men, who were standing in a doorway, was attracted to him.

"There goes a jay!" exclaimed the taller one of the two; both were well-dressed, and looked like young men of good standing. "I think we can pick him up," he continued. "Go for him, Ikey!"

The second young man, who looked as though he was of German descent, with his light hair and blue eyes, crossed the street, hurried up toward Broadway, then crossed again and came down so as to meet the disguised detective.

As soon as he approached near enough he made a dart forward with extended hand,

"Why, is it possible! Mr. Smith, when did you come to town?" And then, before Joe Phenix could say anything, the young man grasped him by the hand and shook it in the warmest manner.

"How did you leave all the folks at home? Well, really, you are about the last man I expected to see!" the young man continued.

The warning of his assistant, Tony Western, to beware of the bunco men, at once came to the mind of the detective.

With all his experience in New York this was the first time that he had ever encountered the ingenious swindlers known as bunco men, and he took it as a great compliment that he had been able to disguise himself so thoroughly as to lead the sharp-eyed rascals to believe they could make a prey of him.

And, just for the joke of the thing, he made up his mind to let the fellows go on so as to see what they would do.

"You have made a mistake, my young friend," he remarked, acting the character of the simple countryman to the life. "My name isn't Smith."

"Is it possible? Well, I declare! I would have picked you out from among a hundred as my old friend, Smith. How may I call your name?" the young man asked, in an innocent way, and affecting to be much puzzled.

"My name is Horton. James Horton, and I am from Gloversville, New York," the disguised detective replied, giving the first name and town that came into his head.

"Ah, yes; well, I see now that I have made a mistake, and you must excuse me!" Then the young man bowed in the politest manner and passed on.

Phenix proceeded slowly up the street.

The young man who had accosted him joined the other in the doorway.

"James Horton, Gloversville, New York!" he acclaimed, rapidly. The tall, slender fellow drew a small bound book from his pocket.

It was a reference book for the use of business men and contained a list of banks, their principal offices, and the legal firms of the various towns in the United States.

Quickly he turned the pages until he came to Gloversville.

"First National, George W. Clark, and Torry and Torry. That will do!" he exclaimed.

Then, shoving the book into his pocket he tried the same game that the other had pursued. He hurried across the street and went up toward Broadway, and as Joe Phenix was crossing the Street when the tall young man arrived at the corner he met him face to face.

"Why, Mr. Horton, how do you do?" he exclaimed, grasping the hand of the supposed countryman with as much enthusiasm as though he was a long-lost brother. "How did you leave all the folks in Gloversville? Well, I declare, I am delighted to see you! You remember me, of course. I haven't forgotten your face although it is some time since I was in your town. I am Clark's cousin, you know, George W., of the First National. Lordy! How I would like to take another trip up to Gloversville. The folks there treated me so well that I thought I owned the town, particularly the Torrys—the lawyers, you know, I hope that they are all well. I don't think that I ever met a finer lot of men in my life, and I am so glad that I happened to encounter you, for now I will be able to show you that the New York boys know how to treat friends when we meet them.

"You must come right along with me and make my place your headquarters while you are in town. My name is William—William W. Clark, named after my cousin, George W., a fancy of my mother's. You know, I reckon the old lady thought I might come in for a little of his cash one of these days, but I don't think there is much chance of that, eh? Not that I need the money, you know, for I am in the wholesale dry-goods business—got a splendid situation with Claflin & Co.—you have heard of the firm, of course, one of the biggest jobbers in the country, but I tell you what it is, Mr. Horton, I am just delighted to see you!"

And again the tall young man shook the hand of the disguised detective.

Joe Phenix, when he listened to this speech, so adroitly made and fluently delivered, was not sorry that he had gone into this adventure, for it was plain that this bunco man was an extra good one, and he did not wonder that dull-witted countrymen are caught, for the affair is managed with exceeding skill.

Alone, amid the never-ending noise and bustle of the great city, the rustic feels like a fish out of water, for there is no loneliness in the world like that which seizes upon a man alone in a great city, without a soul that he knows to whom he can speak.

The hurrying crowd, strangers all, few of whom even take the trouble to cast a glance at him, the most of them rushing along as though their lives depended upon getting to a certain point in a certain time; it is so different from his home, where he knows almost everybody, and where it is the custom even for strangers to nod in a friendly manner to each other as they pass.

The solitude of the wilderness does not strike that terror to the soul that is felt by the stranger alone amid the crowds of a metropolis.

Under such conditions it is not strange then that when the countryman is accosted by a well-dressed, affable stranger who greets him like a brother, and mentions the familiar names of the big men of his town, that the man makes the mistake of supposing that the agreeable gentleman is exactly what he represents himself to be?

True, he cannot exactly recall the circumstances under which he met him at home. Still, he must have done so, or how would the stranger be so pat with his name?

The countryman almost always forgets that he gave his name and address to another stranger only a few minutes before,

Joe Phenix, being an artist himself in his peculiar line, was quick to appreciate a master-fraud, and such this bunco man certainly was. So he humored the fellow, just for the purpose of leading him on, for he was as anxious to watch the development of this little game as the average first-nighter is to see the display of acting upon the mimic stage.

Therefore he shook hands with the tall young man, said he was delighted to meet him, although it was entirely unexpected; explained in a very candid manner that his memory was a little hazy about meeting him, but "reckoned" that it was all right, anyway.

"Certainly, of course; going up the street? I am bound up Broadway myself," the bunco man remarked.

"Yes; taking in the sights, you know."

"You must let me show you around," the other declared as the two proceeded up the street. "You will not find a man in New York who knows the ropes any better than I do."

The disguised detective replied that he would be glad of a pilot, and he did not doubt that his friend knew the city like a book.

"Oh, yes, I was born and brought up here--lived in New York all my life you know, and if any friends want to see the elephant, I think I will be able to show them the animal in all its glory.

"And that reminds me that I have an appointment," he exclaimed, abruptly, pulling out his watch as he spoke.

"Yes, I have just time to get there," he continued. "It is over on the east side of town. We are going to change our cart man; the man we have does not give satisfaction, and the firm asked me to see about another man, and I am going to meet him. It will only take us a short distance out of our way."

"Oh, that is all right, I am in no hurry," Joe Phenix observed, speaking just as a good-natured, easy-going countryman would speak.

Then the bunco man guided the disguised detective across City Hall Park and up Park Row until he came to what used to be known as Chatham Street, but now transformed into Park Row, a locality where second-hand shops, five-cent restaurants and small saloons abound.

"There is the number on the other side of the street, and it is a saloon too!" The young man shook his head as though he did not like it. "I remember now, he said his brother kept a saloon; and, in fact, about all of these cart men hang out in some saloon. It will not do us any harm to go in, we need not drink anything. I am not in the habit of drinking, you know, although I take a glass of ale when I feel thirsty sometimes."

"A glass of beer won't hurt anyone," the supposed countryman remarked.

"Yes, I agree with you!" the bunco man exclaimed, his face lighting up, for he felt sure he had hooked his fish. "Come in and I will stand treat!"

CHAPTER VI.
THE LITTLE GAME.

The saloon was a dingy-looking little place, with a small bar in the front, and a couple of tables with chairs around them at the back, and in the rear wall was a small door.

There were some men drinking at the counter as the pair entered, and at one of the tables at the extreme end of the saloon, sat a well-dressed, stoutly-built man reading a newspaper.

"There is my man now, I think," the bunco sharp observed. "Come on, and we will sit down so we can drink our beer comfortably."

"All right," replied the detective, fully prepared to agree to almost anything so that the game could go on.

The pair proceeded to the table, and as they came up, the man seated there raised his eyes to survey the new-comers.

"Why, Mr. Johnson, is that you?" Mr. Clark exclaimed, and then he shook hands with the other in the warmest manner.

"This is not the party I expected to see, but an old friend of mine whom I haven't met for some time," he explained, and then, with a deal of ceremony, he proceeded to introduce the man from Gloversville to the other.

This was followed by a call for "three beers!" and the new-comers took seats at the table.

"Lemme see!" exclaimed the bunco chief in a reflective way, "the last time I met your royal highness you were the head clerk at the Fifth Avenue Hotel."

"Yes, but I am not there now; I found that the confinement did not agree with me, I needed a more active life," the other said, acting his part in a really splendid manner.

"Ah, yes, I see," exclaimed Clark, in a sympathizing way. "Well, what are you driving at now?"

"Oh, I am in on a big speculation!" the man exclaimed. "Got right in on the ground floor too. I'm the secretary of the Florida Orange Grove Land Improvement Company!"

And it was with a great flourish he made the announcement.

"Yes, yes, I know all about that colossal speculation!" the bunco sharp declared. "I have an interest in it too. Got one of the tickets in my pocket right now!" and as he spoke he took from his pocketbook a printed slip of paper about the size of a bank bill.

It was nicely gotten up, and the disguised detective, glancing at it as the other laid the paper upon the table, saw that it entitled the holder to ten of the company's ten-acre orange grove farms, valued at two hundred dollars apiece.

"You are in for a good thing!" Mr. Johnson announced. "The ten acres tract, with an orange grove upon it in full bearing, is richly worth a thousand dollars of any man's money!" he continued. "And then there is a chance of your catching a premium too. To-day the drawing takes place, and that is what I am waiting here for. Our office is right on the next street, you know; you go through this back door, and through the little alley, and you will find yourself in the rear of our office."

"Ah, yes, I see, but I didn't know that before, although I knew the office was around the block."

"Yes, I am waiting for the drawing now. This is the big day, you know," Mr. Johnson remarked. "There are ten sections to be drawn to-day. Let's see, you are in number one," he added, with a glance at the certificate.

"Yes, but you can just bet that I am going in on every section!" the bunco chief declared.

"That is where your head is level! I am in from number one to ten!" the other exclaimed.

"This is one of the biggest schemes that has ever been run," Mr. Clark explained to the disguised detective. "You see, this company is going to work on a great scale. They want to get their property into the market as soon as possible and so they are offering extra inducements.

"These certificates cost a dollar apiece, and after a hundred of them are sold the company has a drawing and every tenth number that comes out is entitled to a premium of a hundred dollars and a ten-acre farm, and the men who get left are entitled to take their ten acres by paying ten dollars within a year. You understand the whole idea is to create a rush for the shares so as to get people to settle down there as soon as possible."

"The company only sells half their land in this way, you know," Mr. Johnson took upon himself to explain. "Then, when they get the town started they will put the price up to a hundred dollars an acre, a thousand dollars for a ten-acre farm and that is where they will make their money."

"Yes, I see," Joe Phenix remarked; he could not help admiring the shrewdness with which this trap to catch "suckers" had been prepared.

"Perhaps you would like to take a chance, Mr. Horton," the bunco sharp suggested. "It will only cost you a dollar and you may draw a premium which will be a hundred dollars in your pocket; anyway, you will be entitled to take ten of the orange grove farms, but you have a year to make up your mind."

"Yes, it seems like a good scheme," Joe Phenix

remarked.

He was anxious for the play to go on, for as yet he did not see where the bunco men were going to come in.

A single dollar would be poor pay for all this trouble.

"Have you a certificate, Mr. Johnson?" the bunco chief inquired,

"Yes; just by the luckiest chance in the world!" the other answered. And then he produced the certificate.

Joe Phenix was in the habit of carrying some loose change in his vest pocket, and he happened to have a little over a dollar, so he was able to secure the "valuable" certificate.

Then Mr. Johnson glanced at the clock on the wall, and announced that the time for the drawing was at hand.

"I will be back in about ten minutes, and let you know the result!" he exclaimed, as he departed through the rear door.

After he was gone, the bunco sharp ordered the beer-glasses to be refilled, and proceeded to explain what a big thing this Florida land speculation was.

In much less than ten minutes the other bunco man was back, and his face was illuminated with joy as he approached and resumed his seat at the table.

"I wish I may die!" he exclaimed, "If I don't believe that both of you gentlemen were born under a lucky star!"

"You don't mean to say that we have both hit it!" Mr. Clark exclaimed.

"Hang me if you haven't! For a hundred apiece, too, and I have got the ducats!" Mr. Johnson declared, then took a roll of bills from his pocket and handed it to Mr. Clark.

This gentleman ran the bills over rapidly, flipping them apart with the ease of a bank cashier.

"Twenty fives—a hundred dollars! That is right, and

Johnson, old fellow, I am ever so much obliged to you! But, I say, where is Mr. Horton's money? Didn't you bring it?"

"Yes, I got it all right, but as Mr. Horton is a stranger, the president says that he will have to require him to show that he would be able to pay for ten of the lots called for by the certificates; that is, that he is good for a hundred dollars. As soon as he shows the money, I have orders to pay him his premium. It is just a mere form, you know, as a guarantee of good faith, so as to keep irresponsible men from getting into the company."

"Oh, that is all right! I will guarantee that Mr. Horton is good for a thousand!" the bunco chief exclaimed.

"Oh, I haven't any doubt about that!" the other declared, "It is only a mere form, but the president is very strict, and I have to go by his orders, you know. Just as soon as Mr. Horton shows the money I can pay over the hundred."

"If you are a little short, Mr. Horton, put up what money you have, and I will help you out!" the bunco chief declared, with a flourish.

Joe Phenix saw the game now. This was all a desire to get the countryman to produce his money, and the moment it was displayed one of the fellows would snatch it and run through the back door.

As it happened the detective only had a few dollars in his pocketbook, and he made up his mind to bring it forth, thinking that as he was prepared for any trick, it would be a hard matter for the rascals to get the best of him, so he remarked:

"Oh, I reckon I can put up a hundred without any trouble," and as he spoke he dove his hand into his pocket.

CHAPTER VII.
HERRING BOB.

A look of eager interest was on the faces of the sharpers, and a gleam of exultation in their eyes, but just as they fancied that success was about to crown their efforts, there came a sudden and entirely unexpected interruption.

A medium-sized, but muscularly-built young man, dressed rather roughly, and bearing the unmistakable look of a Bowery boy, had been drinking a glass of beer at the end of the counter. And while apparently not paying any attention to the men at the table, yet, in reality, he had listened to the conversation. When the disguised detective put his hand into his pocket the stranger thought that it was time for him to interfere.

"Say, old man, don't pull out your leather, for there's a cove right behind your chair ready to swipe it the moment you do, and he will give you the sneak out so quick that it will make your head swim, see?"

This speech acted upon the bunco men like the explosion of a bomb-shell, particularly as Joe Phenix drew his hand quickly from his pocket, and glancing behind him saw that there was indeed a man leaning over the back of his chair, apparently all ready to grab the pocketbook and run when it should be produced.

The sharpers understood that their little game was spoiled and their rage was great.

The man who had sneaked behind the chair, a good-sized fellow, with an evil-looking face, was the first to take action.

"You blarsted dog! How dare you call me a thief?" be cried in unmistakable English accents, and he made a rush at the stranger, but that worthy was on his guard for an attack and received the Englishman with a straight right-hander to the jaw which knocked him back on the table, all in a heap, and then he rolled to the floor.

The other two were quick to come to the assistance of their pal, but the stranger seemed to be all arms and he knocked them right and left with as much ease as though they had been a pair of schoolboys instead of powerful, fully-developed men.

The one lick that the first man got had taken all the fight out of him, and when he saw his comrades handled in such an unceremonious way he made haste to retreat by means of the rear door.

The other two quickly followed his example; each man had been knocked down twice, and neither one of them was able to land a blow on the skillful stranger, who either dodged or parried their strokes with the greatest ease.

Just as the men retreated, the bartender came to their assistance with a revolver, which he had pulled out from under the counter, but the stranger was equal to the situation.

He seized a bottle from behind the bar—he was right at the end of it—and faced the barkeeper and his weapon without flinching.

"Johnny, you don't want to pull no gun on me!" he cried, drawing hack his arm, the hand of which gripped the heavy bottle by the neck in an extremely threatening way.

"You can't get but one crack at me before I am onto you like a pile of bricks, and if that one shot don't stop me right in my tracks—and it is a thousand to one that it won't—I'll fit you for a pine box afore you kin say Jack Robinson!"

The barkeeper halted; despite the fact that he was armed with a deadly weapon, and the other man not, he hesitated to bring on a fight.

There was something in the eyes of the other that cowed him.

Besides, the bunco gang had fled, having evidently got all of the stranger that they wanted.

The agile and stalwart Bowery boy saw that he had secured an advantage, and he was quick to improve it.

"Put your gun right away now, Johnny, and be quick about it too, 'cos I ain't anxious to put a dead tumbler-juggler on my list, but I will have to come the bottle act on you if you try any ugly business!"

The bartender was both angry and disgusted at the way the stranger had handled the bunco men, for he would have "stood in to win a stake" if the sharpers had succeeded in fleecing the supposed countryman, but as the stranger had proved himself to be a mighty warrior he was unwilling to test his metal.

"Oh, that is all right!" he exclaimed, but in a way that showed he did not relish the stranger's interference. "I ain't got no call to interfere if some of the boys want to have a little quiet scrap, but if you are going in for to clean out der place, I've got for to try and put a stop to it, see!"

"Oh, you're a gen'leman; anybody kin see that!" the stranger observed, in a rather sarcastic way.

Then he turned to the disguised detective.

"I say, boss, if you are going down the street I will walk along with yer a ways."

Joe Phenix understood that this was the stranger's polite manner of saying that he had better get out, so he rose to his feet and announced that he would be glad of the other's company.

The two then left the saloon, followed by the angry glances of the bartender.

The stranger noticed the looks of the saloon man, and spoke about it with a laugh to his companion as they walked down the street.

"That tumbler-juggler in there don't take his medicine for a cent!" he declared. "You see, if them cusses had got away wid yer leather—that's yer wallet and money, you know--that beer-jerker would have come in for five or ten cases, mebbe. Cases are dollars, you see!"

"Yes, I understand. He was in with the fellows then?"

"Yes, you bet! It is a tough old dive!" the other declared, "I never happened to go in there before, but I know about the hole. The barkeeper stands right in wid these gangs. If it had been night, you know, they would not have taken all this trouble to work the bunco biz; they would have given yer a dose in yer first glass of beer which would have laid you out so they could have got all yer stuff without any trouble."

"A regular house of call for thieves, eh?" the detective remarked.

There was something in the way in which the detective spoke which seemed to surprise the stranger.

He surveyed the disguised detective carefully for a moment, and then remarked:

"Say, mebbe you ain't so big a jay as you look?"

"Well, appearances are sometimes deceptive, you know," Joe Phenix replied with a laugh.

"Now, take you, for instance," he continued. "You don't look like a man who would be able to make such a holy show out of three good, stout crooks, such as those fellows certainly were."

"Say! I guess you are up to some little game. I kin

see now that you ain't half as big a Jay as you look to be. Mebbe if I hadn't come in you wouldn't have been skinned after all."

"Well, the rascals would not have got over five dollars, for that is about what I have in my wallet, but they most certainly would have got that, for the man behind my chair would have been a surprise to me. I anticipated that they were going to work the snatch-game upon me, but I was just on the lookout for one of the two trying it."

"There is always three or four of them in a gang, and this crowd is as bad a one as you will find anywhere in New York. I know'em, although they don't know me, for if they did they would never have tried to stand up ag'in me.

"It is Kid Hiller's gang. That was Kid who came in with you, and the cops say that he is the smartest bunco man in the country."

"The man is away up at the top of the heap in his line. I saw that the moment he tried to pick me up, and that was the reason I came along with him. I had a curiosity to see how they worked the game, but I am a little curious about you too, my friend," the disguised detective added. "I have seen some good boxers in my time, but I never saw any man handle his fists any better than you did to-day."

"That is my little biz, you know," the other explained. "I'm a pug!"

"A pugilist, eh?"

"Yes, I'm in the light-weight division, and though I say it myself what hadn't ought to, I kin stand up ag'in' any of 'em, 'cept two or three coves, like Jack McAuliffe, and men of his class.

"My name is Bob Herring—Herring Bob— every one calls me though, and I got the name 'cos I was

284

brought up by an old fish-peddler.

"I was one of the kids that was born in the street, I s'pose, for I never knowed anything 'bout my father or mother, and the only name I ever had was Bob, until I got to going with the old fishman, and then some of the lads commenced to call me Herring, and the name stuck to me."

"Well, one name is about as good as another."

"That is the way I think, and I ain't kicking 'bout my name.

"I have had a mighty hard row to hoe all through my life, but I want you to understand, boss, that I have always been on the square! I could have gone in with these crooks fifty times, but I wouldn't have it for a cent!"

"That is where you are wise; honesty always pays in the long run, and if you notice these crooks, no matter how successful they be for a while, yet in the end they always come to grief."

"You are right, and no mistake!" the other declared. "Now I don't make much out of this here fighting business, and I would like to quit it, but for a man like myself, w'ot ain't got no trade, it is awful hard work to strike anything.

"This fighting business ain't what it is cracked up to be, you know," Herring Bob continued. "A few of the big guns can make a raise once in a while, when they pull off a successful match. I have fought for as high as a thousand a side myself, and beat my man too. I was supposed to git half the stake, the backer took the other half, 'cos he found the money and made the match. Folks would say, 'Well he's got five-hundred to the good,' but when a cove comes to take his training expenses out—there's the trainer to pay, the board and things, and a stake to the seconds, a man is lucky to have two-hundred left out of the five."

While the boxer had been speaking an idea had come to Joe Phenix.

He thought, "Why would not this young man make a good secret agent? Why not enroll him as one of the six?"

And the more the detective thought of the matter the better he was pleased with the idea.

"You would like to get into another line of business?"

"Yes, I would!" the other replied decidedly. "I am sick of this 'ere kind of life that I am leading now! There ain't any show for a man to make anything in it.

"Now, I am giving it to you straight, and if you don't believe me all you have to do is to go to any of the sporting houses in the Bowery, and they will tell you that what I say goes, every time!

"There's no money in the ring for a man like myself. I'm a dead game fighter, and I have never been licked yet; the nearest I came to it was two draws out of ten battles; but things are so bad with me now becos' I won't do any crooked work, that I am boxing at a sporting house in the Bowery for a tenner a week, and although I am not a drinking man yet the boss expects me to leave two or three dollars a week at the bar, and you kin see for yourself that, there isn't much left for me, and it is all I kin do to pay for my room and my grub."

"Well, you have done me a service to-day and I would like to do something for you in return. Is there anyplace in the neighborhood where we can go for a little quiet talk? Somewhere we can speak freely, without danger of being overheard?"

"Yes, there's a back room in the saloon where I box, and at this time of day there ain't much chance of any customers being in it. The saloon is a hang-out place for sports, and there ain't many of them around except at night; the day business does not amount to any thing."

"That will do nicely."

"It won't take us long to go there, and I tell you boss, if you can get me something to do I will be mighty glad, for I'm sick of this here kind of life that I am leading now."

"I think I can put you on a new road!" the other declared.

The sporting saloon was soon reached, and the pugilist escorted the disguised detective into the "drum," as the English fighting men call such a house.

Chapter 8 is ready for you in your own copy of

Joe Phenix's Silent Six;
or;
The Great Detective's Shadow Guard

from

Dark Lantern Tales

Order It Today!

62779363R00168